*when emotional turmoil takes its toll, leaving is not easy*

# THROUGH THE DARKNESS
## ASTRID FICK

Copyright © 2026 by Astrid Fick

All rights reserved.

No part of this publication may be reproduced, distributed, or transmitted in any form or by any means, including photocopying, recording, or other electronic or mechanical methods, without the prior written permission.

Without limiting the author's right, any unauthorised use of this publication to train generative artificial intelligence (A.I.) technology is strictly prohibited.

The story, all names, characters, and incidents portrayed in this production are fictitious. No identification with actual persons (living or deceased), buildings, and products is intended or should be inferred.

Cover by Stephen Blundell

Book Edited by CJ Editing

Book Formatted by Astrid Fick

First edition 2026

eBook ISBN: 978-1-7638484-1-2

Paperback ISBN: 978-1-7638484-1-2

*For those who have travelled in the dark trying to find a way out. May this book shine a light for you to follow out of the tunnel and find your path once again.*

This books contains themes of domestic violence and mental health — reader discretion is advised.

A list of Australian/Queensland helplines can be found on my website (www.astridfick.com/contentwarnings) and my content warning list can be at the end.

# August 2004

*8 Years Old*

Mrs McConnell was up the front writing the plan for the morning on the blackboard. Her small stick of white chalk scraped along and a hush fell over the room. Except for a few boys on the other side who still proceeded to talk.

I tried to advert my eyes from her signature pink maxi dress and white bolero combination to the writing on the far-left aspect of the room length board. Mrs McConnell had today's word of the day: *decadently*.

*Mrs McConnell dressed far more decadently compared to other teachers.*

Except, while she was sweet to the other students, the butterfly clip wearing teacher had me shaking in my seat.

I pursed my lips and focused on the black board, staring into the chalk haze.

*It looks so pretty today, like smoke in the wind.*

'McKenna,' Mrs McConnell stared at me. My feet remained firmly planted on the worn navy coloured carpet. Every muscle in my body tensed. My heart pounded. 'Stop talking.'

Whispers from the right quietened. My brain couldn't decide if I should run or crawl into a ball and die.

*Why is it always me?*

'McKenna, last warning.'

*What?*

I knew what she was doing, but giving in would only make it worse. As much as I wanted to scream: "I wasn't talking"; the last time I tried to stand up for myself, I was kicked out of class. Instead, I prayed the others would stand up for me. But alas, I didn't have friends in my class, except for Bec, and Bec was useless.

'Alright, get out your pencils, sharpeners and rubbers,' Mrs McConnell announced. 'Science quiz time.'

*Keep your head low and try not to finish too early. You've got this.*

'Put your name on top and you have one hour, starting now.'

I scribbled my name and started going through the questions.

Science was one of my better subjects compared to Maths and English. I found the quiz easier than I thought, but I slowed down my pace, ensuring I didn't make any silly errors. Mrs McConnell's pink dress continued dancing within my peripheral vision. But I remained focused on the task.

Before I could answer the next question, my test paper was ripped out from under me. She raised it up, pointing to a terrible photocopied question I missed.

'Make sure you're answering all questions,' Mrs McConnell said.

*I can't do anything right! I am nowhere near complete. What was the point?*

There wasn't a rule stating that quizzes had to be completed front to back.

*How did McKenna die? "Death by embarrassment".*

A dark cloud overshadowed me. The darkened thoughts should've scared me; instead, I welcomed them with open arms. They brought me comfort in a way that happiness couldn't provide.

*What even is happiness?*

'Right, pencils down everyone,' Mrs McConnell called. 'Pass all your quizzes to the front and get your math books out.'

*Keep your head down, and remember, zip your lips and throw away the key.*

'McKenna, what's one on four plus eight on nine?'

My voice box could no longer produce noise whenever I was around her. Instead, I felt my throat close up. The mottled pattern of my desk was more interesting than facing my teacher's wrath. I hadn't even raised my hand.

'Pay attention, McKenna.'

My name was continuously called, but I stayed silent. My cheeks burned at the thought of having to walk past my classmates again.

*I am not allowed to even get a question wrong.*

I longed for the arms of the clock to point at three, combined with the comforting ring of the school bell signalling for home. Except the day was only beginning. There was nothing I wanted more than my books – my way of escaping life's harsh realities. Give me *The Rainbow Magic Series* any day of the week. I craved for home and sleep, where limitless dreams awaited. Nothing made sense to me anymore. School was supposed to be safe, instead it was my recurring nightmare.

'McKenna, seven times twelve.'

Silence filled the air, as did the sixteen raised hands. Sixteen students who the teacher could've called upon, and yet it was me. It was always me.

*Eighty-four.*

It was like a rope was wrapped around me, as crushing pressure formed in my chest. The tightness extracting every last bit of carbon dioxide from my lungs leaving me to battle for air. I wiped my suddenly wet hands on my rough charcoal-coloured skirt. The words caught in my throat as I choked out, 'E-Eighty-s-six.'

My classmates laughed. Mrs McConnell's face turned red, her eyes burning into me. The rope tightened its hold. Blood drained from my face. My heart was beating rapidly. Beads of sweat formed on the top of my forehead.

'I've had enough,' she said sternly. 'If you don't want to learn, then you can sit outside.'

*Fighting it would only make my day worse.*

My chair grazed against the carpet as I stood up. The feeling of nineteen eyes burning into me sent shivers down my spine. My folded arms pressed as close to my body as possible, the pressure forcing my shoulders to slump forward. I sped out of the room and slammed my back into the cold bricked partition wall. My bottom collided with the cold hard vinyl flooring, hard. The floodgates of tears opened.

'I can't do anything right,' I mumbled into my tear-soaked hands.

*I'd rather die than speak another word.*

# 1

# February 2018

*21 Years Old*

The cool sea breeze blew through the open French doors causing the light fabric of my maxi baby blue dress to flutter. There was not a cloud in sight, only green shrubs and the gorgeous deep blue water of Trinity Beach.

'Eight more minutes,' I breathed, checking the large blue resin clock on the wall in the kitchen.

My chest tightened and stomach knotted. It was my final nursing exam, and there was so much riding on it. Despite having my textbooks and thirteen weeks' worth of notes laid out on my father's mahogany timber desk in the family office. I still felt like I was bound to blunder, even though I was as ready as I could be.

'Thank the universe for open-book exams,' I joked.

The only problem was my boyfriend, Kaleb. Though he was happily immersed in some lengthy campaign of a video game, there was the high risk he'd finish just as I was about to start. It's happened on a few occasions where he'd come in every five minutes wanting sex, food, or me to help solve his boredom.

This time, I had a rule: "Door closed, don't come in. Exam in process".

It was a pretty simple boundary. I needed complete concentration. But exams had become the only time he showed any interest.

As soon as I walked towards the bedrooms I could smell the faint scent of Kaleb's Dior Sauvage. Except, my bedroom door was closed.

My heart dropped to my stomach and started beating faster. The never-ending roller-coaster feeling started up. Time slowed down as I made my way to the office door. Beads of sweat began to form on my forehead, and I wiped my sweat-soaked hands against the skirt of my dress.

I held my breath as I pushed the door open, unprepared for the catastrophe that laid beyond it.

'Holy fuck,' I exclaimed, unsure whether I wanted to cry in defeat or out of anger.

Torn and crumpled pages from my textbooks and study notes were littered all over the floor. What was left in my textbooks were filled with hasty scribbles. The internet cables were askew, and my eyes gazed upon the plug. Its three prongs were out in the open and slightly bent.

I examined the black electrical plug. 'How?'

My phone shook in my hand as I pressed the power button.

*Five minutes left.*

There was no quick fix besides hoping that my phone's hotspot would hold up.

'Why did he do that?'

The timber floor groaned, and footsteps echoed towards the office. I sat up straight and watched on as the door slowly creaked open. Kaleb peered into the room. He smirked, causing me to jump as the exam opened up. 'You're blaming me for being unprepared. Oh, Kenny.'

Over the past several months, Kaleb had pulled back. I thought it was stress that was causing him the slight rift between us, but stress doesn't destroy three textbooks that totalled to three-hundred dollars.

I was running on anger and adrenaline.

*Focus McKenna!*

Acknowledging his presence was only going to screw with my head even more. Kaleb was still glaring at me. I didn't care as I ferociously clicked the mouse and typed in the one-word answers.

*Has he cottoned on to a weakness that I don't know about?*

I could sense the breaking of several boundaries at that very moment.

He squinted at me. 'You're not going to pass, you know fuck all.'

*Why is he saying this?*

But my subconscious caught his lies in its elaborate labyrinth of sticky white cobwebs and lapped them up like a cat with a bowl of milk. It was no wonder why I was exhausted. My energy was being split between university and constantly ensuring my sanity remained strong. My psychological hold was slipping. I couldn't ignore him and still focus on the exam.

*He's getting into your head, don't let him.*

'I know my shit. I can do this,' I repeated to myself.

Whilst distracting myself had become the only way to prevent my subconscious from listening to his baits, I was flying through the exam. I was running on hopes and dreams, but I was also my own worst nemesis. My subconscious thrived on the negative words from people like it was shining a black aura around me.

*Does like attract like, or am I just easy prey?*

Trying to drown out the noise was getting harder and harder as the exam progressed, but I had to push on. Maybe I didn't need my textbooks or notes. Maybe I needed to have more faith in myself. Clearly Kaleb did, otherwise I doubted he would've gone to all this trouble.

My eyelids fluttered closed, and I took three deep breaths to control my panicked state. The next thing I knew, the banging of my keyboard and the clicks of my mouse were the only sounds I heard.

'Why did you do this?' I asked Kaleb as I slammed my finger on the mouse. The blue wheel of death circled in the centre of a white screen.

He flicked his dark brown hair out of his face. 'I don't know what you're talking about.' I held up my expensive textbooks and motioned to the crumpled pages. 'That wasn't me. Will's home.'

'Oh, pin this on my brother?' I chuckled. 'He isn't home, and you know it; you just don't want to take the blame. I'm not angry; I want to know why you did it.'

That was a lie; I was beyond pissed. My anger grew worse by the second as he refused to acknowledge the crime he had committed and apologise.

'They weren't that important. It's just a couple of books. No biggie. You're acting like the world is ending. Besides, if you already knew the material, then why does it matter? You're only trying to find an excuse in case you fail, so fine. Blame it on me.'

'Unbelievable.'

The little blue wheel stopped turning, and the screen flicked over to my dashboard.

89.50%.

Weight fell off my shoulders. I let out a sigh of relief, leaning back into my chair.

'Oh my God!' I yelled. 'I did it! I fucking did it!'

Kaleb threw the door shut, the slam echoed through the house. The walls shuddered in response.

I felt my stomach drop again, once again on that never-ending roller-coaster. But that was life – it was a constant roller-coaster. Only mine had more twists and downhills than I would've liked.

I raced to the door and pushed in the lock. My back slid down the glossy white architrave, landing harshly in the fetal position. Silent sobs filled the air, as tears steamrolled down my face, and my heart rattled against my chest.

*Why would he go to the trouble?*

The permanent rose gold choker around my neck made my blood run cold. He claimed he bought it because he loved me, but was it because he loved me or because he wanted others to know I was his?

*Am I that naive, or am I simply reading too much into it?*

Of course, he'd be the one person who could ruin a fantastic day for me. My near-perfect score would earn me an academic award at graduation and allow me to give the commencement speech. Instead, I was left questioning my entire three-year relationship.

This wasn't even just a rule break. Kaleb broke several boundaries. And judging from the vandalism, and a cracked doorframe from the slam, he also broke a couple of laws in his outburst.

I broke.

'I can't do a-any th-thing,' I sobbed.

'Kaleb's right. How am I supposed to deal with a busy ED, or worse, egotistical doctors on a power trip?' I said, wiping my tears.

The sharp sting of my nails in the soft skin of my palms was enough to bring me back to reality.

'Am I capable of being —' My phone vibrating on the timber surface of the desk pulled me out of my thoughts. 'Shit. I've been hiding for an hour.'

*Shit!*

It was an unknown number.

As much as I wanted to ignore it, my gut instincts told me to answer it.

'Hello, McKenna speaking,' I said, placing the call on speaker.

'Hi McKenna, it's Hazel, the Dean of Learning,' the woman said.

'H-Hi.' My brain halted all thinking momentarily as it processed who I was speaking to.

Footsteps echoed down the hallway. Their silhouette stopped on the other side of the door, blocking the light peeking out from under it. I was hyper-aware that Kaleb was listening in from the other side, but I didn't care. This was bound to be good news.

'I wanted to let you know that we're still very keen to have you as our speaker and to congratulate you on your 89.50% grade.'

*Gee, that was fast. I only submitted my exam an hour ago.*

'Thank you.'

'Also we'll be awarding you the Naomi Bloom trophy award upon passing your next placement.'

'Oh my goodness, thank you.'

'No problem. You've earned this, McKenna. Congratulations.'

'Thank you again, Hazel.'

The call ended, and I sat there dumbfounded. The pages of my textbook and notes were still crumpled on the ground around me.

Another door slammed shut.

My heart started beating faster again, the echoes of the slam causing me to jump. I backed myself into the far corner of the room, in the fetal position between the bookshelf and the wall.

'Please leave my property, Kaleb,' I called out, and I sank deeper into my prime hiding spot, as the distant banging continued down the hall. 'I am safe here.'

The bookshelf, cold and hard, slowly warmed against my body heat. My pelvic bones dug into my muscle.

'What possessed him?'

My fingers found the hem of my skirt, running it between them. The accordion fold was my favourite.

A few minutes later, an email notification popped up on my phone from Hazel, reiterating what we had spoken about. I fought against my facial muscles that pulled my lips upward into a smile, but I was unsuccessful. A large grin was firmly planted as I messaged the family chat with the great news, even though nobody would respond until after work, I knew Mum and Dad would come home with a nice bottle of champagne each.

Against my better judgement, I messaged my friend's group chat to see if anyone wanted to go out to Ray's to celebrate. It was a quiet bar near the university campus that was our form of "uni bar". As expected, I got a series of no's from all six of them, plus Kaleb, even when I asked if another night would be better.

Not even twenty minutes later, Naomi announced her promotion and asked to go to Ricki's. The whole chat said yes, even Kaleb.

*So they're too busy for me, but not too busy for Naomi.*

I messaged them saying, "I'm out", just like they had done to me, moments ago.

They hadn't changed since high school. I wanted to drop them, but they were my only support besides Kaleb. My nursing cohort was more of the "every man for themselves" kind. They were only ever interested in studying together if necessary. I was desperate for friends, and the group chat was my only way of having my phone blow up every couple of days.

I was hooked on the dopamine.

Kaleb banged on the door. 'Open the fucking door, McKenna.'

'So you can do what exactly? Are you going to apologise?' I asked.

He giggled loudly. 'No, 'cause I did nothing wrong. What you did was rude! They're your friends. My God, you're so fucking selfish.'

Kaleb kept banging. The walls shuddered.

I stayed hidden in the corner, only peeking out as I heard the door splinter. With a few more pounds, the crack split down even more.

'Get out of my house Kaleb, or I'll call the police,' I warned.

He stomped down the hallway.

I could no longer hear what he was doing until glass shattered, and metal clanked to the ground. It was like a set of weight plates was sitting on my chest. More piled on by the second. My heart felt like it was going to stop at any moment.

The stomping came back down the hall, and the silhouette of his feet were visible under the door.

'I've got triple zero locked and loaded,' I said.

'You don't have it in you,' Kaleb retorted.

'You don't know anything about me. Do you want to find out?' I baited.

Silence.

I could still see his feet from underneath the door. I was far from safe.

'You're nothing without me,' he said.

'Kaleb, please leave,' I said.

'Do you think I want to do this? *You* made me do this.'

'I didn't make you do anything.'

'Are you really that stupid? Naive? You're pathetic.'

'Get out of my house Kaleb.' This time, I matched his tone.

The front door squeaked, his footsteps quietened. The pitter-patter trudged past the office's window and came to a halt.

'I'm off to Ricki's to celebrate Naomi's promotion. Feel free to join when you're done playing the victim.'

I tilted the blinds and watched him from the shadows as he stomped down the stairs and exited through the gate. I regretted introducing him to my friends. They liked him more.

'What's wrong with me?' I asked as I finally exited the study.

Shards of glass and metal legs sat in a pile on the carpet where my desk should have been.

'I deserved this.'

*How am I supposed to explain this to my parents? Maybe I'm not destined for greatness. Maybe I just give up on nursing. I'd graduate, and that's it.*

My friends hated me. I had no friends at uni. All I had was a shattered desk, a boyfriend who was stressed and embarrassed of me, and a degree that I no longer wanted.

*I don't even know who I want to be anymore.*

# 2

# May 2012

*16 Years Old*

My fingers fidgeted with the hem of my school skirt that sat folded in my lap from being turned into makeshift shorts.

Miss Hunter cringed and got redder by the sentence.

I hated English with a passion. The double period every Wednesday after lunch was my living nightmare.

Maybe it was the dark, manky, old classroom at the other end of the school that smelt like fish and moth balls. Or perhaps it was the fact that Miss Hunter was out for my blood. I didn't understand why. I asked questions and yet was still receiving too many C's, despite having a tutor and help from Miss Hunter. My efforts to pass barely kept me afloat.

To make matters worse, I couldn't prove Miss Hunter's maliciousness without filming or recording her. Both options would've led to expulsion. It was an unfortunate "their word against mine" situation.

Despite wearing a gorgeous white and black polka-dot dress, Miss Hunter displayed a horrid attitude that only came out for me. No other student bore her wrath, at least, that I was aware of. It was once again, the pretty young teacher I had, who saw me as the perfect target for being their metaphorical punching bag. The one you would never think twice of for being strict or malicious.

The bell rang, and the boys and girls dashed out of the room, almost like Miss Hunter timed it perfectly to get me alone.

'Take this to your parents,' she finally said, pulling a paper from her leather laptop bag.

The form was a permission slip for parents to allow their child to transfer down to the Non-Overall Position English. It was the only form in her bag. I didn't want to assume, but this was the only OP-listed class she taught. It was only a matter of trying to find a way to work with Miss Hunter, but there was a string of conspiracy theories I could go down. I didn't want to, but it sure felt like the universe was out to get me.

'Tertiary education … University is not in the cards for you.'

My back hit the back of the chair hard. It hurt, but not as much as the comment that should never have been said. I needed the OP English to be able to apply to universities. Though I was strongly considering finding an alternate path if leaving for the easier option meant leaving her mere presence, but I wanted to make it work. I loved the required reading too much, especially as we were about to do *The Great Gatsby* and Shakespeare's *Hamlet* later this year.

*How could she get away with it?*

It was an easy answer, no witnesses. There was not a single student in sight, nor was there a single recording device.

'What am I doing wrong? This is the only class where I am barely passing,' I asked. 'I can see that I'm hitting some higher marks in other criteria, so how can I improve?'

'Well …' She trailed off, looking back at my laptop. 'I don't see how you'll ever get higher than a C minus.'

*"I don't see how you'll ever get higher than a C minus?" What an odd thing to say.*

My eyes widen and my jaw sat ajar. A teacher shouldn't say things like that. It was a blunt, off-the-cuff comment. I wasn't a senior, I was in grade eleven, and I had plenty of time to improve. In fact, I was actively trying. Every morning these past two weeks, I was in a teacher's office getting further assistance on my work.

*Did she mean that, or did she mince her words?*

I didn't care to ask for fear of retribution. 'Thank you miss,' I replied. 'I have to go; otherwise, I'll miss my bus.'

I closed my laptop, threw everything back into my schoolbag, and raced out the gates. I ran from the other students, and down to the bus stop that hardly anyone used. Tears poured down my face, unable to control my emotions.

Faking happiness every day, there were bound to be cracks in the foundation. I wanted to punch something, throw something, do something to let the anger out. The adrenaline rush I was feeling was more intense than it had ever been.

'10 minutes,' I muttered as the bus rounded the corner. 'I'll be home in 10 minutes.'

I clambered on and immediately sat in my favourite spot by the back door. I tried to stop myself from crying, but I couldn't; the tears were overflowing. I hung my neck forward, pulling my hat far enough down to cover my face.

All I wanted right now was my favourite blanket that Grandma made.

*I keep trying but at what point do I just give in?*

# 3

# February 2018

*21 Years Old*

The door squeaked open as I walked into my bedroom. My heart ached. I longed for a companionship I knew would never come. Compared to his laptop, I felt obsolete. Kaleb was so uninterested in my existence that he was playing an online video game in my bed.

'Can we do something, please?' I asked. 'Like that art show we booked for today. It starts in an hour?'

It was a few months ago when we pre-planned it, and yet, it only came up this morning that there was a gaming tournament.

Another date, another excuse.

Our last date would've been at least six months ago, maybe longer.

Kaleb quickly muted his navy gamer headset. 'No, for the last time, I'm in the middle of a campaign.' He flicked his headset back on. The sound of his fingers banging against the keys resonated in the air. 'Fuck me, Peter! Shoot the fucking bitch in the head!' he yelled into his headset. 'Move Jackson! Dammit, Marv, you fucking shot me! Why the fu—'

'Can we please do something?' I asked again.

He muted the microphone. 'Once again, I'm in the middle of a—'

He turned his headset back on. 'DAMMIT BRODY, FOCUS!'

Kaleb turned it back off; his eyes remained focused on his screen. 'We can do something in, like, four hours?'

'Whatever,' I sighed, and headed out to the back deck.

The brown wicker outdoor sofa sat against the wall, facing out to the bush and sea. The bare skin of my thighs rubbed against the rough fabric of the sofas cream coloured cushions. My denim shorts rode up and tightened around my upper thighs.

Cocoa, the family miniature chocolate labradoodle, bounded down the hall. She may have been an old girl, but she could still act like a puppy when she wanted.

'Come here, girl,' I said, lifting her up onto my lap.

She curled up and started snoring softly.

My free hand went to the permanent rose gold choker; a suffocating commodity that had me gasping for air.

I latched on to my dopamine device and started on my endless scroll on Instagram. Except, dopamine wasn't what I was met with, instead it was cortisol. My phone shook in my sweaty palms, as I was bombarded with posts from my so-called "best friends" on Hamilton Island. Dozens of photos of soft, white sand, crystal-clear water, and cocktails. They were drinking, swimming, and having the time of their lives to celebrate graduation.

I couldn't escape them.

But it was Jack's post that got to me. The full group in the background, holding up cocktails and smiling at the camera. He had captioned it: "Celebrations with the bestest buds".

'Come on!' I exclaimed, throwing my phone down on the other end of the outdoor sofa.

I was merely a fly on the wall. An annoying insect that they just swatted away but I still hung about in the distance, listening, watching. They didn't bother apologising after I called them out on saying yes to Naomi's invite for a drink when I asked first. Watching them have fun was embarrassing, and it was like they were punching me in the stomach, over and over again.

'Why couldn't they just text me?' I asked Cocoa, who was still snoring peacefully in my lap.

It wasn't the first time they'd done this. They took many trips together in high school. The only one that stung was their weeklong trip to Hamilton Island days before our high school graduation. They flaunted it all over social media, and I didn't receive an invitation.

I picked Cocoa up carrying her to the dog bed in the living room. With her safely out of my arms, I stormed into my room, flung open my active wear drawer and put on a sports bra, singlet and leggings.

'I don't have my phone on me, going for a run,' I seethed out to my boyfriend.

Kaleb flung his hand in the air, somewhat acknowledging me, but whether he listened or not, I couldn't care less. I had to get away. More importantly, I needed my happy and safe place.

The feel of my joggers tightening around my feet was comforting, as was the sound of my watch as I started the timer. I drove my feet into the concrete path, thankful for the soft cushioning of my shoes. The cool air lapped at my face.

A smile crept up as I surrendered myself to the salty and cold air. As concrete turned to dirt then turned to sand, I bolted faster, setting into a sprint along the shoreline.

I continued sprinting to my favourite spot halfway along the five-kilometre Trinity Beach. Perfectly sheltered by the trees, big enough to climb and sit in or to sit at the base. It depended on how sore my legs were. Today, it felt like a tree-sitting kind of day.

As soon as I spotted my favourite tree unoccupied I powered through the burn. I climbed up the trunk nestling myself in the fork of the branches.

My breaths were heavy as I relaxed my body from the sprint. The rough feel of the bark under my gluteus muscles and back kept me grounded. I continued to slow my breaths and gave in to my surroundings. The sound of the waves. The sensation of the bark. The scent of the salty air.

This was safe.

This was home.

I didn't know why I still expected my friends to invite me out when they hadn't done so for the past several months. Now Kaleb was hanging out with them and leaving me out, even though he was the one who used to invite me. He had become one of them. Maybe I didn't fit in with anyone anymore.

*Why else would I be overlooked?*

Kaleb was too enthralled by his looks and spent an obscene amount of time with his friends. I was redundant yet needed in so many ways too. There was no in-between.

*This would be the perfect tree to hang myself from.*

I shook my head.

'You don't think like that anymore,' I muttered.

This was the downside to being alone. I had nothing to distract me from my thoughts. Nothing to save me from the very near drop to my relapse of suicidality.

'Hey McKenna,' someone called out from below.

*Maybe I was wrong.*

I looked down to see Lucy, Will's mate's little sister, standing at the base.

'Hey, hon,' I said. 'How is it going?'

'Alright,' she replied. 'Life is hard.'

'You got that right,' I said. 'How's Nate going?'

'No clue, he's off with Will. Ya know what those two are like.'
And that I did.

The boys had been friends since nappies. Our mums knew each other since school, and every coffee date they had, the boys tagged along. Since then, they've been inseparable.

Lucy and I were the odd ones out, but still friendly. I often babysat her when I was younger, and now I tutor her occasionally, acting as much of a big sister as I could be.

'Can I come up?' she asked.

'Absolutely.' I helped the teenager into the large branching zone. 'What's up?'

'My parents are being unhelpful about the classes I should take next year,' she said.

'Ahh, yes, classes. I remember those days,' I replied. 'So, tell me, what would you like to do?'

She didn't know. What fifteen-year-olds truly understood who they wanted to be when they grew up? It was something I was still asking myself. Nursing was great, but I couldn't see myself in the position for a long-term career.

'I have ideas like engineering and maybe like a lawyer, but I don't know.'

'How's your mathematics going?' I asked.

'I get Cs,' she replied.

'How would you go if you did Math B?'

'What does that entail?'

'Unit circles.' The minute those words left my mouth Lucy shuddered. She had a couple of encounters earlier this year and hated them with a passion.

'Okay, well, say bye-bye to engineering.' Lucy laughed.

'I'm guessing law's out too. I can't argue for shit.' Her shoulders hunched forward.

I leaned forward. 'There's plenty of stuff out there. What about something in health care? Business? Education?'

'What are the other options in health care besides nursing and medical school?'

'Oh, heaps!' I perked up a little, and she immediately mirrored me. 'There's physiotherapy, chiropractor, medical imaging, sonography, phlebotomy, plus heaps more. It's not all doctors and nurses.'

Lucy seemed intrigued. 'What does it take for medical imaging? That's X-rays, right? I recall one of my teachers discussing it once.'

I nodded. 'If you look up medical imaging degrees, there'll be heaps. Some will require you to have done physics and Math B in high school. Others are only suggested. But I can almost guarantee it'll be easier at university. I would recommend a designated tutor. I wouldn't be much help in physics or advanced maths.'

'Thanks, Kenny,' she said.

'No problem,' I replied. 'By the way, if you'd like, and with your folk's approval. I could try to set up a day for you at one of my favourite placements here for their radiology department.'

'Really?'

'How else would you know if it's for you?'

'Thank you. Thank you. Thank you,' she said, hugging me before jumping down.

'You're welcome.'

Lucy scampered off. The temporary lightness, slowly faded back to my defaulted, depressed state, bringing along my dark thoughts. I couldn't take it anymore. Being alone was when I was at my happiest. Nothing bad could happen when I was alone, but now my thoughts were my worst enemies once again.

Unable to spend any more time alone, I carefully made my way down the tree. My feet sank into the soft sand with each step I took towards the harder stuff on the shoreline.

# 4

# February 2018

*21 Years Old*

By the time I got back, Kaleb was off his game and lying on my bed on his phone. He looked up at me, his green eyes widened, eyebrows raised. 'Where'd you go?'

'For a run around town,' I replied.

'Why?'

'Because I was bored.' I raised my arms and slapped them down at my sides. 'You cancelled another date just to play – what – four hours of freaking video games. My so-called friends ditched us and are having the time of their lives at the beach!'

He shrugged. 'We were going to that art show, so I said we wouldn't go.'

'You mean to tell me we could be on a beach right now, or even at an art show?' I pinched the bridge of my nose. 'Instead you, what? Decided to waste my time?'

Kaleb sat up and reached for my hands. He stared into my eyes, 'Wanna have sex?'

My eyes widened, and I shook my head. 'No.' My jaw clenched and stomach coiled. I was seething as I descended into the red haze. 'Are you just going to ignore me?'

His hands trailed up my arms. I stepped back.

'What is your problem?' He asked, moving towards me. 'You seem like you need a little stress relief.'

Tension inside me boiled, like I was a twig about to snap. It was all he wanted these days. It was never about what I wanted and all about him getting off. If I was sick, having a bad day and just wanted to cuddle, it was always sex.

'Why is that your go-to?' I asked backing further away so he hands were no longer on me.

'We never do it anymore?'

'We did it last night!' I replied. 'I'm depressed and angry, and you don't even care! You don't see or hear me when I tell you that I am hurt when you keep cancelling! When was the last time we went out and spent time together?'

'You don't mean that. You're just being dramatic. Go have a bath and relax.'

'Oh, but I do mean it.' His hands reached out to stroke my legs. 'I said, "No."' Throwing his hands off me. 'Can't take "no" for an answer? Then ... Then ... Then get out.'

Kaleb exploited my hesitation, he cocked his head to the side, watching me. His hands gently grazed the skin of my arms, slowly going down until his fingers grazed my hips.

'I know you want me.' He smirked.

Alarm bells went off in my head. There wasn't anywhere for me to go. My back against the wall. I subtly turned on the recorder on my Apple watch, just in time to get his hand away from my crotch.

'"No" is a full sentence, Kaleb,' I said. 'Get away from me.'

'You're being dramatic and selfish. My needs are just as important as yours.'

'And I said I'm not in the mood!' I pushed him back.

He sat back on my bed, and I took the opportunity to message the group.

**Me:** *Hope youse are all having a blast. Didn't end up going to that art show.*

'Seriously?' Kaleb asked looking up from his phone. 'Why do you have to make everything about you? Quit playing the victim and being selfish.'

I scoffed. 'Get out of my house.'

Kaleb shuddered at the sternness of my voice. 'Tell me when you've stopped being a dramatic bitch. Don't fucking punish me when you're the one in the fucking wrong.' He grabbed his backpack from the foot of my bed, pausing on his way out. 'And *never* touch me like that again.'

I hit the timber floor with a thump. My eyes rained tears that splashed onto the soft black Lycra that covered my thighs.

'What the fuck?' I asked. Cocoa came bounding in, yapping away. 'I'm okay, honey. I promise.'

# 5
# November 2013

*17 Years Old*

A pile of reading material sat organised on my nightstand. Most of which had been collecting dust on my bookshelf for months. My school uniform was in the wash for the second last time and would be ready for graduation on Friday night.

'Kenz?' mum asked as she walked into my room.

'Hmm,' I responded as I got comfortable on my bed, my back propped up by pillows against the wall.

'Please don't spend all day there. Go out and celebrate! It's your last week as a high school student, my love,' she said.

'I won't. Besides, my friends are busy, and I don't have my Ps yet to go shopping anyway.'

'See if someone else is available then.'

'I'm fully aware, Mum. I just want to enjoy my first Monday as a free woman.'

'Amen to that!' my mum laughed. 'Alright, sweetie, enjoy. Your brother should be home by half past three. Pull something out for dinner.'

'Shall do, love you.'

'Love you too.'

'Oh, sorry, forgot my coffee. Can you grab it off my desk, please?'

'Sure thing,' mum laughed again, passing me my large blue marbled pattern mug. She exited my room, leaving me to set up season five of *Criminal Minds*.

'Coffee has never tasted so good,' I said to myself.

It was the perfect start to my last week as a high school student. I could forget about my shitty grades because of my shitty teachers. But something loomed in the back of my mind. It was almost too perfect. My life hadn't been this ideal since the days of Mrs McConnell.

Coffee was almost completely gone. The episodes passed one by one, and my thoughts continued to nag in the back of my mind.

*Will I ever be happy?*

My mind wouldn't quieten. Not even the dulcet looks and voice of Dr Spencer Reid could stop them. I was in trouble.

Trying my luck with a book wasn't working either.

'UGH!' I exclaimed slamming the book closed, swapping it for social media.

A doomscroll was the only thing that could numb the pain. Instead, it added to it today. A plethora of photos, and videos of my entire friend group down on Hamilton Island blinded me.

'That's like a five-hour plane ride with a bloody layover in freaking Brisbane! What the fuck?!'

The next episode of *Criminal Minds* played automatically in the background, but I didn't care. The overwhelming burst of emotion that engulfed me was all-consuming. I couldn't think clearly. All that I could do was look at the little Post-it that Mum had blue-tacked onto my mirror three years ago.

*I am smart.*

*I am beautiful.*

*I can do anything.*

'Words of shitty affirmation,' I muttered. 'More like, "*I'm an outcast. I am average. I can't do anything*". I stayed at that school for what? An awful education and a great bunch of friends.'

The fact that they posted as if I would not see it made my blood boil.

All of them flaunted their wealth. We all went to private school together, so we knew our folks were rich. While they drove around in European or brand-new cars. I drove around in a second-hand 2004 Hyundai Getz that I adored to no end, even though I couldn't drive it alone yet. It was pedal to the metal for me, zipping around like a Formula One driver.

Not that my friends weren't humble. Though they posted about their lavish holidays in Paris, cruises, you name it. While we went on affordable camping holidays in tents. Just because we didn't go on extravagant holidays didn't mean we didn't have fun.

I was a little jealous. While I appreciated dad was in demand at work, and getting holidays was a luxury for him, he wouldn't say no if we kids wanted to go away on a trip with our friends. He'd gladly pay for our airfare, cut of accommodation, and whatever else we needed.

Dad wanted us to have fun, be safe, and live our lives. That was what it should have been like for a teenager. In fact, my parents opted to not only be the two responsible adults looking after the seven teenagers on their trip to Port Douglas for Schoolies but also paid a large sum towards the accommodation.

Instead, here I sat, watching post after post of all my friends having the time of their lives. Celebrating graduation in the crystal blue waters of Catseye Beach. It was a slap to the face.

'Why the hell did you listen to me!' I screamed to no one. 'Why did you let me stay in the hellhole?'

My parents wanted to pull me out, but I claimed I had friends, and wanted to stay. Without the full picture, they listened to me, a child. A child who was getting bullied in a school that wasn't doing their due diligence in protecting me.

I couldn't blame my parents, I could only blame the school. They had on record, with the school counsellor, how depressed I was. I was a high-risk child and yet they kept me in the same class as my bullies and abusers and never told my parents I was suicidal.

*"But I found my friendship group Mum,"* I had announced to her.

I realised now that I hadn't. Maybe I never did. Perhaps I was forced into socialisation because teachers enforced the social decorum. After all, "a child should not eat alone or be in isolation".

*What bullshit.*

I texted the chat, not really expecting a response. A couple of members read my messages and opted not to say a damn word. They had been planning the trip for a while. Nobody planned a five-hour plane ride over a weekend for what I assumed to be a couple of days' holiday.

I couldn't bring myself to ask the all-important burning question: "Do you hate me?" It was a question I already knew the answer to.

**Jack:** *Hey Kenz, I didn't realise that you weren't invited. Hope there are no hard feelings. Miss you.*

I rolled my eyes, not bothering to respond. 'How can you even say that you miss me when you've known since you all showed up at the airport that I wasn't there? In fact, there's probably a whole other fucking group chat!'

I couldn't stop the tears from falling.

Gunshots echoed in the background from *Criminal Minds* still playing.

'UGH!'

I slammed my laptop closed. My finger latched onto the closed pillow and pegged it only for it to collide with the mirrored sliding door to my wardrobe. The sound of its rhythmic pulse made my hair stand tall as I watched the mirror shake.

# 6

# February 2018

*21 Years Old*

I never realised how uncomfortable I felt being in the home — if you could even call it that. It was always obscenely cold. Not a photograph or artwork in sight. Blinds were almost always closed or opened just enough to let in a little light. There wasn't anything that made it homely except for the seven throw blankets on the sofa in the living room.

There was no evidence that he lived with his mother, aside from the glimpses of her room on the off chance her door was ajar. Other than that, nothing. I found it odd how Kaleb would often dodge the question whenever I asked about his mum, but I never pushed. Over the three years I'd been with him I had only seen his mother a few times.

Kaleb hung around me like a bad smell. It made it difficult to navigate around his small bedroom as I tried to get ready to head out.

'I thought I said that you couldn't go out?' he said as he followed me into his bedroom.

'I'm going out with a classmate to discuss an assignment, what's wrong with that again?' My sass was thick.

His need for control was tiresome, like his nit-picking of my clothes. He practically threw a tantrum over having to buy me a whole new wardrobe a couple of days ago.

'You are not to hang out with a guy by yourself!'

I composed myself as I changed from my daily casual wear to a nice dress and knee-high leather boots. As much as I wanted to throw my stuff on the ground in a huff, I scrunched them into my backpack.

*I won't be coming back tonight.*

'First of all, what makes you think it's a guy?' I asked. 'And second of all, are you saying that I'm untrustworthy? Is that it?'

The only sound that emitted from Kaleb's mouth was his stammering.

'Right, well while you ponder over my questions, I'm leaving.' He followed me out to the front door, but just as I was about to pull it open, I turned back and said, 'By the way, Aster's a girl. I know you stalk my Instagram followers, so feel free to look her up and then apologise to me. I'll be waiting.'

I quickly hurried to my car, unsettled by his change in behaviour. I wouldn't put it past him to chase me. My seat belt remained off, and doors locked until I was up the road where he couldn't catch me. Thankfully, I had never mentioned where I was going.

*Why does he feel like he can suddenly control me?*

My mental health was taking a deeper dive, suddenly feeling sick and wishing I was dead.

*Maybe I don't know him as well as I thought I did.*

Cold Chisel's *Khe Sahn* played softly in the background. The playlist I had going didn't fit my mood. I needed something with a bit more punch, like something from Bring Me the Horizon or Black Veil Brides.

I had no one to talk to about Kaleb and how he made me feel. My mind was running in overdrive, telling me he was abusing me, but I couldn't see it. It was just the stress of his job. He was in the running for a promotion that would come in time for his graduation. Long hours, and a lot more responsibility.

*Do I stay? Do I go?*

'Fuck,' I muttered as I drove past the entrance to the bar.

I circled back around the block and pulled into the driveway just in time to score a parking spot right by the entrance. The visor snapped into place as I pulled it down, checking myself over before I made my way into the building.

As always, I tried not to focus on my awkwardness when I walked in looking for where Aster said she was. "Tucked away in the corner behind the entrance" her text had read.

Aster wanted to meet at the Esplanade bar. It was buzzing with university students and young corporate workers.

I rounded the entrance to the left and sure enough spotted her bright fire-engine-red hair in the corner with two pints of beer.

We weren't necessarily close, we had done a few group assignments together. Though she was a year behind me, she was picking up a few subjects over the summer break to get ahead, just like I had. Aster and I bonded over the handling of a number of lazy group participants with our professionality.

'Are we sure that this is the best thing?' I asked, as I approached her in the quietest spot in the pub. 'Drinking and studying?'

I sat down beside her.

'Oh yeah, I've been doing quite well. Come here once a week and get a whole lot done,' she replied.

'Well, whatever works, I'm not to judge.' I laughed.

'Oh here, got you non-alcoholic ginger beer, as I know you're not a beer drinker.' She moved my pint closer to me, to give herself more room for her laptop. 'Okay, here.'

I took a long swig as I read through. She was right. Even if she was doing the assessments under the influence, what I was reading was near perfection. The creamy sound of the keyboard got lost in the loud chatter and music in the pub.

'So?' she asked.

'Make those changes, and I'd say it's at least worthy of a 90%,' I replied showing her the short list of comments on her document.

'Yay!'

I smiled weakly.

'You okay?' she asked, putting her laptop away. 'You seem even more flat than usual.'

'I'm considering dropping out,' I said holding the pint of ginger beer in front of my mouth.

'But you have one placement left.'

'Yeah, but I think this is for the best. I'm no longer enjoying it.'

'Why?'

'I don't know … I'd rather just—' I caught myself before I said what Kaleb had been wanting me to say for ages. I didn't really want that life, did I? Nursing was what I wanted to do. Right? I wanted to help people.

'Is everything okay?'

'Sorry,' I said, leaving my drink half-finished and headed for my car.

Everything was now up in the air. I wasn't sure what I was even doing at this stage. The Clash had the perfect song for the occasion: *Should I Stay, or Should I Go?* It was now painfully obvious that Kaleb, much to my dismay, was in my head.

# 7

# February 2018

*21 Years Old*

Kaleb had just gotten back to his place as I was about to leave. Aster had been pestering me since I walked out on her the other day. I eventually caved. It was the perfect excuse to get a break from Kaleb for an hour.

I made my way towards him and the exit. Before I could even kiss him, or utter a word, he grabbed my bicep tightly, like a blood pressure cuff going off, only his grip was stronger. My bicep ached and a tingling sensation ran down my arm. 'Where do you think you're going?'

'I'm going out with Aster,' I replied. 'Can you let go?'

His fist didn't budge. 'That boy again? Seriously? You know I forbid it.'

'Once again, I know you stalk my Instagram account, so it'll be easy to spot the only Aster in my friends list.'

'Boy, girl, whatever. I'm coming with you.'

I stepped forward, hoping to shake his grip. He moved with me, blocking the exit, but I ducked and made a dash to my vehicle.

*What is his deal?*

Once again, I locked the doors and forgot about my seat belt until I was a safe enough distance away.

The cloudless sky made way for the beaming sun to shine its light on what should have been a glorious day. Except a shadow covered me that I couldn't shake. Kaleb was wearing me down bit by bit.

I thought about our argument over my final placement.

He wanted me to cancel, but it wasn't an option. It was far too late and posed as the world's stupidest idea when I was so close to graduation. However, choosing to not become a nurse after graduating was a more solid choice, giving me time to figure out what I wanted to do.

As I drove slowly along the esplanade, I saw Aster's bright red hair right next to a great parking spot in the shade. She started to walk towards my car, takeaway mugs in hand.

'Hey, hey!' she called. 'Got us a takeaway. Figured we should embrace the gorgeous day rather than spend it in a café.'

'It's like you can read my mind,' I chuckled.

She handed me my large mocha, and I followed her to a shaded park bench along the esplanade.

Trees danced in the breeze, and the seagulls squawked like no tomorrow. There was nothing better than the smell of the salty air. Quite the change from the smell of sugar cane and compost at Kaleb's, in Redlynch.

'Don't run away on me again, but I am very concerned about you,' Aster said.

'Wow, you really are blunt,' I replied.

'It's just, you're skinny. Dangerously skinny. You and I both know that you'll be on a nasal gastric tube in no time.'

That hit me like a truck. Nobody had said anything to me, but that was Aster. She wasn't known to sugar-coat things.

'You're right.' There was no debate needed. I dropped two sizes from an eight to a four. I wasn't on placements long enough to fully get into a size six because the minute I got back, my weight dropped.

'Honey, talk to me. We're friends, right?'

I chuckled. 'We barely know each other, Aster. We've done a couple of group assignments together.'

'Do you have *any* friends?'

'Sort of. I have a study group, but we don't talk about boys or hobbies or anything like that, really.'

'Then are they *really* your friends?'

My shoulders hunched forward, and I stared out to the ocean. 'No, I guess you're right.'

'If you're looking for more substance before you dump your Kaleb issues. Then ... Let me think.' Aster took a large sip of her iced matcha latte, before continuing. 'Oh, I got it. I'm a crocheter, huge concert buff so you'll see me in Brisbane several times a year, and I'm obsessed with *Criminal Minds*.'

'I love *Criminal Minds* too! I'm rewatching it for what feels like the twentieth time. Preparing for the next season.' I took a quick sip of my mocha, letting the hot caffeinated chocolate concoction slide down my throat. 'I sew. Made this outfit myself.' Gesturing to my sage-coloured spaghetti strapped, midi dress. 'I love crime and horror books. Also, I secretly dance to old *Disney Channel*, nineties and early 2000s songs.'

'Oh my God! That's the best! Should have a dance party, just us two,' Aster laughed.

'Definitely,' I giggled. 'Great way to de-stress, I swear.'

'See? Instant besties.'

'Alright, alright. That we are.' She scooted towards me slightly. 'I don't know, he's giving me weird vibes man. Like he just ... He won't touch me or even look at me unless it's because he's bored or he wants ... It.'

As we continued to talk, it became clear it was possible that Kaleb had given up. Maybe he was feeling threatened. I was at a stage in my studies that he wouldn't be reaching for another year and a half. It had to be a monetary or status issue for him.

Given his shift in behaviour, I could only assume he thought I would be more inclined to break up with him for a doctor or fellow nurse. It was almost like he didn't know me at all. No matter how much I tried to show him I loved him, I still felt a pullback.

'I just feel like I'm going crazy.' I placed my head in my hands. 'He—I will raise the fact that he doesn't put in effort, cancels planned dates or whatever. But then he'll turn around a buy me a gift, or he'll take me out for a weekend or a day trip. He'll make it romantic. I just—'

'It sounds like you're in a cycle,' Aster said.

'Cycle?' I asked.

She didn't elaborate. 'If I were you, next time he tries to love-bomb you, don't accept, no matter how good the gift is.'

Her logic was reasonable. I was in a pattern.

'Is it abusive?' she asked, avoiding my gaze.

'Oh, uh. I'm not sure,' I replied. 'It isn't physical.'

'Doesn't have to be, can be emotional, psychological, financial, or verbal.'

*Right.*

I did learn that during my placement in the psychiatric ward. Guess those on the outside can see the signs that we can't.

'I can almost hear your brain whirring around. Is he? 'cause, as your new best friend, I am telling you to leave him.'

'I-I don't know.'

'I'm here for you if you need to talk,' Aster said.

'Same here.'

I chugged the last quarter of my now lukewarm mocha, looking out at the crystal-clear water. We sat in silence for a moment, taking in the ocean air and view. Joggers ran by for their crazy midday run. How people did that in the extreme humidity and heat was insane.

'Should come with me to my group's game night. It's a night where we don't study and play games to relax,' Aster said.

'Sounds fabulous. When is it?' I asked.

'Tomorrow night.'

'I'm in.'

# 8
# February 2018

*21 Years Old*

Aster wasn't kidding when she said that her place was small. It could still somehow house the twelve nursing students in her cohort for game nights.

'Would you like another gin and soda?' One of Aster's male peers, Greggory, asked me.

'Oh, no thanks, I gotta drive home,' I replied. 'But if you're getting drinks, then just a soda with lime, please.'

'No problem,' he laughed, and weaved through a large group of people.

They were definitely a lot closer than my cohort of twenty which felt more like a class full of high schoolers with a clique-like mentality. This was far from that. It was almost like a family – a breath of fresh air.

Kaleb had invited himself and opted to sit in a dark corner. I could feel his gaze burning holes into the back of my skull as I laughed at a joke that one of Aster's friends, Melody, said. But he also paid no attention to me.

When I got up to go to the bathroom earlier, I watched as he stared at Greggory. He wasn't my type, obvious gym buff with more gel in his hair that he'd admit. Nice enough bloke, but Kaleb had nothing to worry about.

'You okay?' Aster asked.

'No,' I replied. 'Is he still ...'

Aster turned her head slightly.

'Yes,' she replied.

I let out a shaky breath before saying that I'll play the winner.

*Just need to pretend that everything is fine.*

A pair of hands gripped my shoulders tightly. Shivers ran down my spine quickly and I looked up at the person.

'You ready —' Kaleb started as he bent down to my ear.

'Should join us,' Aster cut in.

'Alright.' He squeezed my shoulders sharply, letting his long fingernails cut into the skin as he gave Aster a softened look. My head snapped towards him, unsure of what to make of this situation. Part of me was filled with warmth and desire, but the other part couldn't help but feel like he had ulterior motives.

'What are you doing?' I asked her as Kaleb walked around the couch.

'You'll see,' she replied.

I felt the cushions dip and the warmth and pressure of a hand and thigh on mine. Butterflies circulated in my stomach as Kaleb rubbed my leg while he waited for a controller.

'You're so going down, Kaleb,' Aster announced, her words slurring.

'In your dreams, Aster,' he replied with a laugh.

The butterflies turned into a stampeding herd of elephants, making me forget why I feared him. His laugh was music to my ears and the next thing I knew I was back, daydreaming of a marriage with kids and a house. Maybe he was returning to normal.

'Yes!' Kaleb screamed as he passed, right at the last minute, taking first position.

'Dammit!' Aster exclaimed.

A genuine laugh escaped from his lips that I hadn't heard in quite some time. It took everything in me not to move a single muscle.

'We should probably go,' Kaleb said. 'It's getting late, and we've got quite a walk to the car.'

'Sure thing,' Aster said.

'Thanks for the invite, was a blast,' I said as I slid off the couch.

'No problem should come next week,' Aster replied.

'Count me in,' I laughed as I followed her and Kaleb to the door.

Kaleb made his way down the steps, while I hung back.

'That's one sleazebag you got there,' she said to me. 'He was burring holes into every guy that looked your way from the shadows, all the while checking out a few of the girls. Then he's rubbing your shoulders and agreeing to a game with me? Confusion. It was almost like he wasn't aware I was watching. He couldn't let you out of his sight, but at the same time couldn't stand any of the guys near you. He's very insecure.'

'Is that why you asked him to play?' I asked.

'McKenna! Hurry up!' Kaleb called.

'Yes, just to see ...' She looked past me and down the spiral staircase. 'Any problems hon, call me,' the concern thick in her voice. 'Better go to him.'

I nodded and flew down the stairs, pushing the door open and embraced the cool air. Kaleb immediately wrapped a comforting hand around my back as he led us back towards my vehicle. Trees rustled, the waves crashed gently into the shore, and the sound of cats fighting in the distance.

We strolled slowly along the esplanade in a blissful silence. It felt like I was back in the early stages of dating him where we walked hand in hand, laughing and giggling. We would embrace the coolness of the air and lean into each other for slight warmth.

'Should do this more often, aye?' Kaleb said.

'Was thinking the same thing,' I replied with a smile.

'Wanna sit on a bench like old times before we go back to yours?'

I smiled and led him to the closest park bench on the route, facing the beach.

'Wish the lights were closer to us so we could see the water,' Kaleb said.

'Yeah,' I replied. 'Oh well, at least we can hear it.'

'True,' he replied, wrapping his arm around my shoulders, bringing me closer to him. 'They seemed lovely.'

'Yeah, they did.'

In the early days, after we'd hang out with my friends at a bar, the two of us would head down to the water and just chill. Listening to the waves upon the shore while we made out. It's hard to believe that it was only three years ago since those days, now we barely do any of it.

'Ready to continue on the walk?'

I craned my neck to look at him. 'Bored already?'

'Oh, of course not. It's late McKenna.'

It was just after nine o'clock, according to his watch. He has stayed up all night before playing video games.

I nodded sadly against his chest, wishing he'd at least kiss me before we left. Or maybe that was something only teenagers did. Perhaps I had read one too many fictional romance stories. Then there was another alternative, maybe he had changed in more ways than one.

'You okay?' he asked.

'Yeah, just um, thought you would've kissed me.'

Kaleb didn't reply, instead, dropped my hand from his and started to pick up the pace.

**Aster:** *You'd tell me if you're safe yeah? I'm still surprised Kaleb joined in, he was burning holes into the backs of everyone's heads* *all night. He looked at you like a piece of meat, and still checked out every girl ... sleazy. Very sleazy.*

**Me:** *Of course. I don't know, his laugh was genuine. We cuddled on the park bench like old times.*

'You're on your phone? Come on McKenna!' Kaleb yelled.

'Well, you're kilometres ahead, and Mum texted asking where I am. It *is* late out, and you decided to come at the last minute that I forgot to tell her.'

Kaleb seemed to have bought it and continued to walk three steps ahead of me, while I struggled to keep up.

# 9

# October 2006

*10 Years Old*

Bec, Harriet, and I sat at our usual table under the shade of an old Golden Penda tree.

'We're going to the small oval to play sticks again,' Bec announced.

'I can't today. I've got touch footy training on the main oval,' I replied.

Bec's face dropped as the words left my mouth. She loved going to the small oval to play sticks or some other game, like red rover. I rarely got a choice, and when I did, I'd always opt to play a game of soccer or basketball. That, or I was playing touch football with the boys and a couple of girls.

'You do this every week. You are playing with us, and that's final,' Bec said.

Harriet just sat there quietly, fearing that if she spoke up she'd be sitting out once again.

That was the difference between us. I still got to play, but I'd be emotionally blackmailed or physically forced to do so. Meanwhile, Harriet was kicked out. No matter how hard I tried to stop it, Bec would drag me back, pulling me by the arm or hair.

'If I miss out, I'm benched for the semi-finals!'

'*I'll be benched*,' Bec mocked. 'We don't care, play or you'll end up with broken ribs.' She smirked. 'You'll get in trouble with Mr Truches.'

Mr Truches was a scary Principal, he reminded me of Mr Gomez Addams. He was softly spoken, but get on the wrong side of him, and there'd be hell to pay. It was Bec was who I was truly scared of.

My hands shook as I closed up my half-eaten food, suddenly no longer hungry. They knew how to behave to ensure that they weren't the ones who got in trouble.

The teachers' whistles echoed through the school, signalling that us children could play. Harriet and Bec headed towards the bathrooms. Despite their threats, I seized the opportunity and grabbed my hat and bolted.

There was not a care in the world for the "no running on concrete" rule. This was my only chance at freedom. I had commitments.

*Sayonara.*

I embraced the rushing wind through my hair. Its whistle was music to my ears. I was a sprinter and a damn good one. If they tried to catch me, I'd be gone before they could even drag me away.

By the time I got down to the oval, Mr Elliott had finished setting up a makeshift football field.

'Right, warm up, then we'll mix teams,' Mr Elliott said.

'Time to channel my rage,' I muttered.

'Kenna, you gotta join us!' Bella called just as I finished stretching my quads.

It felt great not to be the last picked for something, it made me feel like I had other friends besides Bec's toxic nature.

'Mind if I sub first then?' I asked.

'Not at all,' Bella replied.

As the game started, it quickly dawned on me I shouldn't have let myself be a sub. I felt heavy, and my blood ran cold.

*How could I be the sub when this would've been the first place where Bec would look?*

'McKenna!' Bec called.

And sure enough, my thoughts were right, as always.

The hair on my nape stood tall. Goosebumps lined my arms and legs. My heart pounded against my chest, and the blood drained from my face. I couldn't deal with this, not now, not ever. I didn't think I could ever leave her. No matter how far I went, Bec was in my head, and I kept going back. She was doing all the right things to keep me "happy".

'Y-y-yes?' I turned to face Bec.

The tall, muscular girl towered over me.

*If she wants to make me feel small, she isn't getting the joy.*

'I thought we told you that we're playing sticks. Come now!'

Without thinking, I yelled out to Colby and ran onto the field, subbing in for him. Bec wouldn't be stupid enough to follow me out onto the field and pull me away.

My eyes were focused on the ball. As soon as the dummy half touched it, I pounced off the defending line, heading straight for the ball in play. I grabbed it mid-flight and sprinted down the field. The terrasphere cones outlining the try-line were nearing. Rachel was gaining, and I pushed harder, driving my feet right into the grass like my life depended on it.

I dove into the try-zone, scoring the first and only point for the training session.

'Yes!' Tristan called from the other end of the field. 'Let's go!' I ran to the sub-box while both teams made their way to the mid-line for the next set. I smiled, proud of my first-ever try being scored by an epic intercept.

But my celebration was cut short as I felt my right arm being tugged backwards.

I stumbled and fell right onto the side of the concrete bleachers. Air escaped from my mouth as a sharp pain from my right shoulder blade to my diaphragm made itself known. Tears pricked my eyes as I continued to be dragged.

My chest heaved, trying to get as much oxygen as I could, but it hurt to do so. My right shoulder was mere seconds from being yanked right out of its socket.

'Rebecca. Please?' I cried.

'No,' she said.

Mr Elliott didn't act. The two teachers on duty made eye contact with me, but they continued to laugh and chat with a group of students.

Betrayal.

*How could teachers look at the state I am in and neglect their duties?*

'Please, please, don't tell Mr Neu,' I pleaded.

It was an irrational fear, but I knew Bec could easily concoct a story. Though Mr Neu could smell bullshit a kilometre away, he still never reprimanded Bec.

She continued to drag me back up to the eating area. I felt the girl flinch as the bell echoed through the air.

'Ugh! See what you've done?' Bec yelled. 'Wasted a whole lunchtime!'

I didn't care about missing out on playing with them. I did care about my lack of ability to breathe, and the pain and tingling feeling down my right arm. I stopped pleading for safety, focusing on ensuring my watering eyes did not give us away to passersby.

Bec refused to let me go, even when we waited in line to return to class. The grip was now on my bicep and judging by the sheer pressure Bec had, I was scared it would bruise.

'McKenna,' Mr Neu asked. 'You okay?'

I nodded, not wanting my voice to betray me.

'Rebecca, I suggest you remove your grip from Miss Carrington and hang back for a moment,' Mr Neu said.

The pressure released from my arm lessened. And I followed my classmates into the building.

# 10

# March 2018

*22 Years Old*

It was cold in the Adelaide Airport, my arms crossed over my chest in an attempt to keep myself warm.

*I should have listened to Mum.*

That was my naivety, thinking it'd be an ideal temperature in the airport and that the sun would be delightful.

'McKenna?' I heard my name called from the other side of the conveyor belt.

'Aster?' I muttered, as I spotted her fire-red hair.

Like a game of Temple Run, I dodged and weaved my way over with a backpack full of what may as well have been bricks. That was on me for thinking it was wise to take a binder instead of just using my iPad for my notes.

As I neared closer to her, she had switched her signature mid-length black mesh skirt for a deep turquoise velvet skirt, tan knee-high boots and a matching tan turtleneck jumper. Her outfits were always something to admire. Aster was known to be a little outlandish with her outfits. She was often shopping for unique patterned clothes.

'You going to Calvary Central?' Aster asked.

'No, a public one on the northern side of the city, like Salisbury or Greenwith.'

'Damn, was hoping we'd get to have at least one placement together,' she pouted. 'You're staying in Mawson Lakes too?'

'No, I'm staying in Salisbury, so it's not that far. Just a suburb over.' I spotted my teal suitcase beginning its round on the conveyor belt. 'My bag's here. We'll talk soon. Maybe meet up for coffee or dinner?'

'Absolutely.'

I quickly made my way over and picked it up just in time before it popped back through the plastic strips. The click of the handle resonated in the air. Off I went alongside every businessperson heading to the waiting area for taxis.

'Seventy-five dollars?' I muttered.

Parking fees were looking good right about now. Maybe there was a point to pay for a rental car and parking fees and fuel.

As I quickly placed the eye-watering taxi, it arrived. It was a young man who looked like he was about my age, maybe slightly younger. Can't have had his open licence for more than a couple of years. As always, I texted my parents and Kaleb.

**Me:** *In a car*

**Kaleb:** *You don't need to tell me every time. Rideshares are safe!*

I wish I could believe him, but I may or may have not seen one too many *Criminal Minds* and *Bones* episodes which may have sparked a little paranoia. Coupled with the fact that I had trust issues. If I couldn't even trust my friends, why a stranger?

'Ya okay back there,' the young driver asked.

'Uh, yeah?' I replied.

*Am I?*

'That one of 'em permanen' necklaces?' He ran his fingers through his curly sandy blonde hair.

'Yeah,' I said, trying not to divulge too much information.

'You bough' i' for yourself, righ'? I can't help but wonder why the padlock charm.'

'No, my boyfriend.'

His eyes widened, showing more of the watercolour green eyes, before he frowned in disgust.

'Hon, are you safe? He isn't hurtin' you, is he? It's just a boyfriend getting a permanen' choker with a padlock ... I hope you're okay.'

Steam was surely coming out of my ears.

'What?' I remarked. 'What are — No. Please drop me off here.'

He pulled over to the side of the road. 'I'm sorry.'

As I exited and took my bags from the boot of his vehicle, I couldn't shake the perplexing feeling. Maybe the dude was right.

*What is the meaning, Kaleb? Why did you pick these specifically?*

I didn't understand Kaleb sometimes. One minute he was proud of my accomplishments. The next he was telling me that nursing wasn't a viable career choice. There was always something.

*Why do I continue to stay?*

Cars beeping snapped me out of autopilot, and I realised I had walked six hundred meters from where the taxi had dropped me off. According to maps, I wasn't that far from the hotel, about eight-hundred metres. It wouldn't take me long at all.

The wheels of my suitcase went over each crack in the concrete with a click, as I walked to a building to pause momentarily to call Aster. Almost immediately, she picked up.

'What's up? Everything okay?' she asked.

'Uh, no.' I replied. 'I had to get out of the taxi when he accused my boyfriend of putting a collar on me.'

'What coll — The necklace?!'

'Yeah.'

'Is everything okay? You wouldn't have let it bother you unless you thought — You agree, don't you?'

I breathed heavily into the microphone. I didn't want to believe it. Even she thought it was weird. The change in his behaviour and how I showed signs of surprise at the games night a week ago.

'Look, Kenz, you don't seem to enjoy being with him in the short time I've known you. When was the last time he swept you off your feet?'

'Uh, seven months?'

*Seven months seems too short since our last date. Maybe it's been longer?*

It seemed that all we did was fight. Kaleb still wanted to believe that he was right and that I was a dumb bitch who would be a stay-at-home wife. That wasn't what I wanted, though. I wanted to be a nurse, a doctor.

'Maybe it's time you thought about yourself,' Aster said. 'Seven months is a long time to go without a date. I say plan it as a surprise for him, as a "just-coz", and see how you feel. Or are you just going to end it?'

'I don't know. I'm working on a hunch, and this asshole driver opened my eyes to the fact that this bloke may have ulterior motives.' I came to a T-section, and I realised I was probably lost. I'd been walking north for about ten minutes. 'Hang on, let me just check Google Maps really quick.'

I took my phone off my ear. I was nearing the section where I needed to make a left turn.

'Alright, back,' I said. 'Got another ten-minute walk.'

'Yikes.'

'Eh, I needed this. The driver was out of line.'

'Yeah, but ...' Aster trailed off, and I raised an eyebrow, hoping she'd continue her thought. 'It is a little strange, hon. I didn't know that it was a gift from him.'

'Aster,' I warned. 'You met him once. You can't make that deductive conclusion. He has his good moments.'

'I'm sure he does.' There was a long pause from her end. 'Look, if you ever need to talk, I'm here.'

'Thanks, hon, shall keep that in mind.'

I ended the call after saying goodbye and rounded the final corner.

The hotel was in my sights now. It was a lot smaller than I thought and had the modern-looking exterior aesthetics.

My legs burned as I headed up the short flight of stairs, eager to get inside, get my room key and relax in front of the TV. Drown my thoughts out with a few episodes of one of my many comfort shows. Kaleb couldn't keep occupying every thought in my head. I couldn't keep up with the push and pull.

My hand went for the rose gold chain, playing with it between my fingers.

*Is this domestic violence? Is that what this is? Kaleb isn't violent with me.*

I didn't know myself anymore. I was so mentally exhausted that I was living my life zoned out, operating on autopilot. Yet I couldn't talk to my parents about it. It was downright embarrassing. A taxi driver noticed. That was just insane. I'd been wearing that choker for almost a year, and all anyone could say was how pretty it was.

It was a collar no doubt about it.

# 11

# March 2018

*22 Years Old*

The first day of placement was always the most nerve-wracking experience. You don't know anyone or what was fully required of you. It was always my least favourite day of any placement. However, that was also the beauty of it, I got to learn how the teams operated.

As I entered the staff room closest to the Ward that I was to work in, a middle-aged male nurse, dressed in hot pink scrubs, approached me.

'You must be McKenna.' he said, holding out his hand. The sleeves of his scrubs were tight around his biceps and the bags under his eyes made him appear older than he was. 'I'm Murray, one of the unit managers.'

*Show enthusiasm, but not too much.*

'You would be correct,' I replied. 'It's lovely to meet you. I read over the email, I'm in Ward 2D today.'

'Slight change of plan.' I was accustomed to changes around the nursing stations. In fact, I welcomed it. 'I've got you in the Ortho ward. Listed as 3A.' He led me out of the staff room and up a flight of stairs. 'I'm not sure if you're familiar with other hospitals, but our Wards are numbered by the floor, and the letter, well, best to check the corresponding information. You'll get the hang of it, once you move between sections.'

*Excellent, a new speciality.*

'You'll be with Caitlyn and Mary today. They'll look after you.'

'Thank you.'

As we moved throughout the hospital, I noted how small it was and yet it still bustled with staff, patients and visitors. The bright sterile hallways were filled with people standing around chatting or in beds and wheelchairs as they waited for the elevators and services.

'Caitlyn, this is McKenna,' Murray said to a middle-aged woman in light blue scrubs. 'The fourth-year student, I told you about.'

'Awesome. Thanks, Marz. I'll look after her,' she replied, and off he went. Caitlyn turned to look at me, her blonde hair tied back in a bun. 'So, you'll be all good by yourself then?'

'Yes. Once I know the station, where everything is, and your protocols, I'll be good.' I replied.

'Excellent,' she beamed. 'Right, well, pop your bag in one of the lockers and follow me, I'll show you around the ward.'

The metal clinked together as I shut my handbag and lunchbox into the small cube and followed her out to the nurse's station. It wasn't long before a patient pressed the buzzer, and Caitlyn sprung into action, with me hot on her tail.

The patient was a seventeen year old with a leg suspended slightly.

'Cait, my parents here yet?' he asked.

'Not yet, Benson, they should be here soon,' Caitlyn replied. 'Do you need anything? I might be able to smuggle an extra jelly cup for you.'

'No thanks. I'm alright.' The young boy turned his attention to me. 'Hi, I'm Benson, seventeen, had a bicycle accident that landed me here.'

I took a step back slightly when he mentioned his age. I hadn't seen a paediatric not in a Children's Ward before — though I knew it happened from time to time, mostly due to hospitals without a designated children's ward, a lack of beds or sometimes the doctor. From looking at the name on the white board upon entrance, Benson was under the care of one of the best orthopaedic surgeons in the hospital.

'Nice to meet you, Benson. I'm McKenna, a student nurse,' I replied. My peripherals glimpsed a small Formula One car. 'Formula One fan?'

'Oh, heck yeah!' he laughed. 'I'm a massive Ferrari and Mercedes fan.'

While I checked his vitals, Benson told me about how his dad took him to see the Melbourne Grand Prix when he was five and he fell in love instantly.

The paediatrics were always my favourite patients. They were super chatty once you got them on a favourite topic of theirs. Benson beamed as he talked about F1, despite the situation he had gotten himself into.

'I believe your parents are here, Benson,' Caitlyn said.

'About time,' he laughed. 'Thank you for speaking with me McKenna.'

'You're welcome Benson,' I said as I pumped a decent amount of hand sanitiser into my hand. As I exited, I rubbed the sharp ethanol scented substance over my hands.

'You were a natural in there,' Caitlyn said. 'How would you feel if I let you off by yourself?'

'I think I should be fine, just need you to sign off on meds still, so aside from that I'll be good,' I replied.

She nodded and led me back to the station and introduced me to their systems.

Being at "work" allowed me to focus on something other than Kaleb. He never got a single thought whilst I was on the clock, and rarely during my breaks — often too exhausted to even pull my phone and food out of their respective places. My focus needed to be on the patients, one slip and that could be a mistake that could take a patient's life. Health care was not an industry that took mistakes lightly. It was why I was so hypervigilant took the notion of "don't bring home problems to work" seriously, otherwise, I'd be a mess every day.

The university expelled a peer of mine over an error. Whilst she rectified it, the damage was already done. Nobody needed the full details, we know that if a patient is being taken back to theatre it's usually because of a complication that happens shortly after. In this instance, it was a few days after surgery, and the patient was in some form of shock — most likely septic, hypovolemic, or cardiogenic. Though, I did question the oversight they had. Was that supervisor also reprimanded for failing to provide guidance, especially to a second-year nursing student who should never have been left alone?

Since it was slow, I got a lot of things I needed to get done for the uni. As well as organise what I needed to be trained in and graded on by the end of the six weeks.

As I got permission to do so, I headed off to the office to read each patient's chart in the ward. Ensuring I was familiar with their case when they ring their bell. This was my favourite part of the placement, providing patient care when needed. If there was one thing I hated most about being a patient, it was when nurses didn't read my chart and prepare themselves. I was often decked out in orange for being a known fall risk after anaesthesia, and yet they didn't pay attention. Even when busy, one must have to have a keen eye for detail especially when you're caring for another person.

Just as I predicted, the bell rang for Mrs Helen Watson who was here for a hip replacement.

'Hello Helen,' I said as I entered, promptly squirting hand sanitiser into my palm. 'I'm McKenna, final year nursing student. How can I help you?'

Her facial muscles cringed as she tried to sit up to greet me. A drainage tube was lodged into her side taking care of any potential blood clots.

'I'm a little uncomfortable, lovie. I can't move without causing myself pain,' she said. 'Robert's gone to get himself a coffee. Otherwise he'd be here helping.'

'Not a problem, Helen. Do you have an ideal position that you want to be in?'

*What a stupid question.*

'Preferably one that takes some of the pressure off,' she tittered. 'And maybe some more pain meds if I'm allowed.'

'I'll check your chart once we get you into a better position.'

She had the replacement less than twenty-four hours ago, and the physiotherapist was coming around later today to start her mobility. Until then, I needed to mitigate her pain as best as I could. I adjusted the bed a little and popped a thin pillow behind her back, allowing her to relieve some of the pressure.

'How's that?' I asked Helen.

'Mmm, much better, thank you,' she said.

'No problem.' I pumped the hand sanitiser into my palm again. 'I'm going to review your chart and talk with the team about some meds for you.'

'Thanks, dear.'

I tucked the chart under my armpit and started to rub another squirt of sanitiser over my hands as I made my way back to the station.

'Caitlyn? Do you have a minute?' I asked.

'Absolutely.'

'Mrs Helen Watson, in 73. She is in pain, but I'm not sure on the med situation. I know she's had an opioid a few hours ago, can we give her paracetamol to tide her over?'

Caitlyn reviewed the chart. Her lips scrunched and moved side to side, pondering as she read. 'I'd hold off for now until the doctors come. Luke — Dr Holden — should be here in ten minutes with the physios. I'll note it in her chart though.'

'Sure, I'll let her know.'

I headed back down the hall to Helen's room. The elderly lady still frowned in her new position but was now reading.

'Helen?' I asked knocking upon my entrance, another pump of hand sanitiser ready to coat my hands.

'Ah, yes, dear, come in,' she said putting down her copy of *Wuthering Heights*.

'I've been advised against, however, Dr Holden should be here in the next few minutes with the physios to discuss treatment. We have some fast acting paracetamol on standby if we're given the all clear.'

Her mouth pulled into a tight line. 'Ah, that's okay, lovie. The pain's easing off anyway. Thank you.'

I smiled. 'You're very welcome. Buzz if you're still in pain and we'll see what else we can do for you.'

No other patients needed anything, so I hung around the nurses' station filling out charts and ensured that everything I was allowed to manage was stocked up. Taking the initiative was what I was taught throughout my degree. I would clean, and stock, like my life depended on it.

'Oh my goodness, it's so clean!' Caitlyn exclaimed as she walked out of Benson's room.

'I just did a bit of tidying, checked over your to-do list. Hope you don't mind.'

'Absolutely not! I've never had a student actually go to the trouble.'

# 12

# March 2018

*22 Years Old*

A few days later, after an hour of sitting around watching as doctors came and went, Caitlyn got a call.

'Have you ever dealt with coma patients?' she asked, holding the phone against her chest.

'Yeah, a little,' I replied.

'Would you be comfortable if I send you alone to the ICU for one patient?'

'Uh, yeah.' I hesitated. 'What do I have to do?'

She repeated my question to the person on the other end, before turning back to me, the phone back on her chest. 'Just like any regular patient, change sheets, dress wounds, that sort of thing.' Caitlyn took the phone back up to her ear before placing it back in the holder. 'They're a bit short staffed there. I was going to manage it with you, but if you're comfortable?'

*There's always a first time for everything, better now than when I'm officially a nurse.*

'Yeah, that's fine,' I replied.

Caitlyn nodded and asked me to follow her to the ICU, which was just across the hall.

An older woman, with platinum grey hair pulled back in a bright pink claw clip that matched her bright pink glasses, sat at the nurses station.

'Rubes, meet McKenna, she's a fourth year RN student, she'll be tending Mr Roberts,' Caitlyn said.

'Sounds great!' The older woman exclaimed. 'I'll show you to his room. By the way, my name is Ruby, but feel free to call me Rubes, everyone does.'

The room was dark, aside from the light emanating from the ventilator and the heart rate monitor. Both machines stood proudly, against the wall on either side of Tony's head.

'Meet Mr Tony Irvine,' she said. 'Twenty-seven-year-old male victim in a car versus motorcycle accident.'

The road rash went from his right arm to right leg. His dented crash helmet and cracked visor sat on the table under the window with a view of the hospital courtyard. His scraped clothes were left folded in a plastic bag beside the helmet. It was surprising to see that he was still alive, but to what extent, nobody could know until he woke up.

'Here's everything you will need. If you need me, I'll either be at the station, or in another room,' Rubes said, handing me the sheets, gown and dressings.

'Thank you,' I replied.

I tended to the catheter and wounds, when a tall male doctor with tanned skin and curly brown hair waltzed into the room. He looked no older than I was. For a second I thought he was an intern, until I saw the intern posse behind him.

*A Trainee? Resident? How is that possible? The undergraduate programs are like five or six years.*

I started to prep my space to tend to Tony's wounds. I double checked that Rubes had given me everything I needed, from saline, to gauze, to bandages, to the medications.

As I got set to tend to the wounds, I glanced up to see the doctor now standing merely a bed width from me. I could smell a strong woody cologne. hints of bergamot and cedar tingled my nostrils. As the man shifted, I caught a glimpse of his name, "Dr Dylan Atwood", embroidered in white on his teal-coloured scrubs. I tried to remember Kaleb's scent, his favourite cologne Dior Sauvage, but this was, slightly more mature.

*What am I doing? Stop it.*

'How do you check the neurovascular status of the limb?' Dr Atwood asked the group of interns.

*He's British? Oh dear. McKenna, focus.*

He looked twenty-five, maybe twenty-six, there was no way that he could be a resident or registrar in Ortho. They required a three-year post-graduate stint before they could even apply. Each specialty had their own requirements before you could apply. Some had just the internship, others required a little more training. Even then they only offered places to a handful of trainees. This one must have friends in high places, or he is exceptional at what he does if he is only in his mid-twenties.

*How did he swing a first-year traineeship in ortho?*

Yet, the group looked at him like deer in headlights.

The silence was deafening.

*Well isn't this comforting.*

The sheets rustled as I continued to look after Tony. I gazed up, and Doctor Atwood was eying me as I worked, smirking towards me with endearment.

*Come on, this is fundamental physiology 101.*

As I got up to grab more gauze, I watched as Dr Atwood was about to answer for them.

Something in me ignited and I piped up, 'You check for the pulse, capillary fill, temperature, and colour.' He stared at me, and my mouth went dry, but I continued. 'If the patient wasn't in a coma, you also ask the patient if they can feel the sensations. You should also do a small basic motor function. Wiggling their toes, for example.'

'Nurse practitioner?' Dr Atwood asked, I shook my head.

*Good lord, do I look that old?*

'RN?'

'Close,' I replied. 'I'm a fourth-year nursing student. This is my last placement.'

The doctor's eyes widened before turning to his interns. 'I suggest the lot of you brush up on your knowledge. You have a lot to learn from soon-to-be RN ...'

'Carrington,' I filled in for him. 'McKenna Carrington.'

He smirked at me, my heart pounded heavily in my chest causing vibrations to shake my ribs.

'Befriend the nursing staff if you feel like you aren't going to succeed in your time here in ortho. They know a lot more than you think.' The group of interns raced out of the room, leaving Dr Atwood to sigh in anger and partial relief. He covered his mouth but I could still hear him mutter, '*Lord help me.*'

'They don't seem to listen to you,' I said, placing the rubbish in the bin.

'No, they don't,' he replied, running a hand through his curly chestnut brown hair.

'May I offer some advice?' I went back to Tony, tending to the remaining wounds.

'Yes.' Dr Atwood nodded. 'Please, absolutely.'

'I've been on many placements, met a lot of doctors,' I replied and stopped fussing with the gauze. 'As much as I hate being singled out, there is a benefit. It prompts competition, so try picking someone out instead of waiting like you did before. If they don't answer, open up to the group. If they still don't get it, tell them the answer but prompt the studying, and try again with the next patient.'

'Good point.' He smiled. 'You'd make a good doctor. You have the leadership and knowledge bank that put those interns, and me, to shame.'

'I put *you* to shame?'

'Well you did offer advice to better my teaching technique.'

'Oh my god, I'm —'

'No, no, it's perfectly fine. Actually, it was fantastic advice. I don't get a lot of help on my teaching skills, so advice is always welcomed.' He made a turn to leave but doubled back to face me, leaning against the door frame. 'Seriously, you should consider medical school.'

He left with a wink, leaving me watching myself standing in the light of the machines.

My job isn't to know why the patient isn't awake after his surgery, but I want it to be. It's why I still sat the UMAT every year — the masochist in me did it for fun knowing that I'd never get past 2100.

Maybe it was time I ditched the whole "woe is me" attitude. I hadn't even checked my GAMSAT score from last September's sitting. The practice exams hadn't been going well, neither had my first sitting in March. I automatically assumed it was another poor attempt.

'Fuck,' I muttered.

My heart started beating faster. I forgot where I got up to regarding Tony.

*What am I doing? I should go for it. I need to go for it. I'll apply when I get to the apartment, the cut-off would be in a few days! Shit! Shit! Shit!*

'You okay McKenna?' Rubes asked, coming into the room.

My back snapped straight, and I quickly turned to face her. 'Huh?' I responded. 'Oh, uh, yeah, sorry, just finishing up now.'

'You sure?' I nodded, but Rubes stayed, helping me clean up the room. 'Did Dr Atwood say something to you?'

'Oh, no,' I replied.

*Just that he has me rethinking my career plans.*

There wasn't anything I needed more than to warm up in my hotel room after that weird day. I changed into my matching grey cotton loungewear set, my gaze set upon the cream-coloured popcorn ceiling as I collapsed onto the bed. I tried to ascertain what I was feeling, but no words could form a coherent sentence. Doctor Atwood made a good judgement call, but whether or not he was actually right, was another story. He didn't know me, all I did was answer one question and gave him one piece of advice. Kaleb, on the other hand, knew me.

My phone buzzed beside me and lit up with Kaleb's face.

'Hey, hon,' I said.

'Hey.' He sounded cheerier than usual. 'How was placement?'

'Yeah, great day. Got to look after an ICU patient on my own. How was your day?'

'That's amazing.' There wasn't any sign of feigning in his voice. 'Yeah my day was alright. Same old shit, different day. So tell me more about this day of yours.'

I sat up straight, unsure if I should 'Oh Kaleb it was fan-fuck-ing-tastic! Motorcycle accident, poor bloke. But being trustworthy enough to go between departments was unbelievable. They're short staffed there.'

I prattled on.

'Any nice doctors at this one?' he asked.

'Yeah, actually, Doctor Atwood,' I replied. Sure there were a few toxic staff, but the hospital as a whole was great. Everyone worked as a team, departments chatted between each other. Over the course of my eight placements, this was by far my favourite, topping the medical imaging clinic earlier in my degree.

*Careful now. You know how Kaleb is with other men.*

'Said I have the teaching ability and knowledge bank that'd make me a pretty good doctor.'

'Oh wow, should go for it.' he replied.

Something in me stopped working and I choked on my own saliva.

*Is he being serious right now?*

'Oh—'

'I know how much you want to go to Griffith for med school. You should go for it.'

'Yeah?' My mouth pulled into a wide smile, cheeks aching, but I couldn't stop beaming. 'Alright. I'll um, I'll have a think about it.'

'I gotta go, big presentation tomorrow. Was a last-minute thing ...'

'Okay, best of luck.' I paused before adding, 'I love you.'

'Love you too, Kenzie' He never said it back, but this time he did.

Kaleb hung up, leaving me staring at a painting of the Adelaide's cityscape.

'What just happened?' I asked it.

My backpack was tossed haphazardly on the desk in the hallway. As I pulled my laptop out, it scraped along the deep purple nylon fabric of my backpack like nails on a chalkboard. I sat down on the uncomfortable wooden chair, gnawing on my fingernails as I pulled up my September GAMSAT results.

'I can't look.' The internet in the hotel was slow. It was working in my favour, giving me time to shove my premade chicken risotto into the microwave while I waited for the screen to load.

With the ding of the microwave I pulled out the glass container, mixed the risotto around before placing it back in. I walked the five steps to the desk slowly.

The screen still loading.

A second ding from the microwave took my attention as did the smell of the now piping hot risotto.

'Damn, I'm a good cook,' I muttered as I swallowed a mouthful. The screen had loaded and right before my eyes was an overall competitive score of sixty-nine. Seventy in each section. 'Fuck! I can apply for medicine.'

**Me:** *I can apply to medicine, Kaleb!*

**Kaleb:** *Knew you could do it. Congrats babe*

# 13

# August 2014

*18 Years Old*

My whole body shook as I opened my UMAT results. The chance of poor score was high, and blame could only be on me.

My fingers shook violently as I clicked on the email.

2000

'That's alright, a fine attempt, nonetheless,' I muttered. The undergrad pathway to med was ruthless and it was only my first time. 'Not as good as a 2500 though. Maybe it was the pressure, like it is all the time. Maybe I'm just —' I held my head in my hands. My vision became a windshield in a rainstorm. No matter how much of an overachiever I was, I scraped through every exam in high school, narrowly passing. 'Oh well, I didn't have the OP, anyway.'

Except it was my GPA that mattered, and I had a straight run of high distinctions that gave me a solid "7.0", so there went the pressure theory.

*Maybe there's hope after all?*

'You okay?' Mum asked.

'Just failed the UMAT,' I replied sadly. 'I could still get an interview, but the chances are slim. Most look at uni grades and UMAT, or it's the UMAT more.'

Mum rubbed my back. 'Well you could keep on hoping, and applying?'

'I just don't think it's for me.'

Mum said nothing, only sitting on the unmade bed, watching me intently.

*It was my education. That's the issue.*

Both primary and secondary jilted my learning and caused such self-esteem issues. Now at eighteen-years-old, I still believed I was stupid. I was no stranger to the identity crises that the schools caused me to have on multiple occasions.

*Who am I?*

'Honey, you can sit those exams as many times as you would like. Try again for the next seating and see how you go,' Mum said. 'Your father and I are happy to pay as much as we need to.'

I stared blankly at the score, hoping it would change if I looked at it hard enough. My blunt fingernails danced on the glass surface of my desk.

All my life I dreamed of becoming a paediatric surgeon. But there was also nothing wrong with becoming a paediatric nurse. Save lives, that's what I wanted to do. Not to mention, the constant medical developments and breakthroughs were fascinating.

A puff of air escaped my pursed lips. 'I know it's not ideal, but if I can become a paediatric nurse, it's better than trying to find something else.'

'I'm glad you see it that way. Sounds like an excellent compromise.'

Mum had been my rock since the days of Mrs McConnell. I believed her, but yet she was limited to what she could do. Now I was reaping the effects, and I needed her all over again. There was this child-like thought pattern in my mind that was begging for my 'mummy', and I couldn't shake it.

As if she knew what I was thinking, mum's maternal instincts kicked in. She immediately pushed herself off my bed and embraced me. Tears that clouded my vision streamed down my face. They splashed onto my crossed legs and burned into my skin.

# 14

# March 2018

*22 Years Old*

The ICU was unusually quiet. We were understaffed once again, leaving Timothy, today's head nurse of ICU, and myself the only nurses on the floor.

Timothy was a tall middle-aged man who looked years younger. He joked it was due to his lack of grey hairs and "young person" lingo. He wasn't wrong there. When I started working with him a week ago, I pinned him for thirty-five at least, maybe forty. Turned out we had a lot in common, mainly old music and movies like AC/DC and *Nightmare on Elm Street*.

The phone rang and Timothy answered, hoping it was someone coming up from theatre or another ward. Except the look on his face said otherwise. As he placed the phone back in its cradle he sighed towards me, 'They need you up in the paediatric ward, McKenna.'

'Oh, sure, any reason?' I asked.

It was a fair question. Usually I'd go to another ward, no questions asked, but I liked Timothy and given he was alone I thought he'd try to keep me with him.

'Low on staff, and you're the most experienced student in paediatrics. Plus, you're wanting to go into the area in a few months, would be good for you to get more experience.'

I hadn't been to the children's ward here as of yet, despite having dealt with a few paediatric patients. Though, the heads knew that I had spent a considerable amount of time in children's hospitals and designated wards for other placements. I smiled brightly. 'Ah so you're letting me?'

'Maybe.' He shrugged. 'Just go before I change my mind.'

I raised my hands up, 'Going, going.' I grabbed my things from the staff room and headed to the paediatric wing on the other side of the hospital.

As I entered the paediatric floor, it too was obscenely slow. Maybe because it was only one o'clock in the afternoon, or it was just a random silent period — they happened on occasion, usually the calm before the storm.

As I walked towards the nurses' station, a tall, tan woman dressed in pink heart scrubs ran up to greet me. 'Hi, you must be McKenna. I'm Bianca, and this is Natalie,' she said, pointing to her shorter blonde colleague decked out in teddy bear scrubs.

'That I am. Nice to meet you both,' I replied.

'Oh hon, we gotta get you out of those scrubs and into the fun ones,' Natalie said, pulling me down the corridor to the cupboard filled with spare scrubs. 'You look to be about a size six. Give these a whirl.'

I swapped my bags for the flower scrubs and headed to the staff bathroom. They wouldn't be my first choice, but when it came to kids, it was more about making their day less scary. We wielded the power of distracting them from beeping machines and their pain and suffering.

'Oh my goodness, they look so good on you,' Natalie said as I walked back into the hallway.

'Not what I had in mind for my first set of fun scrubs, but I like them. Less scary.'

'That's why we wear them,' Bianca said with a smile.

'What interests you about paeds?' Natalie asked.

'I don't know, I love kids, and I love making a difference in their lives. It's a different experience ...' I trailed off. 'Sorry, just thought of a quote from *Grey's Anatomy*.'

'Oh I think I know, love the show,' Bianca replied. 'I got you. We get to shower them with magic and take their pain away as best we can.'

'Yeah,' I beamed. 'I enjoy brightening their day, easing their parents' minds. The doctors I had met during my placements wanted to be a team. They took everything into consideration to ensure the child was safe. It's been a real pleasure to see such teamwork.'

'We're like that too here,' Natalie said. 'Now come on, let's take you around the ward.'

The ward was decorated in decals of flowers, rainbows, dinosaurs, stars and much more. Each signed by a volunteer from the hospital's volunteer program. Children's drawings were placed on the doors, stuck on with blu-tack. It felt like a welcoming environment, acting like a home as much as it could be.

'Wow, this is gorgeous,' I said. 'Inviting, despite the connotations of being in a paeds ward.'

'Escapism at its finest,' Natalie said.

'The volunteers do them with the kids,' Bianca explained as we got back to the nurse's station. 'A lot of parents work, some go home, the volunteers do what they can to support them and us.'

The bell dinged and I immediately walked over to the room.

Margaret 'Maggie' Stroll, her chart read. She was in for complications from a bacterial infection. Her parents weren't in the room.

'Hi Maggie, I'm a fourth-year student Registered Nurse McKenna.' The bitter smell of hand sanitizer filled the air as I rubbed the thick substance over my hands.

'I don't feel well,' Maggie said.

I noted her pale appearance. She had her vitals done an hour ago by Bianca. 'And how don't you feel well? Like you're going to throw up?'

'No, like I haven't eaten in days.'

'Ah, so ravenous. Got it,' I replied with a chuckle. 'Let me see what I can do for you, Maggie.'

As I looked through the notes left by the girls and headed to the secret patient food storage in the office.

'Maggie ready for food is she?' Bianca asked.

'Yeah.'

'Awesome, she seemed to be doing a lot better when I saw her.' Bianca pointed to a few snacks grouped together with a rubber band. 'I got a stash ready, all within her dietary requirements, feel free to double check.'

I grabbed the stash that Bianca was pointing to. 'Thank you.'

'You're about to make her one happy kid.'

I laughed and headed back out, checking the list of ingredients.

*Yep, all within the requirements.*

'You're in luck,' I said as I entered the room. 'Last strawberry.'

'No way!' She sat up and pulled the table closer to her. 'Thank you!'

'No problem.'

Per Natalie's instruction, I called her mum to inform her that Maggie was eating and had a bottle of apple juice she was happily sipping on.

The day got slightly busy but ran efficiently. It was clear that Bianca and Natalie had set up quite the department, better than any ward I've been in anywhere.

'Ya know, we're looking for someone to start working with us full time next year,' Natalie said. 'You'd be a great asset to the team. The kids love you, and you've had glowing reviews across the hospital.'

'Oh,' I said. 'I guess I hadn't thought about —'

'It's up to you, of course, but just thought you should know.'

'Thanks,' I replied. 'Means a lot.'

Aside from Kaleb and my parents, there wasn't anything tying me to Cairns. I always said that I'd rather move, but I also thought it'd be to Brisbane in one of their major hospitals like the Royal Women's and Children's, or the Mater Children's. Adelaide was in a whole other state and on the southern coast of the country.

'Hey, Nat?' I asked.

'Hmm?' she replied, taking her eyes off her computer for a moment.

'Can you send me the application, please?'

'Of course.'

# 15

# March 2018

*22 Years Old*

A few days later, after working with Bianca and Natalie, I had somewhat become part of their friendship group.

After my final shift for the week, Bianca came into the staff room. 'Nat and I are heading to the pub for dinner, want to come?'

'Sure.' I followed her out of the ward to the elevators. I hadn't spent a lot of time with them, but when I did, I fitted into their workplace banter and friendly chitchat as if I'd worked there for as long as they had. There was an odd feeling that the two women gave me, sort of similar to how Aster made me feel. It was almost as if I found my "people", where the meaning of friendship actually felt true for the first time in my life.

'Welcome to the best duo of the paeds ward,' Natalie said, running into the elevator just in time. '... Now trio.'

'Thank you,' I replied.

As the elevator door opened out to the lobby, the cool air graced us with its presence. My crossed arms kept my tan cardigan closed and tight around me, as I braced for the cool March air.

'Holy shit,' I said, shivering. 'Will never get used to that.'

'You're so obviously from up north, girl,' Bianca laughed.

'How far is the pub, walking wise.' I shivered.

'Not far, maybe a minute?' Natalie said.

I nodded. There had to be a catch to moving down here, and it was one hundred percent the weather. Didn't think I'd ever see the day that I would say that I missed Cairns, but I miss Cairns.

'Here we are,' Bianca said, as we neared closer to an old rundown red brick building. Though it was dark I could see the rotting timber bar that lined the footpath.

*No wonder nobody is sitting out here, plus it's freezing.*

'Don't let the building dissuade you, it's quite luxurious inside,' Natalie said.

She wasn't kidding. As we walked in, I couldn't help but consider it gorgeous. The interior was styled like an old pub — dark mahogany timber with dark forest green accents. Chandeliers bedazzled the pressed tin ceiling, shining light to the finer details of the patterns in the tin.

We slid into one of the free booths, immediately reaching for the menus.

'So, what do you do in your free time?' Natalie asked me.

'Watch F1 and read. Despite what you may see at work, I am quite the introvert at heart,' I tittered.

'Aren't those races late?' Bianca asked. 'I'm a fan myself, but I just watch it when it's in Melbourne and keep up on the rest via the news.'

'Oh, yup, but I figured, my sleep is already skewed, so really it has no impact.'

The girls laughed.

'Fair enough,' Natalie said. 'Right, I'm getting a drink, it's on me, what would you ladies like?'

'Just a lemon lime and bitters, please,' I said.

'My usual beer,' Bianca replied.

'Coming right up.'

'So, what do you do outside of work?' I asked, glancing up from the menu.

'Spend it with friends, my fiancé, Michael, and just lounging at home. I try not to work the double shifts, if I can help it. I've done my time.'

'Ah, the pure relaxation thing, I get that,' I replied. 'And fair enough, can't think of anything worse than constant double shifts when the newbies should be doing their time. I can't wait, then once I'm seasoned, I can opt out.'

'You'll be wishing for death and coffee in an I.V. in no time,' Natalie said, coming back with the three drinks.

'Oh well, at least I'll have you two for at least one of those shifts,' I replied.

'Don't you know it,' they laughed, clinking their glasses together.

The evening was quite a different story to what I'm used to. Natalie and Bianca were nothing like my other friends. They wanted my opinions and asked questions about me. My stomach ached and tears spilt out of my tear ducts from the constant laughter.

# 16

# March 2018

*22 Years Old*

I sat at the desk in the dark corner, squished between the entrance wall and the pantry, WhatsApp opened up in a minimised window in front of the job application had sat in a pinned tab for the past week. I may have had time to apply considering it was a graduate program that wouldn't start until January next year, but Kaleb was another story. He knew that I've thought about leaving Cairns, but always for Brisbane. Only this time, his stress levels were casting out daggers through the phone. Every text was a jab to the heart. I started to worry about him while I was working, exhaustion was setting in as I tried to help him as best I could despite the distance between us.

*How would he take it?*

His dishevelled and unshaven face popped up on my screen, and my attention was drawn away from that single pinned tab.

'Hey baby.' He adjusted his screen as he spoke. 'Sorry, I just—Haven't had time to shower or anything really. Work again.'

'That's okay,' I replied. 'I had a bit of university stuff to do.'

'Good, good.' Dark circles formed under his brown eyes. His ginger hair sticking out in all directions. 'Not sure if I told you, but I'm in front for that promotion after graduation.'

'Oh my God, Kaleb! That's amazing!'

I couldn't recall what he did, something to do with data analysis. He never really spoke about what he did, only that it was confidential. What I did know, was that with his Bachelor of Criminology and I.T. they were going to send him into a bigger role at the firm.

'Yeah, so uh, time will tell.' He held up crossed fingers, 'I should know soon. So upon graduation in February or whatever, I'll be starting.'

'Either way, hon, congratulations,' I said.

'So have you made any friends, yet?'

'Yeah, yeah, Natalie and Bianca. Nurses. Plus a few other acquaintances in other departments. Now I'm primarily in paediatrics with Nat and Bianca.'

'Oh brilliant, Kenzie.' Kaleb ran a hand through his hair. 'What are they like?'

'Super friendly, and into Formula One. They're very supportive and funny.' I paused, looking down at my hands in my lap. My fingers picked at the skin of my thighs, grabbing a chunk and rolled it between my fingertips. 'In fact they suggested I apply for their graduate program.'

The anger that I anticipated never came. Kaleb's face softened and he readjusted his screen and lighting to get himself out of the dark.

'You should go for it McKenna!' he exclaimed and I tittered. 'I'm serious. I can work and study remotely with the occasional travel around the country. If you want to do it, that's no problem. So tell me about the job.'

He leaned forward and rested his chin on his clasped hands, listening as I told him about the application. At some point during our conversation, he started sending me through apartment listings in Adelaide and added me to a Pinterest board that he was actively filling with gorgeous apartment set ups and aesthetics.

*Maybe everything is all in my head, and everyone is wrong. I know him better than anyone.*

'How's the stress of the job?' I asked, changing the subject. 'It's obvious you're not okay.'

'I'll be fine, once we know who's won the promotion, my stress should go away.' He ran a hand over the growing stubble on his cheeks. 'I'm sorry if I've been angry and short with you.'

'It's okay, you're just stressed.'

'Well, anyway, I apologise, and I've sent you something that should come later today as a token of my apology.'

'You didn't have to, Kaleb.'

He shrugged. 'I gotta go, text me when it arrives.'

With that he hung up. No "I love you". No proper goodbye. Just a blank screen.

Several minutes later, I'm called down to the lobby to collect a huge bouquet of gorgeous blood red roses.

*Dear McKenna,*
*Sorry for being a twat. Here's a rose for each day I've been a jerk to you. (forty stems btw)*
*I love you.*

I carried the large bouquet of forty flowers to the elevators. The smell overwhelming. While they may not have been my favourite flower, the fact that he had done anything at all to demonstrate how sorry he was, meant more to me than the gift itself.

**Me:** *They're gorgeous, Kaleb. Thank you. You really didn't have to do anything.*

**Kaleb:** *Nonsense. I've treated you like shit for the past month and a bit. I love you. Thank you for being supportive.*

**Me:** *Same to you. I'm just about to submit my application to the hospital.*

# 17

# April 2018

*22 Years Old*

The buildings and streetlights blurred together as my driver drove through the suburbs. The thick residue and fog not making it easy to focus on something other than the sound of Kaleb yelling in my ear. My driver, Bobby, flashed his concerned green eyes to me through the rear-view mirror. He motioned to me to see if I needed help. I waved my hand back at him politely, as he took a wrong turn.

*Great, now I'm going to be late.*

'Sorry miss, traffic ahead,' he said in his Irish accent.

*Like hell there is, I can see the map. All clear.*

I left it, still trying to get a word in with Kaleb.

'Ka—' I tried.

'Oh, for fuck's sake McKenna! Just fucking stop!' Kaleb yelled into the phone. 'Who the fuck are these people, Nat and Bianca? You've known them for like five seconds and you're already uprooting your life for them? Where are your loyalties McKenna? To the five second freaks, or to me, your boyfriend of three years?'

'What?' I replied calmly. 'I explained it to y-'

I shook my head.

*What is his problem?*

It was almost like he woke up this morning and chose violence. He was in agreeance last night, sending me apartment listings even.

'I'm conf- '

'I don't want to hear it, McKenna!' He sighed heavily in my ear. 'Did my bouquet of forty fucking roses fall on deaf ears? Do you know how much that cost me? Four hundred fucking dollars!'

It felt like misplaced anger, and for me, it was too early to deal with it. I was running on three hours of sleep and one cup of coffee. 'Did something happen at work? Are you getting passed up for the promotion?'

The man was silent. All I got was more heavy breathing. Even through the phone, I felt his anger.

I fidgeted with the constant awful reminder that I was his. It might as well had been a wedding ring. Except that it was the innocent, loving symbol of joining two people who love each other together. The chain wasn't a beautiful thing. It was a symbol of a wild BDSM play made to look like a fashion statement to everyone else.

Dylan saw right through it. He was the only person at any of my placements who gave a disgusted look when it peeked out of my scrubs.

"I've never seen that before; permanent necklace?" Dylan had asked.

"Yeah," I replied. "Kaleb bought it for me."

His eyes darted to it, widening as he stared. "We're friends, right?"

"Of course."

"You'd tell me if he was hurting you, wouldn't you?"

"Dylan, it's fine. It's just a necklace."

He knew what it was and questioned if I was okay.

'Go to hell McKenna,' Kaleb said and hung up.

Repeated texts started to come through on my phone. The string of endless notifications were derogatory in nature.

*Clearly whatever has sparked his sudden outburst has really gotten to him. It's fine. He'll calm down in a few hours.*

Except it was a dance that I couldn't keep up with, nor wanted to. Why was I expected to?

The driver took another wrong turn, thinking I wouldn't notice. 'Mate, you took a wrong turn, hospital's the other way.'

Dylan beamed as he approached from the opposite side of the car park. 'Good morning McKenna.'

I gave him a tiny wave with a slight smile. 'Morning.'

But no matter how cheerful I tried to be, I couldn't move from the resting bitch face. I wanted this placement to be over and to get back home to sort things out.

He took one look at me and said, 'Another one?' I nodded. 'Talk about bad luck, how many drivers is that now?'

'Like five? I don't know, one too many, Dylan.' I didn't mean to be short with him.

We neared the hospital entrance. 'I could drive you home, if you'd like. The hotel is on the way to my parents' place.'

'If it's no trouble,' I said with a hint of eagerness, but I didn't care.

I was sick of the assholes, and if Dylan made a genuine offer, I wouldn't pass it up.

'Not at all. I finish around the same time you do, so I'll come by Ward ...'

'3B,' I finished for him.

'Ward 3B, after my shift.'

'Thank you, Dylan.'

He smiled and headed towards the theatres, and I made my way to the staff room closest to Ward B to drop my bag into a locker.

With over fifty texts from Kaleb, I didn't have time to sit and go through them all. I let him know that I would text him when I got home. "Phones away" was student policy; had your phone out and you'd be risking a failed placement. Dealing with a stressed out and angry boyfriend was not worth ruining my graduation, nor my GPA. If I responded now or focused on my phone anyway, he was going to impact my work, and that was the last thing I wanted for my patients.

*Keep home at home, and work at work. Self-regulate. Deep breaths.*

As I took in my first deep breath, I tossed my phone into the locker. The device clashing with its metal floor sending the steel into a vibration. With my exhale, I slammed the door shut, the sound of the metal clanking together echoed through the staff room.

'Self-regulate McKenna. Don't let him do this.'

I stood still, leaning against the cool beige painted metal cupboard, taking in my final two deep breathed. With a quick one-eighty turn, I stormed towards the exit, the rubber soles of my black leather Asics joggers squeaked. I caught my dishevelled reflection on the television on my way out. My blonde hair a mess, strands falling out of my once picture-perfect ponytail. A thick black line of mascara outlined the bottom of my eyes.

*I don't remember tearing up.*

'I'm a right disgrace,' I said. 'Terrible. Pathetic. Why do I let him do this?'

I dashed to the bathroom, running a tissue, I grabbed on my way in, under the water and removed the mascara. The hair tie pulled at my hair as I yanked it out and smoothed the strands the best I could without my brush. It bubbled in places but looked better than it did moments before.

I leaned against the bench, staring at my somewhat better-looking reflection.

'Can I continue to blame stress anymore?' All I hoped for was that he'd get over his stress and go back to the man I fell in love with. There were glimpses of him, but I was starting to think he'd never come back. My work phone buzzed with a message for Murray asking where I was. 'Shit.'

# 18

# April 2018

*22 Years Old*

Conversations were muffled in the distance while I laboured over my final chart of the day. My eyes were glued to my screen and ears were concentrating on the crisp clicking sound of my keyboard. Nothing could break my focus.

That was until I smelt him.

I basked in the scent of sandalwood, sage and salt, the perfect combination where land meets sea. It reminded me of Cairns and my running route from the backyard to the beach. I could see it now, the dirt turning to sand, and the shrubbery slowly thinning out to the glorious view of Trinity Beach.

Dylan's fingertips danced in my peripheral vision. 'Hey, are you done with your shift?'

'Huh?' I hit submit and logged out of the system. 'Oh, uh yeah, just finishing up a chart.' I pushed myself away and finally looked up at him. He'd changed out of his scrubs and into jeans and a t-shirt.

'You still want that lift to your hotel?' he asked.

'Yeah, please. Absolutely.'

'Awesome.'

'Let me clock off.'

He nodded and I quickly scanned my to-do list and patients. All handovers had been done. I dashed to the staff room off the nurse's station. Clocked off at the tablet to the side of the door and grabbed my belongings from the locker.

'Is that cute resident waiting for you?' Bethany, one of my supervisors, asked.

'We're just friends,' I replied.

What they weren't aware of was a crappy long-term relationship that I had to be mindful of. Until I was sure I wanted to leave Kaleb, I was still in a relationship. Part of me still loved him, deeply, but Dylan was opening my eyes to what I was missing out on — chivalry. He would hold doors open for me, buy me coffee, and now he was waiting for me so he could drive me to my hotel. This was what I had always seen in the movies, and read in books. I had settled for someone who I thought could treat me like any guy in a romcom, but he was more like a wolf in sheep's clothing.

'Ready?' Dylan asked. I nodded and led the way out of the building.

The cold April air had more of a bite in Adelaide than when I was in Melbourne this time last year. I was rugged up as much as I could be, but I was still cold. I kept my arms crossed in front of my chest, trying to keep them and my chest warm, silently hoping we'd be at the car soon.

'Maybe I need to keep an extra jacket on me just for you,' he joked.

'Oh hush, it's that not cold.' I chuckled.

'Hmm, sure, that's why your arms are crossed.'

I regretted choosing to bring a short-sleeved t-shirt with me. It was freezing cold, fifteen degrees Celsius. Sure to Dylan, this would've been nothing, but April in Cairns was like twenty-two to twenty-nine.

'Right, here we are,' Dylan said, pointing to a black 2010 Mazda MX-5.

A laugh escaped my lips, and my hands quickly flew to my mouth. My laughing stopped. 'Oh my God, I am so sorry.'

'It's cool. Most girls have that reaction. Probably why I don't get a second date.'

'That's a shame.' I patted his shoulder in a sad attempt of comfort. 'If it's a reliable car, then what's the issue? I, myself, am a proud owner and driver of a 2004 Hyundai Getz.'

'And it's still going?'

'Oh, and how? I even drive it like I'm a Formula One driver.'

Dylan opened the passenger door and closed it behind me. 'Ah, a pedal to the metal kinda girl. Never would've thought.'

Once he got into the car, I replied, 'Should come go-karting, then you'll see.'

'Oh, you are so on!'

He clearly knew that his car was going to be around for a long time. A brand-new touch screen had replaced what would've been the original CD/cassette and radio. A 2010 car had a state-of-the-art Bluetooth network. 'Fancy little setup you have here,' I stated as he set up music for the twenty-minute drive.

'Why, thank you,' he replied. 'Any requests for the drive?'

'I actually have a full playlist for night drives.'

'Spotify?' I nodded. 'Here, search it up on my phone.'

Dylan passed me his phone, and I typed in my username.

'I prefer more mellow songs for laid-back drives. Unless you want me screaming every Taylor Swift or My Chemical Romance song?' I cheekily hit the follow button not only on myself but on the playlist, too.

Dylan laughed, 'Nah, laid back sounds good. So you literally have a variety of music?'

'Absolutely. I grew up on a lot of rock' n roll from the 60s to 90s. Then branched out with my taste.' I hit shuffle and *Daddy Issues* by The Neighbourhood played softly through the speakers. 'So if you look in any of my playlists, you will go from *Highway to Hell* to the soft rock of Cigarettes After Sex. Then to some form of screamo before diving into the plethora of Taylor Swift.'

'Now that's a wild taste in music.' He started laughing. 'I'm the same, except instead of screamo, it's jazz. Instead of Taylor Swift, it's Keith Urban.'

'Not to genre shame, but jazz is even worse than screamo.'

Dylan rested a hand on his chest. 'What do you have against Jazz?'

'Gotta be the saxophone and the syncopation. Can't stand either.'

He burst into a fit of laughter, and sure enough the contagious noise caught on. My eyes watering and stomach aching. As it died down, a strange feeling entered my chest and stomach, growing as we got further away from the hospital. It was foreign to me. I knew it wasn't a feeling associated with heart attacks in women, nor anxiety. I couldn't put my symptoms to a potential diagnosis. Was there even one?

'Behind your seat is a jumper,' Dylan said.

'What?'

'You're obviously cold. I would put the heater on, but it's broken.'

'You keep a jumper in the car?'

'Yeah, for times like these when the heater doesn't work.'

I turned to look at him, deadpanning as best I could. 'Oh, so you get cold too.'

'Ha. Ha,' he replied. 'Yes, but I'm not cold now. I'm acclimatised to the weather.'

'How long have you lived here then?'

'Uh, well let's see, my parents moved us from the UK to Brisbane when I was thirteen for Dad's work.'

*He must be pretty close with his family if they moved down here.*

'Ah,' I replied and smirked. 'So jeans, not slacks, because …'

'I find them comfier, plus show my figure more,' he replied with a wink.

A weird sound involuntarily escaped from my lips.

*Did I just giggle?! Oh fuck!*

'And you're how old now? If you don't mind me asking,' I said, trying to change the subject. 'You seem quite young to be a resident.'

'Maybe.' Dylan shrugged. 'I did an engineering certificate at TAFE whilst I was at school, grade ten, I started. Then in years eleven and twelve I did another qualification which gave me the ability to knock several courses off my Undergraduate degree thanks to work experience and education. So I finished in two years thanks to the summer terms, whilst also knocking subjects off for Med School. So I completed that in three and a half years. Then I made the right connections to enter ortho early.'

I turned dramatically in my seat. 'Wow, so you're like mega smart?'

'You know it.' He winked. 'Wouldn't recommend it though, I'm exhausted, and I fear that I haven't given myself ample time to fully decide on a specialty. I enjoy Ortho, but I'm no longer one-hundred percent sure.'

'I'm sure you'll work it out. You'll be a great doctor no matter what you do,' I replied.

'Thanks.' He turned the wheel towards the loading zone out the front of the hotel. Dylan's eyes locked onto mine. Our gaze held for a few seconds too long before I turned away, clearing my throat.

I quickly gathered my belongings from the floor. 'Well, uh. Thank you for dropping me off.'

'No problem.'

I exited as fast as I could and headed into the lobby without a second glance back to his vehicle.

# 19

# April 2018

*22 Years Old*

My back hit the cool metal wall of the narrow elevator that would have sent a claustrophobe into a panic.

'McKenna, you stupid bitch!' I exclaimed. 'Think about Kaleb, for fuck's sake!'

*It is just a crush. That's all that this feeling is. I had it when I first met Kaleb. It means nothing. Tomorrow's my day off, so it's all good.*

A gust of cool air greeted me as soon as the elevators opened. Concrete floors, rendered walls, and instead of windows, it had a fence to stop guests from falling. I'd been here for almost three weeks and was already sick of it. The only benefit and excitement for my brisk walk to my room was the fact that I could preheat it.

My key was in my hand, ready to insert into the doorknob. The mechanical click of the door unlocking echoed, and I was graced with the warm air. I tossed my bag onto the desk chair and took off my scrubs.

It was an odd feeling not having assessments after placement.

*This must be what it feels like to have a full-time job.*

I was exhausted, but it was certainly not the same as being university exhausted. It was almost blissful-like. 'Now, sleep, shower, or eat? What to do?' My stomach growled. 'Well, there's my answer.'

I pulled the butter chicken that I had premade a couple of days ago, from the freezer, dumping the contents of the Tupperware container onto a plate. The door of the microwave clicked shut and started to whir.

*The beauty of meal prep.*

I grabbed my phone out of my bag to let Dylan know I had arrived at my room, but Kaleb bombarded my phone. Several missed calls from my parents, and the man himself.

*So much for my peaceful evening after a busy day.*

**Kaleb:** *We had a deal! You text me on your break. It's noon, you should be on your break now! Every day at 12.30, you have lunch.*

**Kaleb:** *ANSWER ME DAMMIT! What the fuck is wrong with you?!*

**Kaleb:** *Have you died?*

**Kaleb:** *Hello?*

**Kaleb:** *If you don't answer me in 1 hour, I'm calling the police.*

'What deal is he banging on about?' I quickly searched through our prior text messages and nothing. 'Fuck!'

As I sifted through the hundreds of text messages, I found that he had called the hospital. 'Don't bring home to work, and don't take work home; and he's fucking brought it to work!'

*Whoever answered the phone, why didn't they tell me that my boyfriend was on a rampage?*

Kaleb had contacted my parents, and whatever he said concerned them, despite them knowing I was on placement and don't touch my phone during the day. I barely get a lunch break sometimes, and the minute I can eat, I do so in peace, without my phone.

'What is he doing?'

Panic rose in my stomach, and my airway constricted. Tightness wrapped around me. What little air I had left in my lungs escaped through a forced, sharp exhale. I battled for oxygen, but the air felt thin. Black spots clouded my vision, like an old television losing reception.

*Why is he doing this? This is taking the piss!*

I didn't know what to do, but I knew I had to do damage control.

'The only supervisor on for the night shift is Cassandra. What do I even say? "Yes, hi, my boyfriend was just concerned"? He knows I'm a nursing student and how inundated nurses are.'

*Hospitals almost everywhere are short-staffed, so what was he bloody thinking? When did I even agree to a deal?*

My head was reeling. The microwave dinged, and I stood there, staring at the black box. It dinged again. I didn't move. All I heard was the constant sound of annoyance, until a knock at my door broke me.

'He hasn't come here has he?' I mumbled as I shuffled towards the door.

My fingers shook against the button of the microwave, opening it up and quietly as I could. As I peered through the peephole, I saw a bearded man dressed in the familiar blue uniform, police.

'Fuck me,' I mumbled.

I grabbed my white hotel robe from the bathroom, rubbing my sweaty palms down the length of the soft plush fabric. My hand shook as I reached for the doorknob, twisting it open.

*Why is he here?*

He stood there with thumbs looped under his belt. I dug my fingers into the robe, bunching as much as I could in my fist. My heart was beating like a drum.

'Ms McKenna Carrington?' The officer asked. I could only nod. 'I'm Officer Langdon, and I'm here to perform a welfare check on you.'

'Uh, on what grounds?' I asked stepping aside to let the Officer in.

'Just so you're aware, Ms Carrington, I am wearing a body cam. I'm here on the grounds of out-of-character behaviour.'

I laughed.

*He can't be serious. This has to be a prank.*

'Sorry, it's just – Is this for real?' I tittered.

'Yes.'

'My boyfriend ... I don't know why he's done this, but I'm a nursing student. I've been flat out all day and haven't touch my phone since this morning.' My breathing slowed as I talked. I looked down to my fist, my knuckles were as white as the. 'We're just in a fight, is all. I can assure you, this wellness, welfare, whatever check was a waste of your time. As you can see, I am perfectly fine. He was probably concerned, things got a little heated was all.'

My feet danced along the rough surface of the old navy carpet.

He hummed as he pulled out his notebook. 'Can you tell me more about this fight? Which may have prompted him to call??'

'I got in about 10 minutes and only just saw a string of text messages.' I slid my phone off the counter and showed the officer the messages.

'Do you mind if I go back a few days?'

'No, go ahead.'

I collapsed to the comfort of the bed. Officer Langdon scrolled through the endless supply of messages. His eyebrows furrowed together. I watched as the corners of his mouth twitched.

*He must be pretty bad at poker.*

My heels kicked the side of the bed. I hunched forward shifting in my seat.

*What can there possibly be in those messages?*

My stomach was in knots. The smell of the butter chicken enticed my gag reflex. I turned away from him, leaning on my elbow on my knee.

'I've seen enough, thank you.' He passed me my phone showing me a tirade of messages from a few days ago.

**Kaleb:** *Where are you, you're not at the hospital*
**Kaleb:** *Call me ASAP*
**Kaleb:** *If you aren't at work, why are you ignoring me?*
**Kaleb:** *Are you with another guy?!*
**Kaleb:** HEY TALK TO ME YOU FUCKING BITCH!

'These text messages are of particular concern. The messages from today, too. He's showing extreme force of control. Potential emotional abuse.' He kept talking to me, but all my mind focused on was the word "abuse". It had been used a lot recently. Aster, that first driver, and now I had a police officer.

*How long has this been going on?*

'It's up to you, and there may be more to the story, but this looks to me that you are being abused. I can leave it for now, if you wish,' the officer said.

'A-Abused? Sorry, I don't understand. It's just a fight. He's stressed. It's really no biggie.'

*"It's just a fight". Am I seriously downplaying his behaviour ... again? Why am I protecting him?*

'What you've shown me is gaslighting. The texts are forceful and signify the need for control. He's threatened you with police and has followed through. And by the number of texts and missed calls, he's harassed several people.' He paused for a moment. 'Look, think about it. By the way, the body cam has recorded his messages. If you wish to file a complaint, let them know that there is police evidence already concerning this case number.'

Officer Langdon passed me his card with the file number already listed on it.

'Thank you,' I replied.

My brain was empty. It felt like I had officially malfunctioned and was now like Windows XP or Internet Explorer. The officer left, leaving me to sink to the floor in a puddle.

**Me:** *Hey, are you off your shift? Kinda need to talk. Face to face, preferably. Can you come to my hotel, or I can come to you.*

**Aster:** *I'll redirect the Uber, be right there.*

Ten minutes later, I'm down in the lobby of the hotel dressed in rust coloured trackpants and my favourite black hoodie. My foot tapped against the salt and pepper specked epoxy floor while I sat on one of the hotel's ocean blue armchairs. My fingers dug into the velvet of the armrests.

Aster waltzed through the door, still in her university scrubs, her red hair thrown up in a messy bun. She rushed over, 'What happened?'

'I — He,' I stumbled over my words. 'How do I?'

'Okay, okay, let's get you back upstairs,' she led me towards the lifts. As we entered, it felt like the lift was smaller than I thought. A mirrorless shoe box. I hit my floor number and the elevator dinged on my floor, and I led her down the cold concrete path to the hotel room. We were barely inside before I started bawling.

'I-I-I ...'

'Shhh,' Aster whispered in my ear while she helped me to the bed and held me as the tears flowed, pooling on my track pants. 'I got you.'

'I. Know. You. Do,' I replied through sobs.

'What happened?' Aster asked.

'I-It's easier if I show you.'

I grabbed my phone off the desk and passed it to Aster, letting her scroll through Kaleb's messages.

'I love him, Aster, despite everything, I love him. Why?' I asked. 'I should — I should hate him. Loathe him. Break up with him ... It's just stress, I know he – he lo–loves me. I think?'

'Because he wasn't always like this, and your brain is hooked on the good times,' she replied. 'Breaking up is a personal thing, but as your best friend, I urge to leave him, and if you won't … yet. Then I will be here for you, even if you flip flop, like you're doing now, I'll be your voice of reason.'

'*You* will be my voice of reason?' I joked.

'Oh, ha ha,' she laughed. 'But in all seriousness, no matter how angry he makes me, I will support you. If he tries to split us up, I'm dragging your sorry ass away from him and going to the police. Understand?'

'I understand,' I replied with a salute.

'Love, he's as cunning as a fox. No wonder you didn't pick up on the abuse, take your own screenshots and seriously think about leaving.'

I smiled at her. 'Wanna stay the night? I got an extra butter chicken in the freezer. Or you back at placement?'

'Yeah, sure. Tomorrow's my day off, so I can stay, especially if it's your butter chicken.'

She looked over to the right, next to the door to the back deck sat my dead bouquet of roses. 'A gift from him?'

'Yep,' I replied.

'Please throw them out.'

'Nah, it's a reminder of the fact that love doesn't last if it's not deeply rooted in healthy, loving soil.'

Aster cringed. 'That was cheesy and fucking bleak. Just get rid of them.'

I laughed. 'Hold the door for me then, please.'

Aster opened the apartment door, while I tried my hardest to not drop any of the falling petals that had since wilted and turned to a dark crimson.

# 20

# May 2018

*22 Years Old*

It was my last full day in Adelaide before I headed back to Cairns. All three of my new friends had a day off together, and Dylan thought it was a grand idea to organise a trip to an indoor go-karting track. It was a great distraction from my not-so-great boyfriend.

Yesterday I had mentioned I got the job for next year, and Kaleb stopped communicating with me for nearly twelve hours. It troubled me slightly, but he had been off for a while. One minute he was sending me apartment listings and glad I made friends, the next he was sending a police officer to my hotel room.

*Maybe he's taking time to cool off. Maybe he's seen that he was completely unreasonable, given that I had mentioned it to him. Besides, it isn't like I had accepted it.*

As I danced into a pair of jeans, I couldn't help but feel an eerie bout of zen. There was no unnecessary worry. I layered my white short sleeve t-shirt with my burgundy turtleneck jumper. My reflection beamed at me with a flushed face. I fluttered my eyelids against the wand of my mascara. There was no greater buzz. Days like these didn't come around very often, especially before I met Aster.

As I walked back into the tiny hotel suite, Aster's ringtone blasted through the air. I pounced for my phone, trying to catch it before it sent her to voicemail.

'Hey girl,' I answered just as I landed on my stomach, the mattress of the bed cushioning me.

'Any word from that dickward?' she asked.

I sat upright. The hair on the back of my neck stood up.

*Name calling isn't ... It isn't okay.*

'Do you have to keep calling him horrible names?' I asked. 'And no, he's gone radio silent for almost twelve hours.'

'As long as you stay with him and he treats you like shit, he's getting shitty names. Seems only fair.'

*Can't argue with that logic, I guess. Still, it doesn't make it okay.*

'Ugh, whatever.' Leave it to Aster to be blunt and ruin a perfectly good mood, but she was unfortunately right. 'Now what's up. You called, not texted, so what happened?'

'I think I met someone. I don't know. Nothing's happened ...yet. He's a physiotherapy student. We met when he was doing one of his practical exams.'

A notification sound pulled me away momentarily, as Bianca messaged to let me know she was on her way.

'I'm listening. Just getting ready for a day of go-karting,' I said to Aster. 'But that's exciting. He cute? Oh how about the massages?'

'So good! And yes he's freaking cute! Try Christian Bale in *Little Women*.'

'Holy shit!' I stopped mid lipstick application, picturing a young Christian Bale lookalike. 'Bro, you at least got his number right?'

'You know me, slipped it to him as he was leaving. I, unfortunately, had to hang back for other students. They stung man.' I chuckled slightly. 'Not funny bro, they hurt. They left bruises!'

'That's shit, well at least you look tough now. Nobody will want to mess with you.' She laughed. 'Well, so tell me. Has cute guy messaged?'

'Yeah, he did actually. He's really smart. He's looking at getting a PhD and starting his own specific clinic, can't recall in what area. I'll tell you when I find out.'

'Sounds great, I'm so happy for you!' I sang.

'Thank you.'

'Hey, I gotta go. The girls will be here soon. I need the details when I get back.'

'Sounds good, coz I'm actually going out with him now. He messaged me asking me for coffee.'

'Shit. Enjoy!'

'I will!'

My hand gripped the doorknob, I felt an intense darkness wash over me. The hair on my head stood tall. Beads of sweat started to form. I shuffled towards the balcony door. As I peered over the balcony railing I saw him. My stomach was doing somersaults. Kaleb was walking towards reception.

*This isn't what I needed today.*

After the police incident a couple of weeks ago, I had no desire to hear from him, let alone see him. This took the cake. I wanted to run but the chances of him seeing me were high. There was only one entry and exit without triggering the fire alarm through the fire escape.

**Me:** *Boyfriend decided to show up unannounced, so I won't be coming. Raincheck on the karting.* <3

**Bianca:** *Why? He can come too. I wanna meet him, he seems nice. Very handsome.*

**Me:** *I really don't want to get into it. We're in a fight and this really wasn't what I needed.*

**Dylan:** *Everything okay?*

**Me:** *Yeah. Everything's fine. Have fun.*
It was a half-truth.
*They will never know.*

I quickly phoned down to reception to inform them of the unwanted guest and to not let him past them. But I was too late, they had let him in. In a matter of seconds, he'll be pounding on the door, and I'll be trapped.

I hid the chats in time for the pounding to begin.

*Could he know I was in the apartment?*

'I know you're in there!' Kaleb called.

My breathing hitched. My heart pounded in my chest, vibrating my ribcage.

*I had to get out, but how?*

A lump formed in my throat, constricting my airway. 'Panic attack, I'm safe here' I locked myself in the bathroom. 'What do I do?'

I tried calling down to the front desk, but nobody picked up. The last thing that I wanted to do was to call the police. Kaleb was a genius when it came to twisting the truth. It would end up being that whole "Rational Choice" theory, I remember hearing one of my friends talking about it at uni. I knew that Kaleb would weigh up the costs and benefits and lie to the police.

I have to acknowledge what I am in. I have to.

'McKenna!'

*Bang, bang, bang.*

My heart started beating harder and faster. It wanted to burst out of my chest. My phone slipped side to side in my sweat-soaked hands as I tried calling the front desk once more.

Nothing.

I had to face the music, or maybe if I waited it out, he'd give up.

'Think, Kenz, think,' I whispered to myself.

A brilliant cunning plan concocted in my head.

Kaleb had been blowing up my phone for the past five minutes. I ignored him and tried the front desk again. Finally someone answered, a lady by the name of Hannah.

'Hi, my name is McKenna Carrington, I'm in room 104. Someone had let my boyfriend into the complex, he's not a guest here, only me' I whispered. 'Can you hear the banging?'

'Yes,' she replied.

'I'm hiding in the bathroom, he is not a nice person. He followed me from Cairns.' I heard her gasp on the other end. 'Can you please remove him from the premises so I can get an Uber out of here. I was supposed to check out anyway tomorrow, but I found an earlier flight.'

*How the fuck does that happen? Surely they have policies put in place to prevent such actions. Isn't this trespassing?*

'Absolutely, security will be up in two minutes. I'll stay on the line and let you know when he's gone.'

'Thank you.'

'I'll also help you to the car.'

I stayed on the line, trying to listen to the commotion outside. The banging stopped but muffled yelling started.

'They're calling the police,' Hannah said. 'He's being difficult.'

*Good. Hopefully that will scare him.*

The commotion wasn't dying down. He was putting up a massive fight.

*How did McKenna die? Death by embarrassment.*

'You doing okay?' Hannah asked.

'Yeah, can they move him or is he ...'

'No, they're trying. They're keeping me updated. He doesn't know you're in the room.'

'Good, good.'

I felt safe enough to move out from the bathroom. The commotion was louder than ever.

'Just so you know, I've moved out of the bathroom,' I said to Hannah.

'Excellent. The police are nearly here, they'll sort him out.'

'Thank you, and if you can pass this incident to your manager and your colleague who spoke to him ...'

'Yeah, absolutely! I've made a report. I am terribly sorry that this happened.'

'Not your fault. Nobody's fault really.'

My ear was glued to the cold timber door. All I could get was Kaleb's muffled voice about the officers.

*Is he trying to prove his innocence? Why aren't they just getting him to move on?*

Nobody should scare you into a false sense of a livelihood. Nobody should make you feel you don't matter. People who do, should have everything they have taken away. Rot in a cell. Be struck with a record that will haunt them for the rest of their life.

Kaleb deserved everything that was coming to him. I didn't deserve the life I had. I couldn't get justice against my teachers for the psychological and emotional abuse. But I could get justice against Kaleb.

'You there hon?' Hannah asked.

'Yeah,' I replied.

'They've arrested him for trespassing. They're removing him now. I'll hang up and come up as soon as they've taken him to the car so we can get you out of here.'

I breathed a sigh of relief.

'Thank you, thank you so much!'

'You're welcome, see you in a bit.'

She hung up and I packed up the rest of my belongings.

Everything was tossed haphazardly into my suitcases. I didn't care if anything got crushed. I needed to go. He was escalating and I needed a safety plan. There was no telling what his capabilities were, this — the stalking, the police and threats — would've been untenable to comprehend a month ago, now I needed a plan, and fast. Except, how could I when I still couldn't bring myself to admit that this very well could be an abusive relationship?

# 21

# March 2017

*21 Years Old*

Kaleb didn't give me much faith when he took me to a rundown house in the middle of the suburb of Redlynch. The small dark blue shack-like house sat between a modernised Queenslander and a Contemporary home. Its painted timber cladding was peeling, exposing the hard wood underneath.

My eyes fixated on the white rusty Holden Commodore. It sat underneath a gazebo made out of old carport poles, a tarp and rope. I tried not to judge, but of all the places that Kaleb could take me to, this was by far the most unsettling. Rubbish sat in very full bags spilling out from the bin by the front chain fence. Remnants of rubbish littered the small patch of gold lawn beside the driveway.

'What are we doing here?' I asked.

'I told you, it's a surprise.' He looked giddy with excitement, and I wasn't about to burst his bubble. I could only assume he had ordered something online, and the owners of this quaint home were getting ready to move out.

'I get that, but please tell me that this isn't the house,' I said.

'It is.'

I breathed out shakily.

*I cannot judge. It's okay. I'm reading too much into it.*

'Kaleb, until you reassure me that you aren't getting me killed, I am not getting out of the car.'

He took both of my hands in his and kissed the backs of them. 'I love you, and I promise, nothing bad is going to happen to you.'

His reassurance didn't help to settle my nerves. My legs bounced as I waited for him to come around to open the passenger side door of his 2001 Ford Falcon.

*I've seen one too many episodes of* Criminal Minds.

'I really don't like this, Kaleb.'

'If at any point you feel unsafe, say "Pythagoras".'

It was a weird safe word, but I guess that was the point. 'Sure.'

As his arm snaked around my waist, drawing me closer to him, I relaxed slightly. My muscles still tensed as he walked across the road and up the driveway to the front door.

*Why would he put me in harm's way if he loved me?*

Kaleb rang the doorbell, and a young woman, with various gold facial and ear piercings, answered the door. Her gold ring covered fingers gripped the door and the architrave, peaking her head out of the shadows.

'Hello, can I help you?' she asked.

'I'm Kaleb, I believe we may have spoken on the phone.' Kaleb held his right hand out.

'Ah, yes.' She let go of the architrave. The sunlight bounced off her gold chain belt that sat loosely around the waist of her mid-length black asymmetrical dress. 'Come in, come in. I'm Beth, short for Bethany.'

We followed her through the derelict house. Furniture was broken or worn, with a light layer of rubbish sitting on top of everything. A path had been cleared to a little room at the back of the property.

My germophobia was going ballistic. The stench of old food wafted throughout the house causing my gag reflex to engage.

'Pythagoras,' I choked out to Kaleb under my breath.

'Not yet,' he whispered back. 'Just give her a minute.'

She seemed nice enough, but my germophobia wasn't making the situation easy for me. Kaleb pulled me closer to him, but I remained prepared to run.

'Here we are,' Beth said, opening a door to a small room.

Inside was plenty of stock of permanent jewellery. Behind the desk that sat in the middle of the room was an older woman dressed in orange pants and a white and orange striped top.

'Hi, I'm Jolene,' the woman with her red ginger hair in dreadlocks said.

The room was a stark contrast to the rest of the property. It was clean, bright, and had the inviting scent of rosemary and lemon.

Jolene came to shake both our hands and started to show me around. She stopped at the bracelet section of her stock, 'Was there something you had in mind?'

I didn't know what to say. The wall of stock was overwhelming, and permanent jewellery wasn't exactly popular, nor was I a fan. Kaleb, on the other hand, was a different story.

'Oh, she wants this,' Kaleb piped up, pointing to a dainty rose gold chain. 'And can we get these charms?'

He was like a teenager when they're in a 7/11, or a grocery store, going straight for the confectionery section.

'Is that what you want, sweetie?' Jolene asked me.

Her question caught me off-guard and behind her was Kaleb, nodding his head excitedly. I looked back at her, smiling weakly, 'Y-yes.'

Despite my clear hesitation, she sat me down in the chair opposite hers. Jolene wheeled her stool behind me and held the long chain around my neck, assessing the length I wanted.

'A choker,' Kaleb said.

Jolene obliged.

I felt the cold metal wrap around my neck and my fear receptors started going off. The sensitive area of skin above my major blood vessels was a no-go – I immediately felt like she was choking me. My fingers looped under the fine chain, stopping her in an instant.

'Yeah no,' I choked putting a slight resistance onto the chain. 'Can it sit so it dangles just below my collar bones?'

Jolene smiled at me in the mirror and moved with me as I held it down to my collar bone region. Kaleb scowled but I didn't care, it was gorgeous. I could envisage the charms now, sitting between the medial aspect of my collar bones.

'I love it,' I said.

'Awesome, I'll start soldering it,' Jolene said.

I watched as she cut the chain and started to prep her workspace.

'Happy birthday, Kenzie,' Kaleb said, kissing the back of my right hand. 'I love you.'

'I love you too,' I replied.

# 22

# May 2018

*22 Years Old*

The crunch of the leaves from the bush out back was music to my ears as I jogged through the path to the beach. The sandy opening got wider the closer I got. Its picturesque view reminded me of why I loved coming out here, even if I didn't want to. Not a single troubled thought ever entered my mind. The crashing of the gentle waves and the feeling of the salt in the air touching my bare skin was heaven for me. It was as if the breeze blew away all my troubles and replaced them with freedom. The wind powered through me and sure enough I was on the last two hundred metres to my tree. My legs burned, aching for a break.

*I should've stretched first.*

But as I neared closer, an eerie feeling kept me moving forward. I headed further and further down the beach, my legs no longer burned. My heart raced. Beads of sweat formed on my forehead.

*I gotta get back. I have to chuck a uey. I can't be out here. I should've brought my bloody phone.*

As I made my way back to the tree. I slowed and locked onto the dark figure that stood watching me at the base of the tree. Its gaze followed me as I kept on running. Just as I was about to lose sight from a bush, the figure stepped onto the beach.

The tall figure became clear, and I bolted. My legs burned as I sprinted as fast as I could. My heart felt like it was about to explode. There was no way that this was happening.

*Kaleb.*

I hadn't seen or heard from him since the hotel. That was four days ago. Part of that was being in police custody, and quite possibly the flight home. His silence for the rest of the time was probably planning for retaliation. I was anticipating that whatever it could be, it was bound to be extreme.

I couldn't risk continuing my run. I couldn't.

*Push. Push. Push.*

'Oh. My. God,' I huffed as the sand turned to dirt. I was almost home.

A few metres ahead was the concrete path and I drove my feet harder and harder into the hardening ground beneath me.

I fumbled at the coded gate, unsure what Kaleb's capabilities were. For all I knew, he drove his way over and was around the corner, ready to choke me out from behind.

*He isn't violent. You're worrying for nothing.*

I thought back to the other week, how he behaved. My blood boiled, and I slammed the gate shut behind me.

As soon as I was in the safety of my own bedroom, I tossed my phone on my bed and collapsed on the ground. Chest heaving. My clothes clung to me, beads of sweat still rolling down my body.

My phone had been sounding away the minute I fell to the ground. I crawled on the hardwood floors to my bed, my legs still feeling like jelly.

**Kaleb:** *Knew you'd be on a run today, just had a feeling*

There was an attachment sent. My hands begun to shake, as I tapped on the file, sure enough, it was me, in my Mercedes F1 team jersey and black leggings.

**Kaleb:** *Aww, did I scare you?*

**Kaleb:** *I didn't mean to. I'm so sorry. I just wanted to talk.*

**Kaleb:** *Damn girl, didn't know you could run like that.*

A video file popped up after the string of texts. There was a bitter taste on my tongue, a wave of nausea washed through me. He has reached a new low.

'He filmed me!?' I yelped.

I ran out of my room and to the bathroom, heaving puke into the toilet bowl.

'Everything okay sweetheart?' Mum asked as she ran to the bathroom.

'Yeah, just pushed myself too hard. Didn't help that I didn't give myself enough time to digest my food.'

She nodded and headed back out. I pushed the lock pin in, scared she'd come back around.

I couldn't tell her. The embarrassment was real. Too real. Like a siren blaring that ignited panic from deep within. There was nothing left of me anymore. I felt like a shell of a person.

I collapsed to the ground, horrified at his lengths, as yet another image came through.

*He was in the trees? What was his deal now? Hasn't he done enough with the police officer for a welfare check or showing up at my hotel? What do I do?*

**Kaleb:** *Pay back is a bitch isn't it. Never call the police on me again.*

**Kaleb:** *Do you understand me?*

**Kaleb:** *I said, do you understand me?*

**Kaleb:** *Hello? Bitch?*

My phone shook violently as I tried to open the collection of images he had sent. As I maneuvered my hand around my phone, my sweaty palms reared the one-handed task almost impossible.

'Fuck,' I muttered as I almost dropped my phone on the tiles, gripping the phone with both hands before it hit. Keeping a death grip on the phone in one hand, I shakily tapped the collection with the other. Only to find multiple photos of me from a boudoir photo shoot I did for him in the early stages of dating. There was only one thing that I could do.

**Me:** *I understand.*

I left the bathroom, tail between my legs as I headed back to the comfort of my bedroom.

As soon as I had crossed the threshold, my door was closed and locked. I pulled my late grandma's crocheted blanket over my shoulders and wrapped it around me. The soft mattress shifted under my weight as I moved to sit against the wall, letting myself stare out the window to the bush behind the house.

'I was wrong, so wrong,' I whispered.

I was well and truly in danger now. Kaleb had stooped to a level I didn't think was possible. Yet, my heart and my brain were not united.

'Logically and realistically, I should go. He's threatened me. The police would ... But I love him.'

*You were taught to obey with a smile, not to disrupt peace. This is your own fault, McKenna. You disobeyed him.*

I opened the blanket up and pulled my legs to my chest, wrapping myself back up in the comfort of my grandma's memory.

'The officer's wrong. This isn't abuse, it's just punishment.' The words tumbled out like vomit.

> "Sit there until you decide that you are done lying," Mr Ohm, my grade seven teacher, said.

"Yes, sir," I replied, my head hung low.

I looked over to see Harriet mouth "I'm sorry" except 'sorry' meant nothing. She could've backed me up, said to Mr Ohm that I wasn't lying, that Bec were bullying me. Instead, they stood there smirking at me.

'Punished for standing up for myself is an absolute joke,' I muttered. 'Keeping my mouth shut worked, why didn't I — Why didn't I just stay a selective mute with him? Why?'

*'You deserve this,'* Kaleb's voice echoed in my head.

'I do deserve this,' I repeated. My fingernails dug eight little crescent moons into my calves with every deep breath I took. The stinging heat was a comforting feeling, my muscles relaxed.

There was a knock on my bedroom door.

'What?' I called.

'You okay honey?' Mum asked.

*No, my boyfriend is emotionally abusing me, stalking me, blackmailing me. I need you.*

I dug my nails back into my calves as I said, 'Yeah, everything's fine, ma.'

*That was too convincing.*

My stomach churned again. I dug my nails further into the skin.

'Okay, Kenny,' she said. 'Want me to make you a lemon and ginger or peppermint tea?'

'No, thank you, mum, I'm just going to chill for a while.'

I shakily reached for my phone and saved the images, videos and conversation screenshots into a hidden folder labelled: "For when I decide it's time".

# 23

# May 2018

*22 Years Old*

I was cosied up with a cup of orange juice with a half shot of vodka in the corner of Kaleb's L-shaped sofa. The sound of the hail hitting the roof sent a high-pitched ding echoing through the air. Shivers ran down my spine, and I wrapped the blanket around my head, providing more comfort while I stared at my laptop screen in my lap.

'McKenna?' Dylan said through the computer screen.

'Huh? Sorry,' I replied. 'What did you say?'

'Doesn't matter, you okay?'

*Am I really okay?*

If he could see the state I was in beyond the screen, he wouldn't have needed to ask me that. Kaleb was instilling fear into me. Whilst the storm brought me comfort, every sound made me jump in fear that it would be him.

A large hail stone hit the shutters, I flinched causing my laptop to fall off my legs.

'Yeah, yeah. I'm fine.'

'I may have only known you for a short time, but you're most certainly lying.'

I drew my lips into a tight line, unsure if I should even raise my true thoughts. Dylan had become a great friend in a matter of days during my last nursing placement. That wasn't enough for me to fully trust him. Though if I didn't ask, I never would know.

'Did you really mean what you said when you thought I was a med student?'

'Yeah, it looked and sounded like you had been in the industry a lot longer than four years as a nursing student. You're the only person in health care in your family aren't you?'

'Yes I am,' I said proudly. 'I've just been thinking more and more. Nursing isn't really for me. Don't get me wrong, I love it, but I ...'

'You want more responsibility in the decisions?'

'Sort of. Also, nurses have major responsibilities too, Dylan.'

'Oh I am very much aware.'

'But I — I don't really know. Medicine is definitely something I want to pursue. I love patient care that nursing provides, but it's the problem solving that comes along with medicine.'

I may have wanted more in my career, even if I did enjoy nursing. Except, the more I thought about starting my job, or post-grad, the more I thought about medicine. It was a challenge, no matter the specialty or sub-specialty I was to undertake, it wouldn't be easy.

'It's a tough road, I get abused by consultants most days of the week. It isn't for the faint of heart, especially when a patient dies.'

'You trying to talk me out of it?'

'Just making sure you have the full picture. Most people glorify medicine and do it for the ego or God-complex. Then they can't handle getting yelled at by the consultants, who, for the most part, are on the same ego trip.'

I laughed. 'I've come across some of those consultants. It isn't fun as a nurse either. Some of the higher ups, dish it back because they won't stand for the abuse. Us younglings? Oh we need to keep a clean slate for sure.'

Doctor Andrew Houton was my first egotistical consultant. He swore at me because how I dressed a wound wasn't how he liked it. Not one supervisor I was with warned me about him. Probably an initiation tactic even though I was a student not a graduate. I was so scared and embarrassed that I demanded to learn what standard of practice he wanted, in case it wasn't something we were taught in school.

'If med's the goal and dream, I say go for it. You have the eye for detail. Heck! I'll vouch for you to get a placement in Adelaide, study under me.'

'Thank you,' I replied, toying with the chain wrapped around my neck.

'Why do you wear that? It's like a tag, as if he's saying you're *his*.'

'Dyl, come on, it's a nice gift.'

'Is it?' From the frown that quickly consumed his facial features, I could tell that it came out harsher than he intended, but I stopped his apology before he could say it.

'I —' I cut myself off.

'I'm sorry if I overstepped,' Dylan said.

'No, no. It's fine. I, uh. I gotta go.'

I closed Zoom and suddenly realised how alone I was. Listening to the continuous pings of hail hitting the roof wasn't the same as it used to be. After the final day in Adelaide, anything was now possible. Maybe I was that naïve after all and Kaleb really has been this way for a long time.

'I haven't paid for my applications yet, I have time,' I whispered. I looked at the open tabs to GEMSAS and every private application.

They taunted me, causing a downward spiral into an existential crisis of what did I really want to do? What direction was pulling me harder than the rest? It wasn't too late to back out of my applications, they were more like drafts. Maybe I was an academic masochist. Maybe I was my own biggest enemy.

The minute the money leaves my account, it'd be too late to pull out.

Considering I'd sat every year without fail, only to obtain a score less than fifty in one or all sections of the exam. This was the first time I had a highly competitive score for the GAMSAT with an overall score of 80. I'd be a fool to let that go.

Maybe Dylan had a point. If I had an aspiration, I should just go for it. Spending a life where I solely people pleased would be boring and depressing.

That was my life.

*Sometimes you need to be a little selfish; this is the time for me to step away from giving people what they want.*

'Kenz!?'

'Crap,' I mumbled, quickly shutting down all my tabs but Netflix. 'In here!' I called from the dining room.

# 24

# May 2018

*22 Years Old*

Kaleb walked out from his bedroom with a slight bounce to his step. He was soaking wet from the storm outside considering he rarely ever used the front door. He always opted for the private patio entrance to his bedroom.

'I had the best day ever!' he said. 'Just got offered a promotion for when I graduate.'

'That's great hon,' I replied, trying my best to hide the fear in my voice with fake enthusiasm.

'Yeah it is. I'll be making up to six figures and since you hate nursing, we can easily live off my pay, no reason for you to study or work.'

'What?'

Dumbfounded. Rage. Confusion.

So many emotions ran through my body.

I couldn't tell whether I wanted to scream or cry. I wanted to have a career. There was no way in hell that I was going to give that up to be a stay-at-home wife. I had no desire to become one, especially to Kaleb.

"I'm going out for two hours, got errands to run," Kaleb said, as I handed him the takeout coffee I picked up on the way over.

"Okay?" I replied, taking a sip of my takeout coffee. "If you said that you were going out, I could've come over later."

"The dishes need to be done, clothes need to be washed and hung out while I'm out. Thanks bye."

No kiss, no 'love you'.

Doing chores was fine with me, but I hadn't been at his place in a week, maybe ten days tops.

The place was a mess, clothes everywhere and dishes stacked next to the sink. It was like he waited for me to arrive, so he didn't have to do any of it. Even the rubbish in his room had started to stink up the place.

If I did buy into this stay-at-home-wife thing, I wouldn't be looking at a partnership. This wasn't about gender roles or being a traditional wife. This would be him getting to do as little as possible and being looked after like a parent to a child. That wasn't a partnership I wanted. I wanted one that works together. Who love each other and who wants to be a family-unit raising the next generation.

'I'm actually planning on pursuing medicine, I told you that,' I said. 'I told you I was settling for second best with nursing. That doesn't mean that if I don't get into medicine I'd drop my degree entirely. You were ... supportive.'

'Well this is news to me.'

'We — We had a conversation about it, just last night,' I whispered. 'We've had multiple conversations.'

"Kaleb, can I talk to you?" I had asked.

"Sure thing," he replied.

He was in a much better mood after the whole Adelaide ordeal, he even took me to dinner and bought me an amethyst pendent to make up for it. My fear and concerns had gone out the window. He just wanted to protect me.

"Great," I said, sitting down beside him on the sofa. "I've been thinking more about pursuing medicine. I have a competitive GAMSAT score of seventy-nine, so I think I want to apply."

He laced his fingers in mine and leaned over, kissing me on the lips. When he pulled away, he smiled.

"I think that's wonderful!" He beamed. "Should go for it. I know how much you wanted Griffith University, should apply Kenzie."

'No we didn't, that conversation never happened!' his baritone voice bellowed in the air.

His face went red, and his mouth pulled into a tight frown. I was trapped. I pulled the blanket that was around me tighter, covering more of my head, to form a barrier from him.

'What's the point of this then?' he shouted as he pointed between himself and me. 'I thought we had a plan.'

'We did, and I thought we were on the same page and now apparently, in your words, we aren't,' I said. 'It was never my dream to be a stay at home anything. You keep bringing up kids and marriage, but I don't even know if I want any kids myself.'

That was a lie. I wanted kids. But not now. I was only twenty-two with my whole life ahead of me and a career I so desperately wanted. This wasn't a man I wanted to be tied down to for the rest of my life. I couldn't do that to myself, not when I had things going really well for me.

I barely knew myself anymore.

But fear held me back. What he was capable of could've been far worse than I could ever had imagined. Would he murder me? He had the balls to stalk me and call the cops.

Under the blanket my nails dug deep into my palms trying to signal to my sympathetic nervous system to cool it. I felt my face flush, heat consuming me. My nails dug in deeper, stopping myself from lashing. If I let it slip it would be another thing he'd turn back to me.

'What the fuck has gotten into you?!' he exclaimed.

The sudden input of the explicative sent shivers down my spine.

'I need to get out of here,' I said slowly.

The blanket fell off me into a crumbled pile on the couch as I stood up, taking my laptop with me.

'Fuck you, McKenna. You clearly don't fucking love me anymore.'

'Who said I didn't?'

I was face-to-face with him now. His warm breath hit my cheek as he continued to huff.

'Well you're going back on your plan,' he breathed.

'No, I'm adjusting the plan to fit who I am, not what everyone wants me to be,' I replied.

But that was the thing. I kept saying that I am becoming myself, but truth was, I still didn't know. Lost was an understatement, but that was the only way I could fully describe how I felt. My brain wanted to succumb to the need for routine, not wanting to change its ways.

'What's that supposed to mean?'

'It means.' I stopped dead in my tracks, holding my open backpack in one hand, and I took a deep breath. 'I am over people telling me who I am and what I am supposed to do.'

'That still doesn't make any sense.'

'Kaleb, I have always wanted to be a doctor.'

'You're a dumb fucking bitch, how are you supposed to be a doctor when you have to look after our kids?'

'I don't want kids now, I don't even know if I want any in the future. I'm twenty-two for crying out loud. I can barely look after myself.' I shoved my belongings into the bag and hurried toward his sliding door. 'Oh and, F.Y.I., I am not dumb, I completed my degree with a GPA of 7.0. Check your facts before trying to insult me.'

I stormed out, closing the sliding door with force, but not quite a slam. My legs carried me as best they could though they felt like jelly. The rain drops felt cool against my bare skin, washing away the anger as I hightailed it to my car.

'I can't believe I did that,' I said to myself as I pulled out of the driveway with my seatbelt still resting beside my seat.

My throat started to feel tight. I gripped my Bluetooth device, yanking it out of the cigarette lighter. I tossed it to the floor of the passenger front seat along with my belongings.

'Why the fuck did I do that? Of all things! He's going to make me regret it. Fuck!'

I banged the steering wheel with the one hand that wasn't steering the car towards the road. Once I was a safe distance away, I pulled on my seat belt. My windscreen wipers danced side to side quickly as the rain poured down.

It seemed to be easing up. The hail had finally stopped. Though I wouldn't have minded to drive in the hail. It would've been better than remaining in the house with Kaleb, where I was at risk of further losing more of myself in this battle between my heart, true self, and brain.

Driving was the best way to clear my head, but tonight it only continued my internal spiral. I knew I couldn't stay with him but now I was more afraid to leave. But I had to leave. I just didn't want to on account of normalcy.

*This is normal, isn't it? But those images.*

I shuddered. Every time I closed my eyes, I saw them.

I was wrong. So wrong. Physicality was becoming near, but how far would he go?

My heart raced and tears stung my eyes, but I kept focused on the road.

I no longer had a partner that was in my corner. Instead I had a stranger. Kaleb was showing more of his true colours. Tonight, he scared me more than I wanted to admit out loud. I never wanted to repeat it at all. But it was getting too hard to hide now. I had watched as he had his balled fists, the vein in his forehead became prominent.

Dylan wouldn't treat me this way. He even wants to aid in getting me a placement in Adelaide. But he could just be saying that before he leaves me in the lurch like Kaleb.

I wanted to talk to people — not just my parents — about my tug-o-war in my brain. As much as I valued Aster and Dylan, friends were the worst backstabbers of my life. I lent on them more than my folks back in the day, and they were just as quick to leave me or throw me under the bus. I felt more lost than I ever had.

'What do I do?' I asked the rain. 'I want medicine, I want to be a nurse, but I love him. Even though I shouldn't. I do. Oh, what do I do?'

# 25

## August 2013

*15 Years Old*

I sat at the foot of my bed, my nan's blue and white blanket she crocheted for me, wrapped around my shoulders. The sound of the harsh storm was a comfort to my depression and got me into a heated bate. Darkness washed over the house, and I greeted it like an old friend. Unlike my parents, grandparents, and friends, it didn't lie to me.

"Are you having a blonde moment," Mrs Hatti had said earlier in the week.

The thunder clapped overhead.

I had asked a question about how to approach one of the more difficultly worded problems in next week's math content. Except, Mr Barnaby scrunched his face and said, "That's a silly question. McKenna, you should know that by now." Only to answer my friend, Lilly, who asked the same question.

Lightning cracked like a whip as lit up the sky for a couple of seconds.

*I sat with Mr Johanus to get insight into one of my assignments, hoping to do better for my next assignment. Instead, of a pleasant smile that he had given many of my pees before me, I was met with a stone-cold look. "If you followed the task and criteria sheets, this wouldn't have happened," he said. I watched as my classmates succeeded, while I went backwards, confidence dwindling.*

I knew I wasn't good enough. My teachers thought so. All of my efforts to do better than a C-average went unnoticed. They saw more of my academic talent than my parents who only aided in my homework if I asked. So why should I believe the words told by my folks when they're not the ones grading me?

My four-page *Romeo and Juliet* monologue assignment felt heavy in my hands. With a quick flick of the wrist, I watched on as the pages scattered, knowing that nothing I do would make them a killer monologue.

*Medical school is my goal, but if I don't have what it takes, then why should I even bother trying to apply? I could sit with the truth that my teachers were right.*

I spoke to the rain, 'Better I know now than trying to apply to university and failing. I guess.' The windowpane cold against my tear-stained cheek. 'I'm not smart enough for anything.'

My parents made me believe that I was brave, strong, and smart, but I knew better than the lies. I wasn't brave, or smart. I had it on good authority. How could my parents think that private school education and standards were the right fit for me? I was falling further and further behind as my mental health continued to plummet.

Schools these days were supposed to have a zero-bully tolerance. Yet Sunnydale College did nothing. Rocks were thrown at me. No one was reprimanded, despite several witnesses, and it being caught on camera.

I wasn't protected.

My parents did what they could, entrusting a school's word against their own daughter's. They also didn't want to pull me out with only one term to go. Though changing schools was definitely an option, but was it though? Moving from primary to high school, didn't protect me from the wrath of students and teachers.

I longed for the escape to a fantasy land, I was still waiting for that bloody letter to whisk me away. It was nothing more than a mere dream. I let myself escape into the deep realms of "fandom" Tumblr, pretending to be someone I'm not.

I turned my gaze to the sky. 'Will it ever get better, God? Why should I continue to talk to you if none of my prayers have been answered? All I want is a signal as to why you've allowed me to be bullied. Why, God?'

Like always, there was no response. My faith was hanging by a thread. Unsure where to turn.

'What's the point of believing in something if nothing good ever happens to those who should deserve it? Karma is bullshit because good things always happen to the shitty people.'

I grabbed the closest throw pillow, drew it to my ear and shoved it like a shotput ball towards the wall. I watched as it hit the framed picture collection of my friends and me on a boat on the Great Barrier Reef a few months ago. They fell, the glass shattering and ripping into the pillow.

'Fuck,' I muttered. 'Oh well, it was a shitty pillowcase anyway.'

Only it wasn't, I had grabbed the sentimental piece of craftwork that Mum and I had done together. My sobs filled the air mixing in with the storm outside.

I continued to sit in the cold darkness, staring at my reflection in the mirror. The walls felt like they were closing in. I continued to feed her brain more lies, letting myself embrace the 'dumb blonde' mentality that my teachers inflicted.

'How can they get away with telling an impressionable child?'

How nobody could answer that, I had no idea. It was a shitty stereotype, yet one that I wanted to succumb to.

*Why not become who they want me to be?*

To me, teachers were untouchable, like police officers and paramedics. No evidence could be obtained without jeopardising yourself.

I always thought my destiny was medicine or something in health care, like nursing, but now, I wasn't so sure.

'Maybe I'm not supposed to live past fifteen.'

My last string of sanity went out the window.

The thunder's roar grew louder, shaking the house. Nobody goes six years of bullying and abuse without the string snapping. Without meeting rock bottom.

The last straw for me was getting told, "You won't get higher than a C," by one teacher when all I asked for was help. Though it was painfully obvious that I was so close. I had a B minus to B's in other criteria but missed out significantly in the heavier areas. She couldn't even lend some advice, while I listened to my best friend get help when he asked the same question. Mind you, he was getting A's as it was.

It was almost like I was a beacon for negative energy. Nobody else, at least that I was aware of, got the same treatment; I was picked out of 23 kids per class. I was over it.

'I hate it here. What's the point anymore?'

With the bullying getting worse and being left out academically, I was losing sight of myself.

*Who am I if I'm not meant to be a doctor?*

There were so many other great options out there. At the rate that I was going, all I was destined for was an Arts Degree or finding a job without needing a degree. Nothing wrong with that, but I had plans. Why were they getting squished when I was putting in the effort?

*Is the plan to die at the ripe age of fourteen?*

As soon as the thought crossed my mind, I stood shakily towards the mirror.

'Do I want to die?' I cocked my head to the side, just like my dog, Cocoa, did whenever she heard her favourite word; "walk". It was the anticipation as I studied my reflection's expression.

Thunder clapped loudly above.

I jumped at the sudden noise, and the thought of death went away, replaced with harm. I pressed my long fingernails into my skin as hard as I could go. I looked over to the words of affirmation Mum stuck on my mirror and envisioned them burning to the ground.

I dug my nails in further, letting out a chat of grunts, 'Lies. Lies. Lies. I am stupid. I am ugly. I am an imposter. I hate it here. Nobody loves me. Nobody wants me. What's the fucking point?'

A sharp fiery pain in my palms caused me to stop. I immediately pulled my finger nails out, only to see thin streaks of red drops coming for the cuts. Blood drained from my face and blackness started to cloud my vision. I quickly laid down on my bed feeling grateful for the first, and only, time for my extremely painful period cramps and fear of blood.

Except, I found an alternative.

After tending to the wounds on my hands, the thought of my dysmenorrhea inspired me. The withheld orgasm replicated my excruciating period cramp. Except this time, I was in control. Orgasms were supposed to be a good thing, a reward, but how could I have anything good when I deserved nothing? As soon as my muscles stopped spasming, I smiled wildly as the lightning cracked loudly overhead.

The storm outside wasn't letting up. With my parents and brother still out, I walked to the bathroom and pulled out Mum's box blonde hair dye.

'Well. If they wanna treat me like a blonde. Then they're gonna get a motherfucking blonde.' I pulled up a YouTube video and read the instructions. Once I was confident, I started to prepare the dye. 'How hard can this be?'

The smell of bleach filled the air as I started to lather it on. There was certainly no going back now. The dye was applied just as the YouTube video said.

'Goodbye McKenna, Kenz, Kenna, and Ken. You will be missed.'

My scalp tingled.

There was nothing left for me now. I had nothing to lose.

*Why should I have pleasures? Why should I be allowed to live in a world where I am seen as worthless?*

Another crack of lightning sounded.

'Yes! Feed off my motherfucking anger!' I screamed to the storm.

Hail pelted at the windows. The thunder continued to roar. I laughed manically as I waited for the time to tick over half an hour. It was time for them to see what they've done to me.

# 26

# July 2018

*22 Years Old*

With hesitantly placed step, I stood proud in my emerald-green midi-dress and two-inch black stilettos, as I treaded through the cobblestone courtyard of grand hall of the university. Ankle high rope fences outlined the pristine green grass patches, creating a trip hazard.

My family trailed behind, and I stopped just shy of a cream canvas tent, secured 'Come find us once you're out and we'll get the photos,' mum said embracing me in a hug, to which I returned.

Before I turned to head to the tent, I went to hug Kaleb. His arms stayed stiff his side, his head straight ahead and refused to look at me. 'What's the matter?' I asked.

He ignored my question. His eyes widened, and he pushed me out of the way 'Franklin!' he called out to a guy I hadn't me. 'Mate! What are you doing here?'

My heart grew heavier by the minute. I reluctantly headed towards the tent, ignoring the pang in my heart. I dodged the few families and their graduates on my way to the cap and gown area, trying to not let my emotions show. After all, today was about me, and my monumental achievement.

Though I was allowed to be upset. Why would my boyfriend choose to ruin one of the biggest milestones in my life? Unlike Dad, who was likely stuck in traffic, Kaleb made the choice to be distant.

I was about to pull myself away from the line-up and make a dash for the bathrooms, when I heard one of my classmates call out.

'Oh, my god! That colour on you!' Melody cried, giving me a hug.

I quickly tried to blink away the water in my eyes before turning to face the overly positive woman.

'Thanks,' I replied, eyeing the gorgeous ruby red dress she had on. 'Loving the red on you, hon. Powerful.'

'The Christmas graduates,' she laughed.

'That'd be a great IG caption.'

The two of us laughed into the line-up.

Eight rows of hundreds of gowns lined the entrance. It was hitting me that I was only an hour away from crossing the stage. It was an overwhelming feeling. I never thought I would ever get to see myself graduate, and yet, there I was, getting helped into the gown and hood. A true honour.

'Feeling ready?' Melody asked as I got to the mortarboard area.

'Yes, and no,' I replied. 'Overwhelming.'

'I know right! Imposter syndrome is kicking in.'

She wasn't wrong. This was a tremendous deal, and I felt like I didn't belong. Though I earned my grades fair and square. I was about to read a speech to thousands of people, which also included high school alumni.

'Congratulations,' the lady giving me the mortarboard said.

'Thank you,' I replied. She was the third helper to congratulate me since I got in line.

Melody passed her phone to one of the other graduates and the two of us posed, showing off our gowns and dresses. Enjoying the moment. It really was fleeting. It was real now. I could feel the weight of the gown push my shoulders down, but it felt soft against my bare skin.

Once enough photos had been taken, Melody had dashed out into the sea of shiny gowns and proud families.

I weaved through the crowd towards where my family should be. Immediately, feeling relief washed over me as I spotted Dad sitting with Mum and Will, right where I had left them. As I got closer and saw that Mum was already tearful, I quickly pulled a tissue from my purse.

'Don't ma, I don't need mascara running down my face quite this soon,' I said.

Kaleb was nowhere to be seen. Though, I didn't care. He could leave for all I care. This was my day.

'Holy crap! You look amazing!'

'Aster!' I exclaimed, turning around to see her running graciously in 5-inch stilettos. 'Okay, tell me your secret. I can barely walk in these two-inch heels.'

Her laugh was contagious, but it came to an abrupt stop when she noticed Kaleb was nowhere to be found.

'Where —?' she started. I shook my head.

The four of us headed up to the photo booths for the professional photos. I tried to see if I could see him in the crowd, but I couldn't. It was just a complete sea of hundreds of graduates and their parents.

**Me:** *Where are you? We're at the photo booths*

'Is he coming?' Aster asked.

'Not by the look of being left on read,' I replied. 'Let's just go. I don't need him in the photos.'

It was already dawning on me that I was dating a Class-A narcissist. He was miserable if something wasn't about him. Being here would be making him miserable, and yet he still came. I couldn't tell if this was a ploy of manipulation or if somewhere deep, deep down, he actually cared about me.

Well, Kaleb won't be getting any more attention from me today. I won't feed into his game. I don't even know why I still let him come after the incident back in July. That was probably the worst day of my life to date. Besides finding out that this bloody necklace was a collar.

*I'm a person! Not a toy.*

'I sent the Adelaide folk the link so they can watch it live,' Aster said.

'You're too kind,' I replied.

'We're so proud of you, honey,' Dad said, kissing my cheek. 'Might want to lose the loser though.'

'Planning on it,' I replied.

*Just a matter of "when".*

I wasn't entirely ready to ditch him, nor did I have enough to really stick it to him. There was a lack of evidence of the abuse. I really wanted to show him just how strong I am, make him pay for the hurt he's caused me over the years.

The line was moving faster now, and we were sent to the far station of the professional photo booth line-up. This was my moment. My cheeks ached from how widely I smiled. I was beaming. A metaphorical glow surrounded me, almost like a pregnancy glow, or the glow after just having the best sex of your life.

Mum was tearing up again. Dad tapped her arm, handing her a tissue. Will was as still as a statue; expressionless. I knew deep down he was proud of me. He just didn't like to show it, after all he had a reputation to uphold.

My leg bounced ferociously, but I kept it at bay, trying to not let it be seen from afar.. I could barely make out the crowd through the darkened auditorium and the heads of staff and a few fellow graduates.

*Come on, come on.*

Names were called for those who scored a GPA below the distinction and high distinction line. I smiled and applauded my peers as they walked past me. Twiddling my thumbs seemed to work, hidden from the cameras that pointed towards the full stage.

'High distinction, and school medallist for the School of Nursing, Midwifery, and Social Sciences, McKenna Carrington,' Professor Sav Greggory, said.

I rose from my seat and doffed my mortarboard as I walked towards Vice Chancellor Ruby Smeltz, shaking her hand.

My cheeks ached as I beamed brightly. It stayed even when I walked back around to my seat, testamur and medal in hand. My leg was back to bouncing while I watched the rest of the graduates get theirs, itching to get the speech over with.

'We will now present awards to some of our graduates and honorary guests,' the speaker announced.

I waited once again for my name to be called front and centre. Several fellow award winners walked past me.

'The Bloom Unity for nurses – Naomi Bloom trophy is awarded to one graduating nursing student who has excelled in their studies. On placements and practical assessments, they always maintained a high aptitude of dedication, grit, empathy, and autonomy. It is my great honour to present this trophy to McKenna Carrington in the graduating class of 2018.'

I walked across that stage like I owned it. My parents and friends yelled from the audience as I crossed the stage once again. My smile did not falter once. My head held high.

'Thank you,' I said to the Vice Chancellor as I shook her hand once more, taking the trophy and certificate from her.

*Goodbye Imposter Syndrome.*

The air felt thin. A kaleidoscope of butterflies fluttered around my stomach. I was on cloud-nine.

'I'd like to now invite McKenna Carrington to the stage to give the student commencement speech,' Sav said.

I rose from my seat and pulled the neatly folding pages from my bra, taking my place downstage right. Normally, looking out to darkness brought me warmth and safety, but this was different. My hands grew clammy, and I fumbled, scrunching my speech rather than smoothing it out. I glanced up to the darkness, and my mouth dried up.

For the first time, the dark scared me; I wasn't alone.

I turned away from the microphone and cleared my throat. The paper took my focus rather than the people.

'Esteemed faculty, friends, family and, of course, the graduating class of 2018. Today marks the start of the next chapter of our lives. Whether we're off travelling the world. Starting that new job or heading straight into post-grad.' I took a slight step back to swallow the large amount of saliva. 'My name is McKenna Carrington, Bachelor of Nursing and as of today—' I moved my tassel to the left. '—A qualified registered nurse. Fellow graduates, we made it. Overcame challenges and maybe tried many degrees. Either way, you ended up exactly where you were meant to be today.'

I read the next line in my head and paused momentarily. Looking up to the section I put my family, and Kaleb and Aster in.

'I almost didn't,' I continued. 'My life wasn't exactly the easiest. Being up here today is like a dream I didn't think I'd get to live in real life. Not to mention, my high school grades almost weren't enough to get me into university. Yet, as soon as I started my degree, I met the most nurturing and supportive tutors. I saw my grades become as high as they have ever been. Thank you to my wonderful educators who helped me get here. To my group of friends, aka the best group of now qualified nurses, and soon to be qualified RN.' I saluted up to Aster. 'May our game nights live on, whether via zoom or in person. And finally, to my parents. I honestly don't think there's anything left to say that I haven't said over the past four years. This day is as much your day as it is mine. Thank you for being the best practice patients and really testing me. I don't think I ever could have done it without you.'

Their screams from the left side of the auditorium said it all, and I chuckled.

'Oh and how could I forget my statue of a brother.' Laughter erupted from the auditorium. 'Not a single tear or smile shed today. Funny, two graduates in one year. You're welcome for obtaining the best biology tutor you could find.' I pointed to myself, earning me laughs from the crowd. 'And thank you for letting me ramble about human anatomy to you. From the sounds of it, I think you may have benefitted. Doh. I think I just got you into university.'

More laughs erupted, and I waited for them to die down before continuing, 'On a more serious note. I really wouldn't be up here pursuing my dreams if it weren't for the help of my teaching team and my family. I threw myself into the deep end, taking up every opportunity I could handle.'

The papers shook as my fingers grazed the edges, turning over to the next page.

'Now to wrap up my long winded and quite self-centred speech. Oh look, halfway to being a doctor, just need the shocking handwriting.' The crowd's laughter was music to my ears. 'Fellow graduates, go out there and be the absolute legends we were taught to be. Some of us will be up for promotions, PhDs, awards, and so much more before we know it. I part you with these words, explore outside your comfort zone. Take every opportunity that comes your way. You never know what may happen if you take it. We can all achieve great things if we seize every opportunity. Congratulations, class of 2018.'

As I made my way off the stand, I grabbed the rough fabric that covered the tip of my cap, doffing toward the Vice Chancellor and to Sav.

'Splendid speech,' Simon said, turning around to face me as I sat down. 'And well done on the prize, you've earned it.'

'Thank you,' I replied.

I looked out to the crowd once more, as we filed off the stage and out to the hallway. My clammy sweat-drench hands held my achievements in death grips; scared I'd drop them.

*Today I got the last hurrah.*

As I continued to mosey around the lobby looking for my parents, I saw old girls and boys from my high school. Whether they were fellow graduates, siblings or friends of graduates, it didn't matter. Cairns may have had a population of approximately 165,530 people, but yet, it felt a lot smaller. It was their shocked faces that made me smile, and my already great day turned even better.

My parents, Will and Aster came down the steps from the upper levels. With my head held high, I walked towards them with a death grip on my testamur, certificate and trophy.

# 27

# November 2015

*17 Years Old*

I sat in the darkest and coldest corner of my room. My ears had gone numb from wearing my headphones for hours, with my emo playlist blasting through them.

My last week as a high school student ruined. Not one person cared that I wasn't there at graduation rehearsal, or that I shied away from online socialisation and the final school held celebrations yesterday.

I was so caught up in my own feelings that I didn't hear mum shouting my name. Instead I felt my headphones getting ripped off my head.

'Hey!' I exclaimed.

Mum moved into my vision. 'I've been calling you for ages. Everything okay?' I shrugged. 'Well, I just got a call from Mr Domelio asking if you're going to attend your graduation tonight.'

'Depends. Do you want me to go?'

I had my own views on the school that made me lose my faith in God and almost cost me my life. However, with a supporter like mum, this was just as much her moment as it was mine.

She turned to face my neatly hung-up uniform for a moment. When she turned back to face me, there was a look of sadness in her eyes.

'I don't need you to walk across the stage if you don't want to,' she said. 'Your father and I are very proud of you no matter what you want to do.'

'That isn't an answer mum.'

The phone calls she would get from the school. The discussions we had over coffee and arrowroots. She could see the pain I was in, but she was in the dark. There were so many opportunities for the school to give her warnings, especially me being a high risk of suicide.

*If only you knew. If only they did their due diligence. You never would have let me make a big decision if you knew more than just the bullshit they fed you. If only I told you the truth, not half.*

'Honey, I —' She stopped herself, not giving me a clear enough response.

I sighed. 'I won't go unless you want me to. You deserve to watch at least one of your children cross the stage. You know damn well Will won't show up to his own graduation.'

I watched her fight a smirk. 'You'll regret it either way.'

'Only way I regret it, is if you lie to me and say "no".' I was happy with my decision to wait for Mum. After yesterday's school leaving ceremony, I felt a sense of relief.

Sure, there were some happy memories, like the solidification of wanting to pursue medical school and leaving high school behind. But Mum had been through the thick of it all with me. If she wanted to see me cross the stage, then I was more than happy to suck it up for a night.

'Ask me again,' mum said.

'Do you want to see me cross the stage?'

'Yes.'

'Right, then if you will excuse me, I have a uniform to put on, and you have a phone call to make. Tell Will and Dad to get ready.'

She left my room, and I closed my door with my back. I lingered for a second on the smooth glossy white surface, staring at my uniform.

I moved towards my wardrobe, my eyes darting to the right. My reflection stared at me with hollow eyes and an expressionless stature. It was merely a shell of a person.

There were no more tears left for me to shed. All emotions dissipated long ago.

As I took the blouse and skirt off, the hangers dislodged and clattered to the dark stained timber floor as if they were my hopes and dreams.

The candy cane striped blouse was rough against my skin. Even after three years of laundry cycles and fabric softener, it was still like I was wearing cardboard, looking far bigger than it was on me. The ensemble's charcoal skirt was softer and extremely worn at the waist band. I grabbed the long crimson fake tie from the picture frame hook beside my door, placing its elastic band over my head, and secured it under the collar of my blouse.

*'The symbol for the beginning of the end,' I said to my reflection as I put on the long tie for the first time. 'Cannot wait for graduation.'*

I stared at my reflection, taking it in that this was the last time that I would ever be in my uniform. The past five years flashed before my eyes. Remembering all the good and all the bad.

'I deserve this,' I choked out. 'I made it.'

My heart swelled, filling with pride. The photos of William and myself in our uniforms throughout the years sat on the buffet. My smiles dwindled little by little each year. Grade eight, I was so excited to wear the knee length grey dress and the short crimson tie. By grade ten, I smiled with my eyes in the same blouse and skirt I had on and the same crimson tie from middle school.

This year's photo, however, the smile was gone from every part of me. Not a single ounce of life reflected in my eyes. I donned the pain, unable to contain it behind my signature fake smile. It was like I was posing for my driver's licence or passport. The stare was uncanny, burning deep into my soul.

'Nearly ready?' mum asked.

'Yeah, just gotta tie my hair up, put in a ribbon,' I called back from the bathroom.

I pulled my hair into a neat high ponytail, slipping the red ribbon through the band. The bathroom mirror reflected a young woman who was conflicted. A young woman who couldn't decide if she was happy to leave a toxic environment or if she wished she was back there.

'What is this feeling?' I asked the mirror, as I shrugged on my red blazer for the last time. 'I thought I was glad to leave.'

Maybe it was because, despite all the mental torture I endured, I did have a couple of great biology teachers and homeroom teacher. For fifteen minutes, at the start of every day, I could laugh until my cheeks hurt. The days I had biology, I knew that I would be seen as an equal. Nurtured academically; not once was I made to feel like I was stupid.

The drive to school was short and the odd feeling remained; like a string was pulling at my heart.

As I watched my parents and brother walk to the auditorium, I bravely entered the classroom where all the students were lining up in their houses. Darkness encompassed me, shielding me from my already thumping heart.

Walking through to my place in the line for my house, Nobbi Dragons. Being a private school, you'd think we'd be named after the founders or notable alumni like many schools around Australia. No, our houses were named after native Cairns creatures. There was also the Snubfin Dolphins, Canefield Rats, and the Saw-Shelled Turtles.

We were definitely a unique bunch.

I passed several of my friends. Not one of them greeted me. Their lips pursed as they watched me trudge on by, the guilty look among them was quite telling.

*At least they appear remorseful for ditching me, now all they needed to do is find the courage to actually apologise.*

I found my place in the alphabetical line-up and like Mikaela and Oliver, on either side of me, I, too, remained focused on my phone.

*Surprise that Oliver hasn't said anything.*

Everyone around me was laughing and showcasing their excitement. Meanwhile, I sat there encompassed by my thoughts and scrolled on Instagram and Facebook. Waiting for the class of seventy-six students to be asked to make their way to the auditorium.

'Shoes, tie, and hair check everyone,' Mr Domelio said.

The heads of houses went from student to student, looking from head to toe. Few girls were handed ribbons, few boys were made to adjust their ties. Several students had to polish their shoes. I stood there in my picture-perfect formal attire for one last time and I was itching to remove it.

*Five more minutes. Just five more minutes until the ceremony. I've got this.*

House by house we exited.

I stood on the back metal stairs that led to the backstage area of our large auditorium. Legs shook like jelly on a plate. My stomach queasy. Maybe it was the rickety old stairs, wobbling ever so slightly in the breeze. That didn't help my anxiety. I wanted this to be over. I wanted to be off the stairs. Across the stage. Then back home curled up on my bed with a packet of dark chocolate TimTams and watching 80's Horror films.

'Reckon the rumours are true?' Mikaela asked down the line.

'Dunno,' Oliver replied. 'I reckon they aren't, why else would these stairs still be standing and room be in use?'

The stairs led to a large green room under the stage, which was now used as storage for old drama props from years ago. Rumours had floated around for decades, where a drama student had been found hanging from a rope. Between the stage and green room, via a trap door.

'I reckon it was made up to scare us, so we didn't do something silly,' I replied. 'It was probably started by a teacher, and students ran with it, blowing the rumour out of proportion. Mass hysteria, like *The Crucible*.'

'Wow, that's deep, Carrington,' Oliver said.

I nodded and smiled slightly at him, before turning around to look out to the school yard while we waited. There was still no apology from him, and yet, he was my closest friend out of the seven of them. It stung knowing that our friendship meant nothing after all these years.

Mr Domelio called for Nobbi House, and I followed the procession down to the seats.

*Let the impatient waiting begin.*

Speech after speech.

Musical number after musical number.

My heart pounded like a drum in my ear. As I went to wipe my hands on my skirt, time slowed down and I became more aware of the roughness of my uniform, and the skirt's elastic waistband digging into my waist. My tie was like a noose against my neck causing my breathing to quicken.

Oliver bumped my shoulder with his. 'You okay?'

I looked at him. 'Yeah, yeah. I'm fine.'

The thought of vomiting on the Principal and Head of House was becoming an excellent idea. The perfect memento for them and me. Both deserved. Considering they never took me out of classes or talked to my parents about the bullying. Not even our little heart to hearts.

'I'd now like to invite our students from Sunningdale to receive their certificates,' Mr Domelio said.

*Finally.*

He called us house by house, and I watched the first row of students stand up and make their way across the stage. I looked down to the audience, and even though I was looking out into the darkness, I smiled in mum's direction.

I was never supposed to graduate, let alone live past the age of fourteen, but I did. Next step would be to get into university, either in nursing or medicine. For the first time, I was excited, despite being back on school grounds for one last time.

'McKenna Carrington,' Mr Domelio called. Whistles from my brother, father and mother echoed through the hall as I walked briskly but proudly to accept my certificate.

Though it was dark, as I got to stage left, the light shifted where I could see Mum waving at me. The nausea slowly dissipated, my legs still shook as I smiled broadly. With the feeling of the stiff, smooth paper certificate in my hand, I stood tall and proud.

I made it. It's over and I'm alive. You can knock me down all you want, but I'll only come back stronger.

As soon as I was allowed to leave, I bolted up to the foyer. Bumping into Mum, Dad and Will on the way.

'Did you want to get photos?' mum asked.

I watched as my friends laughed with each other, we locked eyes, but they went back to chatting and taking photos. I turned back to mum, 'No, I would very much like to leave, and if you let me, I would very much like to have a sip of wine.'

'You're not eighteen yet!' she remarked.

I laughed weakly and started to walk backwards, facing the seven people I once called friends. 'Oh, come on Mum, please? What occurs in our house, the police will never know.'

Mum laughed. 'How about ... sparkling apple juice instead?'

'That's a nicer compromise, I guess.'

Dad cocked his head to the side, his eyes squinted slightly. 'We'll do photos at home. Now, how about Maccas as a treat and celebration?'

'Hell yes! Now we're talking.' For a boy who hardly showed emotion, when it came to food and treats, he couldn't help himself. Will pulled me into an awkward side hug, just as we got to the car. 'Well done, sis.'

'Oh thanks, William.' I tried not to choke up at the unexpected words of affirmation and hug.

'We're proud of you darling.' Dad kissed the top of my head as he opened up the back left car door for me.

# 28

# December 2018

*22 Years Old*

5:03 *am*

'Fuck me,' I muttered after yet another restless sleep. I scrolled through the several notifications, on my lock screen from Dylan announcing that there would be universities sending out acceptances. 'Eh.' I yawned. 'It's the 21$^{st}$, I doubt that.'

I turned my phone off and my eyelids fluttered closed. I tossed and turned for what felt like hours, trying to get back to sleep.

With no avail, I flung my sheets off me and headed out to the kitchen, fixing myself an instant coffee not wanting to bother with the heavy-duty coffee machine just yet. The bitter substance strong on my taste buds.

I padded onto the deck, the hard timber planks rough on the balls of my feet. The sunrise was pretty. Its orange glow danced along the gentle waves. Out in the distance, I swore I saw a pair of dolphins come up to greet the air. But they were too far out. Birds sang, leave rustled, and all I could smell was my coffee. I sat on the brown wicker sofa, curling up on the sandpaper like cushion.

'You're up early,' Will said as he joined me on the couch.

'I might be hearing from Universities today,' I replied.

'Oh, that's exciting.' He sat down beside me, sighing. 'Do you think they're upset that we're both leaving?' Will got into Griffith University's dentistry school a few weeks ago. 'Well you *might* be leaving, but I do think you'll get in, they'd be stupid not to take you.'

'Thanks bro,' I replied. 'It'll be hard at first, but we'll come visit. They'll come visit. They know we're doing what is best for us and our education.'

'True, I just don't want to leave.'

It was a side of Will that I never got to see often, raw and emotive; made him more human than statue.

'It's scary, that I get. I'm nervous too,' I empathised. 'You know, there's always the holidays, and coming back home is also an option after we graduate. Or who knows, maybe they'll move to be closer to us?'

Will chuckled and nodded. 'Thanks, sis.'

A silence washed over us as we continued to look out to the water. Revelling in the sights as if it was the last time we would ever see it.

He headed back to his room, and I felt like the sibling relationship I had dreamed of was slipping away. Maybe I was being melodramatic. He was still a teenager after all, but some thoughts can't be stopped. Though, I cherished every conversation we had, even if they were five minutes tops, like this one.

We couldn't be in the same room for longer than fifteen minutes unless it was dinner. I thought we were getting better now that he had graduated from high school. These past two months had been great. We had been talking more and spending time together.

I headed back inside and made myself a second cup of coffee, and my parents one too.

The loud whir of the coffee machine echoed, and the strong aroma of the fresh hot brew made me think of the quiet afternoons with mum. Our chats on the balcony, or when it was raining, we'd curl up on the couch watching trashy reality TV.

**Dylan:** *Hey, good luck. I know that you've knocked the socks off those medical schools. You'll get an offer I'm sure. Tell me how it goes*

**Me:** *Your wish is my command. Thank you Dylan x*

I could hear dad's heavy footsteps bound up the stairs as the milk finished steaming. Mum followed closely behind.

'What's got you all riled up?' Dad asked as I passed him his coffee.

'Dylan reckons I might be hearing from universities today,' I replied. 'Weird timing but guess they need to start the roll out. Some places have already been filled, so this is the next lot, I guess?'

'You'll be fine,' dad said. 'You have a plan if you don't get in, and a plan if you do. Why don't you sit down with your mum and I to get your mind off it?'

'Gardening Australia? No thanks, I'll go and read or find something funny to watch until I hear something.'

I opted for books. Something I could do all day. But we were all watching the clock.

The GAMSAT group chat that I had joined was blowing up. Several people had heard from universities already. I was watching the spots at most of my top universities start to fill up in real time.

'Griffith's full,' I said walking out to the living room where my parents were.

'Have you eaten today, Kenz?' Mum asked. I shook my head. 'Tim, can you get her an apple, please?'

Every five seconds I was hitting refresh. Flinders hadn't sent out many acceptances yet, but so far three on my list of seven were full.

All three gathered round me as the anticipation crept up. I took a large bite of my apple, refreshing my emails.

Then I saw it. The subject line: *Your offer from Flinders University.*

'Oh my,' mum said.

Words were on the tip of my tongue. My eyes darted back and forth looking over the subject line.

'Click on it,' dad yelled.

The anticipation was getting to him. He beat me to it, opening my email. Will's scream and a pop of a champagne bottle echoed in my ear. I turned away from my screen for a moment to look at Will who had a look of pure admiration in his eyes.

'Okay, you're scaring me, who are you?' I asked Will.

'Oh shut up,' he replied. 'Can't I be happy for you?'

He embraced me in an awkward barely-a-hug hug.

'Yes you can,' I said, as I patted his arm.

I turned back to my screen, staring at it in disbelief.

*No way.*

I hit accept straight away. Mum suffocated me in a hug.

'We're so proud of you honey,' dad said, passing me a glass of champagne. 'You too, William.'

'To our superstars!' Mum yelled, raising her glass up for a toast.

'To us!' Will and I yelled, raising our glasses to join mum and dad's.

The bubbles danced on my tongue.

**Me:** *Moving to South Aus! Flinders Baby!*

**Dylan:** *Shit! No freaking way*

**Me:** IMG

**Me:** *Please see screenshot then XD*

**Dylan:** *When you arrive, we're taking you for drinks! Congratulations future Dr Carrington*

All of my accomplishments have led me to this moment. I smiled into my champagne, enjoying the celebratory dance of the bubbles on my tongue. I remember how amazing it felt to hold that scalpel back in biology, many moons ago. The image of removing the tiny red kidney from the rat was still etched in my brain, my perfect Nephrectomy.

*Doctor. In four years' time, I will officially be "Doctor Carrington".*

# 29

# December 2018

*22 Years Old*

The artificial forest green Christmas tree was gorgeously decorated in gold, white, and red tinsel and bubals – done by yours truly – stood proudly in the corner of the living room. I took my usual place at the outdoor dining table, my back to the water, and view to the kitchen. Though that wasn't my only view, I had the perfect sight of the twinkling LED fairly lights that I had hung up from the kitchen to living room to the veranda ceiling.

Though, what was supposed to be the most joyous time of the year, Kaleb had crushed it the second he arrived. I wanted to tell him the good news about Flinders, instead he was acting more of a Grinch than Will. Kaleb sat beside me, providing nothing to conversation, leaving dad and Will to talk amongst themselves in the growing awkward Christmas air.

Several minutes later, mum called dad and Will in to assist her with Christmas lunch. The two of them couldn't get away quick enough, almost tripping on their exit.

'Why do you do this?' Kaleb whispered in my ear. 'You're a fucking atheist. I'm an atheist. When will you stop jumping on this bloody bandwagon?'

'It's more about family than the Religious component for me,' I replied, murmuring through gritted teeth. My parents loved that I still celebrated portions of the Christian holiday. Besides, they weren't extremely devoted Catholics, we hadn't stepped foot inside a church since 2005. Though, a Nativity scene could still be found in several places around our house at this time of year.

Will and dad came back, sitting down in their spots. Dad at the head of the table, and Will in front of me.

'So, Kaleb, how's your Christmas been so far?' dad asked.

'Alright,' he replied. 'Mum's gone back to work the day shift at the hospital.'

'Oh right. What does she do again?' mum asked.

'She's an enrolled nurse.'

Once again, an awkward silence washed over us. Not even the parodic *Aussie Jingle Bells* by Colin Buchanan and Greg Champ could save us.

The fan on high speed rattled the fly screen in its breeze. My bare legs still stuck to the clear plastic chairs, jilting my movement towards my vodka cranberry. The condensation dripped off the glass, splashing onto my legs, cooling me down as I titled the cup to take a swig. The silence dimmed my light more and more, despite the delicious scent of the Christmas ham roasting in the oven.

Mum walked out of the kitchen, and Will's growing need for food started to show. 'Ham almost ready?' he asked.

'No, another hour,' Mum said.

The conversation went dark once again, and an awkward silence fell over us. We all sighed out heavily. Dad got up and the smell of eucalyptus filled the air as Dad set out the fly deterrents.

'Shall we do presents while we wait?' Will asked.

'Sounds like a plan,' Dad replied.

The five of us left the table and sat around the tree. Kaleb rolled his eyes at me.

'*The ground? Really?*' he whispered lowly in my ear.

I turned away and shifted closer to Mum, taking over my favourite spot by the tree.

'Why is McKenna Santa?' Will asked. 'You're always Santa.'

Being "Santa", or the passer of gifts, was something that had been given to me after Will had decided that he'd become the family's Grinch. He loved us, he really did, but, well, he was a teenage boy who loved video games and hiding out in his room. Family came second.

'Because I find it fun and hello, you're the family's Grinch!' I replied.

Kaleb glared at me, every chance he got when my family wasn't watching. He was supposed to be making it up to me for ditching me at graduation. It didn't feel like it. As I studied his body language it was clear, he thought of this as a chore, an obligation.

I handed Kaleb a small neatly wrapped gift.

'Oh that's from us,' Mum said to him.

'Thank you, Leonie, Tim,' Kaleb replied, flashing her an obvious fake smile as he tore open the wrapping to the game *Red Dead Redemption 2*.

I handed the presents to my parents, leaving Kaleb's gift to me.

It was small, so it definitely wasn't the gift I thought he would've gotten me. The feel of the present under the black wrapping paper felt soft until my fingertips stumbled not what felt like hinges and a small button.

My breath hitched as I tore open the wrapping paper, hoping that whatever it was, would be better than the choker.

In the palm of my hands was a jewellery box, housing a rose gold necklace with a round cut created amethyst pendant. It was gorgeous. I loved it. He was showing me he was trying. It was definitely an upgrade from the usual gift card and chocolates. Both he'd usually pick up on his way to mine or just before I was due to arrive at his place.

A warmth filled my heart as the positive thoughts started to pile on.

*He is trying. Maybe he is coming around. Maybe this isn't even the whole gift? He was looking at books and vintage medical tools I wanted. There were boxes at his place from both sites, so maybe.*

'It's gorgeous,' I said. 'Thank you, Kaleb.'

I put it on, but I was starting to really sense that he was trying to read me. As if suggesting that there was something more to the necklace than him listening.

'You're welcome.' For the first time all morning, he didn't flash a fake smile.

'Ham should be ready now,' Mum said as she got up from her spot on the ground.

'We need to talk later,' Kaleb breathed into my ear.

Shivers ran down my spine.

Dad sat at the head of the table, and Will in front of Kaleb, watched in horror as Kaleb immediately started to load his plate up. Mum and I were still bringing the food over. Kaleb knew that we waited until all food was on the table before we dished up. Then one of us, mainly Dad, would say Grace before we'd start eating. Instead, Kaleb's lack of etiquette was discernible. As soon as mum and I sat down, Kaleb started eating before dad was even able to say Grace. I gave him a light tap on the shin, but he rolled his eyes and continued eating.

My appetite, just like the remaining Christmas cheer and thoughts of Kaleb making it up to me, was gone. As much as I wanted to yell at him to get out, I remained civil, reminding myself of the boudoir polaroids.

The family ate in silence, occasionally glancing up at one another and shared a look of disappointment towards Kaleb. I slowly began eating the delicious food that Mum and I had prepared.

Both chains around my neck felt heavy and burned into my skin.

I felt around for the clasp of the new necklace; pressed the lever and removed it from around my neck, setting it on the table within Kaleb's line of sight.

He drove his foot into my shin, but I didn't react.

*The breakdown is here.*

'I'm going to the bathroom,' I said.

I pushed in the lock. My shin was bright red and would likely start to bruise over the coming days. 'Fuck.'

There was a knock on the door, and I quickly backed away, leaning against the vanity for support.

'You doing okay sweetie?' mum asked.

My chin dug into my shoulder. 'Yeah, yeah, I'm fine, just an upset stomach. I'll be out in a bit.'

'Okay.' I listened to her footsteps die down, leaving me alone with my reflection in the mirror. My lungs were hungry for air, chest heaving. Beads of sweat started to descend from my forehead and my grip on the raised basin started to slip. My heart was rattling in my chest.

Before I knew it, I was on the hard cold tiles. 'Shit.' I hooked my fingers under the choker pulling it off my neck as far as it could go. Trying to keep the metal way from the soft sensitive skin that covered the major blood vessels.

*In two, three. Hold two three, Out two, three.*

My breathing slowed to normal after a few controlled breathing exercises, I finally felt like I could stand back up.

*He's throwing a tantrum in front of my parents. This is how he reacts when it's just us. What is he doing?*

I pulled my phone out from my back pocket and started to go through the evidence I compiled. The two years' worth of content showed that he was escalating rapidly, especially within the last several months. I snapped a photo of the red mark that Kaleb's shoe made on my shin, adding it to my secret folder called "When you decide to leave".

He was starting to lose me, and now I wanted to watch him crumble.

# 30

# December 2018

*22 Years Old*

Since the issue on Christmas, Kaleb was no longer back in the house. As much as I wanted to argue with my parents, the bruise on my shin (that was a nightmare to hide) rendered the argument moot. However, my sleep habits were less than ideal, with arguments up the wazoo.

A few days later, I was in his dark kitchen. The scent of bolognese sauce and pasta filled the small open floor space. I couldn't keep my secret in anymore. He was now aware that we were celebrating something, but I wanted to hold off any hints until we were eating.

There was a risk I was running sharing this news. Especially with his attempts at convincing me that being a stay-at-home mum was a good idea.

'So, what is it?' he asked as he set the table.

'I'll wait,' I replied. 'Want help?'

'No, you just mess everything up. Just move out of the way, McKenna.' I was nowhere near him. He made a pointed beeline towards me, my back against the wall about two metres away from the table. Kaleb stuck his elbows out like chicken wings and poked me in the stomach.

'Ow!' I exclaimed.

'See? You're always in my way.' I flinched away from the hot pot of pasta. The possibilities of his capabilities were limitless and unpredictable. He sat down at the round four-seater glass table. 'Now will you tell me?'

'Sure.' I sat myself down in one of the white leather chairs and loaded my plate up with penne.

'Are you sure you're going to eat all of that? You're just going to add more weight on.' Just for that I loaded more, my stomach grumbling loudly should've given him a heads up. 'McKenna! Enough!' He grabbed the spoon off me, taking a spoonful off and dumping it onto his own. 'You're getting fat. What on earth do you eat on your placements? Maccas?'

'Uh, no, a healthy portion of a healthy meal! You realise I'm underweight, Kaleb?'

'Oh bullshit.'

'I'm forty-seven kilos. I should be in the fifties to sixties!'

Kaleb scoffed, proceeding to load his plate with enough for two servings. I couldn't tell him, not when joyful news for me meant an ego blow for him. It was blow after blow, but all I could think about were the images he had.

Even though he had images, despite everything, I still had a right to share happy news. I did, didn't I?

'Come on, please Kenz. Just tell me.' His face softened as he spoke.

His death grip on the serving spoon was no longer tight. Kaleb almost appeared to act like a normal boyfriend, but he was also known to go from zero to one hundred in seconds.

'I got into medicine,' I whispered.

'What?' he replied, inching forward.

My small plate of pasta provided comfort against his harsh gaze. 'I got into medicine.'

Cutlery clattered onto his plate before clamouring on the floor. A fist came down like a hammer on the table; a crack formed beneath it. 'When I said no, you went behind my back?!'

I pushed myself away, scared the whole thing could shatter any minute. 'I didn't know I needed permission to do what I wanted to do.' Upon leaving, I stumbled over the aluminium leg of the chair. 'I'm sorry, when did we go back to the early 1900s? Besides, you were happy for me when I said I applied.'

His fists slammed the table again, the crack getting bigger. 'You stupid bitch!' My lips quivered, I walked backwards down the hall, putting as much distance as I could between us. 'You a doctor? You're fucking stupid.'

*Is he for real?*

'I'm a straight high distinction student who graduated with a perfect 7.0 GPA. I won a medal and an award! Get your facts straight before you come for my intelligence.'

'Oh, so you're believing a technicality?'

I couldn't believe him.

*Technicality? What technicality?*

I excused myself to his bedroom and started throwing my things into my backpack. There was no point in me staying for the week like I planned if this was how I was going to get spoken to. I couldn't care less about the images now. He could post them and add that to the list for the cops to deal with. Soon revenge porn will be a crime.

*Three years together, and this was what I got? What did I deserve to get such treatment? Maybe Aster was right. Maybe he was threatened by me.*

I graduated before him and smashed through my entire degree. I was offered a job whilst on my last placement, and I took it. That would certainly kill a man's ego if he's desiring a stay-at-home wife.

'What are you doing?' Kaleb asked.

He appeared to have calmed down, but I wasn't going to fall for his tricks again. Kaleb had a remorseful look on his face, but I wouldn't let him off that easily.

'I'm going home,' I said.

'Oh.'

'Well, I will not tolerate you talking to me like that.'

Zero apology came from him as he exited his bedroom. I let out a heavy sigh.

*Has he ever apologised to me and meant it? Or am I only now making that observation?*

He never apologised for calling the cops for a welfare check on me during my placement. Only time was that big bouquet of roses, and now I was rethinking its validity.

With all the items I could fit packed into my bag, I ducked to the bathroom to change.

'Kaleb?' I asked.

'Yeah?' He called from the other side of the door.

'Where is my menstrual stuff?' I checked the cupboard again, but no packets were there.

'You must've run out.'

'I opened a new packet this morning.' He shrugged, but fortunately and unfortunately for me, he was a terrible liar. He smirked despite his face attempting to suppress it. 'Are you kidding me?! I've already bled through, so where did you put them?'

He stayed silent. I pushed past him and started looking everywhere. The few items that were in my purse were gone. I knew I had them in there. Frustration, anger, humiliation boiled through me. I needed to get out. There was no point in trying to find it. He was beyond cunning.

The scent of blood drifted through the air. I sprayed my Victoria Secret "Midnight Bloom" body mist spray, but it wasn't enough.

The two scents blended together. If I had soaked through a pad in less than one hour, the scent would only worsen, especially considering the half-hour walk to the train.

*Of course, this happens when I don't drive.*

Just as I made it to the gate, the bus rounded the corner, and I ran for the stop, hailing it down. It meant a longer ride, but it sure beat the half-hour walk to the train. Plus, I got dropped right at my front door.

Thankfully, the bus wasn't packed, and I sat down as close to the exit as possible. I tried my best to mask the smell with my backpack, but I wasn't sure if it was just because I was aware of it or if it was noticeable. Either way, it didn't matter. I shouldn't be sitting down with nothing besides several layers of toilet paper to soak up the Niagara Falls of blood.

I could hear it squelch with every bump and small movement I made.

*Ugh. Kill me now.*

I was exhausted, yet I could feel the steam bursting out of my ears.

*This is so fucking embarrassing! He's gone too fucking far now!*

I pulled my phone and typed ferociously.

**Me:** *What compelled you to hide things that aren't yours? Not to mention, they're sanitary items for a reason! Is your plan to humiliate me?*

Trees blurred by as we passed lavish greenery nearing the oceanfront. I couldn't wait to get off the bus and into the shower. It was becoming uncomfortable to sit in.

We rounded the corner, and I pressed the button. The large vehicle slowed. I waited for the doors to open before I dashed out. The stain was obvious, as was the smell. Before anyone could say anything, I was racing inside the gate.

# 31

# February 2016

*19 Years Old*

Kaleb's left hand never left my thigh as he drove aimlessly out of Redlynch and through the city centre of Cairns to Trinity Beach.

'You're not taking me home are you?' I asked.

He squeezed my thigh and said, 'Absolutely not.'

He made the turn in the road before my own that took us to Earl Hill; a five-minute drive from my house and had a glorious hiking track.

'I found this little hidden spot, and it has a great view out to the water,' Kaleb said. 'Figured I'd take you for Valentine's instead of doing the typical dinner and a movie.'

Just like books and movies dictate, a sudden warmth consumed me, and my heart skipped a beat. With a gentle squeeze of my thigh, he removed his hand from me and pulled into the closest parking spot near the entrance to Half Moon Bay Beach. The lonesome light shining down a narrow path through the bush and out to the water.

'Let's go,' he said.

I exited his black and white patched 2001 Ford Falcon and waited beside him as he pulled a couple of blankets from the boot.

'This way,' Kaleb said, grabbing my hand and leading me down the sandy path.

The further along the beach we got, the less of the water I could see. Kaleb's torch only illuminated the immediate path as we trudged along the tree line. He lay down the blankets beneath the canopy of the trees. I sat down while he set up the light so we could see out to the water. It didn't do much, but enough to see the small waves break, lapping at the shoreline.

'What made you decide this spot? There's another great one that overlooks the Marina,' I said.

'Smell the air, listen to the trees,' Kaleb said. 'This is you.'

He wasn't wrong. You wouldn't get the same salty smell nor be one with the sea overlooking the Marina. The sound of the water breaking and the rustle of the trees clashed in the air providing a comforting sound.

'You know me so well,' I replied. 'This is perfect, thank you.'

'You are most welcome.'

He leaned down to kiss me softly.

'I love you,' he said when he pulled away.

A nervous giggle escaped from my lips.

This was all too new to me. He was my first boyfriend, but there was no denying how I felt. It was exactly as it was described in books and movies. The electricity, the butterflies. He felt like home. A certain sense of completeness that I had never felt before.

'I love you too,' I echoed.

I leaned into him, kissing him, with one hand firmly planted on the rough surface of the blanket to steady myself.

Kaleb wrapped his arms around me, supporting me as he deepened the kiss. His tongue soft and warm against mine. One of his hands cupped the back of my head, the other on the small of my back. The one in my hair, snaked down to my arse, and guided me so I was straddling him. I buried my hands in his ginger hair, letting my fingers get tangled amongst the soft curls.

'Can't believe it's been like six months since we started dating,' he said, pulling away for a moment.

'I know right?' I replied. 'Time flies.'

Kaleb laughed.

I moved off him and sat next to him, embracing his body heat.

'This has been the most amazing evening,' I said to him. 'Thank you.'

'I'm glad.'

He kissed the top of my head. His hands found their way to bare skin beneath the waistband of my shorts and the hem of my top.

We sat in silence, listening to the sound of the ocean and the trees. It was peaceful. It felt like home. I had someone who gave me butterflies and loved me for who I am.

# 32

# December 2018

*22 Years Old*

I patiently awaited her arrival on a park bench overlooking the water. Savouring my fresh green juice from a café over the road. I could feel the weight of the cups in my hands, and the condensation on plastic dripping into my palms.

The shade of an old Sea Hibiscus provided protection from the afternoon sun while I waited for Aster. Boats floated by, driving towards the marina. The shimmering rays of sunlight reflected off the serene water, creating a dazzling display. It was one of the many reasons why it became Aster's and my favourite spot to sit.

'A little birdie told me you have major news!' A familiar voice called out from my left.

'Well, your source would be correct,' I said, passing Aster her large cup of orange juice.

'So, tell me,' she begged, her breath heavy with anticipation.

'Once you swallow, I'll tell you. I don't want you spilling juice on me.' Aster set her takeaway cup on the bench and swallowed loudly. 'I got into medicine at Flinders.'

'No way!'

'Yes way! You're talking to the future Doctor McKenna Carrington.'

'Aw, congratulations hon! Let's finish our drinks and I'm shouting you to dinner to celebrate. Champagne on me!'

I laughed into my straw, savouring the taste of cucumber and apple.

'I'm serious, Kenna. Let's go and celebrate! This is huge! It'll be an early dinner then we can go back to mine and get shitfaced!'

It was just a further six years of study. I'll be graduating at twenty-seven. It wasn't something to brag about. Sure it was my dream, but I couldn't help but think that I was being callous. All my life I've been a people pleaser and the one time I think about myself, it blows up in front of me.

'What did he say?' Aster asked.

'What?' I replied.

'You've gone quiet, and I can only assume he said something.'

'I —'

*I can do this.*

'He has, but that wasn't all he did,' I said. 'He, uh. He hid my menstrual items, probably threw them out, undoubtedly for punishment, I don't even know. Kaleb, uh. Fuck! He – Dammit.'

The words wouldn't form. I downed the rest of the juice and threw the cup in the green metal bin that was only a few steps away.

'He fucking, slammed his fist to the table and claimed that "I went behind his back".'

I used air quotations as I mocked him, the rage was out of control. I wanted to scream. The feeling was too much. I dug my nails into my palms, but once again, the bluntness of them provided no pain.

'That rat bastard, what?!' She pushed herself off the chair, fist clenched. 'I wanna kill him. How dare he say that to you! What a wanker!'

There was no use in holding back now.

'He made comments about my weight too today, pretty much said being forty-seven kilos is fat ...'

'No honey, you know he's wrong!'

'I know, and I have enough to break up with him.'

'And file a police report!'

'Maybe, I get that it's abuse. But I need time.'

'Hon, this is getting serious,' she said, as she sat back down and hugged me. I didn't know how much I needed one. 'I'm taking you tomorrow.'

'As long as you come with me,' I said. 'I doubt I'd even get to the door.'

'I'll be with you the whole time,' Aster replied. It was comforting to know that I had someone who supported me. 'Okay, you've gone tense again, I don't want to pressure you, but I can tell you need to talk.' Aster was careful with her words.

Medicine was a big deal, but it still felt like a blip in my life. A second degree seemed like a waste, no matter how much I wanted that dream.

*That's just Kaleb still in your head, girl. Chill. Go out and celebrate, you've earned it.*

'Thank you, and I know you're here, but can we just celebrate? There's a lot that goes beyond that man, and I'll share in due time, you have my word.'

'Sounds like a plan! I'll be there.'

It was a short walk along the Esplanade to our go-to rooftop bar with gorgeous views of the ocean, also called *The Esplanade*. There was nothing else quite like it around.

Aster handled refreshments while I admired the view. I quickly grabbed my phone and captured a snapshot of the vibrant scene, ready to share on Instagram.

'Will she be happy to see us?' I recognised that voice and I instantly jumped.

I turned to face the voice, Dylan, Natalie, and Bianca walked towards me. 'It's a dead pub,' I retorted. 'You gotta talk more quietly if you don't want the Doctor to hear what you're gossiping about. Have you learned nothing, Dr Atwood?' My feet hit the floor, and I reached up to hug him. 'Hi.'

He returned my hug, 'Hey.' While I continued to hug the two women, Dylan sat down at the table. 'Also, Aster mentioned you have something to share?'

I knew he knew that I got into medicine, so she must've called for another reason. Me getting into medicine was that sweet added bonus. Bianca and Natalie didn't know though, so this was going to be a surprise for them for sure.

'Of course she did, well take a seat, and I'll tell you.' I saw Aster walking back with a tray full of drinks. The cups shook with every hesitantly placed step, and I raced over to her. 'So you informed them I had news, and why are they here?'

I helped move the tray to a clear table taking a couple of drinks off her.

'I may have mentioned your tough time and the need for support,' she replied.

My breath hitched in my throat. 'When did you call them?'

'A week or so ago.' Aster looked at me, her eyes darting from side to side. 'Don't worry, I said nothing about him, but figured you needed the cavalry.'

'Thank you, but let's focus on my good news tonight. He doesn't need a second thought.'

We headed back over, and I placed one of the gin and tonics in front of Dylan, keeping the other one for me. Aster had two pints of beer and a vodka cranberry on the tray.

Aster pulled out her phone. 'I'm filming a reaction video, no questions asked.'

I acknowledged needing peer pressure, causing me to roll my eyes at her. It was fantastic news, and I knew I shouldn't be thinking otherwise. After today, I realised Kaleb was not deserving of my energy.

'I got into medicine at Flinders!' I announced.

Screams from the girls filled the air.

Dylan came over and gave me an awkward hug. 'It'd look weird if I did nothing. They don't know I know,' he whispered in my ear.

These were the ones I considered my own. Bianca and Natalie were my favourite nursing buddies. Fresh university grads and gave me the best tips to win over supervisor Murray.

'To Doctor McKenna Carrington!' Dylan yelled, the camera still rolling as we cheered our glasses of booze.

My worries went out the window. For the first time in well over a decade, I was with people who lifted the mask I hid behind, and I could breathe in the clean air. No longer was I panicking while sitting in the smog of the unknown, waiting for life to overtake me from my slipstream. In a matter of months, I had a small close-knit support system.

Tension I was holding in my neck and back slowly disappeared, and I slouched into the conversation, laughing with the group. I never thought I'd see that day I would be sitting at a table bursting into a fit of eye watering giggles, drinking and eating over shared interests. It was becoming clear to me that I only stuck with my old friend group because it meant that I had "friends" in the teachers' eyes.

Warmth grew throughout my body, my arms and legs uncrossed and one hand gripping my drink, the other draped across the back of Bianca's chair. I knew I could go to them if I had problems and I wouldn't be shut down. I could tell them about my fabulous news, and this was exactly how they would react.

My phone started buzzing on the table. The screen lit up with Kaleb's face. My breath got caught in my throat and I immediately hung up and turned off my phone.

'Kenz,' Aster said.

'He's not ruining tonight,' I replied. 'He doesn't get that satisfaction, too.'

'Too?' Dylan queried.

'I don't want to go into it,' I stated firmly. 'This is a celebration, and I wanna get absolutely shitfaced. So who's ready for another round?'

I slid off the chair and headed to the bar, ordering a quick shot of Bacardi, before asking for another round of the same drinks for the table.

'McKenna please …' Aster said as she moved quickly towards me

'Aster,' I warned. 'I get that this was an intervention, but after the day I've had, I want to celebrate and not give that. That. That …' I struggled to find a word for him that wasn't crude.

'Dickhead? Asshole?'

'Aster,' I warned again. 'I don't want to give that man any more ammunition.'

'You should at least tell him,' Aster said, pointing to Dylan.

'No! I don't need pity for Kaleb's abuse.'

'It won't be, it'll be support.'

I sighed heavily but didn't want to admit defeat just yet. Acknowledging that I was abused to myself was one thing. It was another admitting it to people who may have been my friends. But

I didn't know them that well to start spilling over my entire story with Kaleb.

She kept pestering, but I ignored and carried the tray back to the table.

On the other hand, I did feel close to all of them despite the short time frame. If I did tell one of them, it would be Dylan. He's had my back a few times when I've dealt with horrible consultants who felt the need to use me for their power trip.

*How would he react though? Would he be as supportive outside of work than at work?*

I was waiting for the alcohol to kick in, desperate for a little liquid courage. It was an army I needed to ensure that I was safe from Kaleb and my own brain, who thought that I desperately needed him. Only, I was proving that this wasn't the case at all.

*I can do this.*

'Dylan, can I talk to you?' I asked.

'Of course.'

Dylan followed me to the smoker's area, which was thankfully empty. It was far quieter out there than it was where we were sitting.

'You're not going to light up are you?' Dylan joked.

'Goodness no, that shit is gross and would be hypocritical as a nurse and prospective doctor,' I replied. 'It's just quieter out here is all.'

'Got it.' He sat down at one of the bar tables and kicked the seat beside him out for me to join him. 'So tell me. Aster called us up for a reason.'

'You were right,' I said as I looped my fingers underneath the rose gold chain.

'No, d-don't say that. I –' Dylan started but I cut him off.

'Kaleb was the reason I came to placement looking like I had limited sleep. Sure the drivers were shit, so were the taxis, but he fought with me almost every day.'

I got that he didn't want to be right, but I didn't need him to go down his line of commentary. It was neither one of our fault for Kaleb's abuse, it simply took me an embarrassingly long time to see the signs. They needed to be pointed out, that didn't mean Dylan could go down the pity route.

My gaze was trained on the timber tabletop and the blue mosaic ash tray that sat in the centre. It was embarrassing, but it needed to be talked about. I had to accept the situation I was in and get out of it as safely as I could. I tolerated so much over the past two years. Now he was letting it all out, except I wasn't so tightly wrapped around his finger like he thought. It took one placement to show me what I was truly missing: true friends and who I actually am.

'I uh. I had a feeling about a month or so before I met you. But his behaviour, over the past few months, solidified it for me.' Dylan reached for my hand as I spoke. My body warmed to his touch, all I've ever wanted was support and I finally had it. I had an army to back me, even if it was only four people, it was more than enough. 'I've researched and compiled evidence to give to the police, but I need help. Besides Aster, all I have are my parents and they – They don't know.'

'You have me, and I'm sure you'd have B and Nat too. You three are unstoppable,' Dylan said. 'Whatever you want to do, we will protect you. Just bear in mind, I'm not exactly a fellow, just a trainee, so I'm strapped for cash, but I will provide the money somehow to bail you down to Adelaide if you need.'

A laugh erupted from deep in the pits of my stomach. 'Thank you. I needed that.'

'You're welcome,' he replied. 'And hey. Thank you for sharing with me.'

He stood from the stool, pulling me into a hug.

*Is it possible for a hug to feel like home?*

I immediately pushed myself back from his warm embrace, shaking my head slightly.

'Uh, we should – we should uh, get back,' I said pointing my thumb towards the door.

'Oh, yeah, yeah.'

We stood there awkwardly for what felt like eternity. Our eyes locked onto each other for a moment before my gaze went to the floor. I tried to navigate around him, but we fumbled. Our feet were in sync with each other as we attempted to head back through the door. He placed a hand on my lower back guiding me. Electricity from his touch shot through my body.

*I really need another drink.*

The humidity in the air was thick, no breeze wafted through the open French doors.

'There you two are, we're all going back to Aster's,' Bianca said.

Dylan nudged my shoulder. I glared back at him.

'Umm, before we do. There's something I have to tell you both,' I said. The two girls looked at me, eager to know what I had to say. 'It isn't what you think.'

The two of us took our seats at the table.

'So you two aren't –?' Natalie asked.

'No, we aren't,' I said, a little too quickly. 'My boyfriend is toxic –'

'Abusive,' Aster chimed in, Bianca and Natalie gasped in response.

'That's why she called you all here,' I continued. 'Me getting into medicine was solely a happy bonus. She wanted me to know that I had a team behind me even if you are like two-thousand kilometres away.'

'Oh darling,' Nat said. 'You should've told us sooner.'

'I'm taking her to the police station tomorrow, and she'll be giving your details over to the police,' Aster said.

'We'll tell the police,' Bianca and Nat jinxed.

'I'll come too.' Dylan said.

'It'll need to be over the phone for us, we got an early flight in the morning,' Bianca said.

'Speaking of, we should probably head back to the hotel and pack, it's eight o'clock,' Natalie said.

'Shit is it?' Bianca replied.

'Crap it is too!' Aster said. 'Did you want to come back to mine for pizza?'

'Yeah sure, discuss this a little more,' Bianca said.

'Agreed,' Natalie said.

I smiled brightly and yet weakly.

They shouldn't have needed to do that. The fact that just like that, they would be willing to come forward to stand up for me was something that my old group of friends would never do. I had my people, an ever-growing group. We all fit together in a way that I never thought I'd experience.

# 33

# December 2018

*22 Years Old*

The five of us sat squished on Aster's worn brown leather three-seater sofa. Eating pizza in a comfortable silence. Her Spotify playlist played quietly through the television.

'Can I ask why you stayed so long?' Natalie asked.

'Nat,' Bianca warned, slapping the other nurse softly on the thigh.

Any previous concerns had gone out the window the second I told them before we left the bar. It wasn't easy looking at them, the girl's tearing eyes, and Dylan's comforting smile warmed me.

'It's okay B,' I replied. 'He wasn't always like this ... Or it was subtle. I guess it's why domestic violence is so complex. It wasn't until I was getting ready to graduate that it became obvious, plus, Aster started to open my eyes too.' Dylan reached around to give my back a comforting rub as I talked. 'Thanks.'

It was difficult to explain the full ins and outs of the relationship I knew was dead. The good memories were overshadowed by the bad. I couldn't remember the last time I truly felt alive with him.

'I don't get it,' Dylan said. 'If he loved you ... why?'

'Don't know, I don't think anyone really knows why,' I replied. 'Could be family dynamics. Could be anything.'

Something had to be said about how each of them reacted. Their kindness and compassion. This wasn't something you could fake. I had baggage, a lot of it. Maybe a moving truck or two worth. This was like what you see in movies, friends comforting each other, lifting each other up. I wanted to cry, but no tears came, only the burn of them as they sat there, blurring my vision.

'Any other questions?' I asked, clearing my throat. "Cause I don't want to give any more air to this man tonight.'

'Just one,' Bianca said. 'Is that why you took the job?'

Dylan and Aster looked at me.

'No, I took it because you and Nat were amazing supervisors and mentees during my placement,' I replied. 'When you suggested I apply, I did so knowing that the placement was the best one I had ever done. Every section I was in, I was well looked after and got along with most people. Some of the doctors could lose the God-complex though.'

'Wait so how will that work with med school?' Dylan asked.

'I informed Murray about it, and he said that if I got into uni down there, I'd be well looked after,' I said. 'No favouritism allowed, obviously, but it means I work casual hours over the weekend. If I have placement that takes priority.'

'Damn, that's pretty decent,' Natalie said. 'I'm jealous.'

'Crap, we better go Nat, it's like ten!' Bianca said, checking her watch.

'When you go to the cops, love, make sure you give them our contacts,' Nat said, giving me a hug.

'Absolutely,' I replied. 'Safe flights you two.'

'Shall do,' Bianca replied. 'Thanks again for the invite Aster, was lovely to finally meet you.'

'No problem,' Aster replied. 'I'm sure we'll meet again soon.'

The three of us walked them down to the footpath and waited for their taxi to arrive.

As soon as we got back into the apartment, I asked, 'Can we please hear more about this Mr Bale, Aster?'

'Oh, there's a guy?' Dylan asked.

'There's a guy,' I confirmed.

He crossed his legs and turned dramatically to face Aster. His shaggy brown hair flopping in front of his face.

'Terrible, the both of you,' Aster said. 'I'm making coffee. You both need coffee.'

'Deflection,' Dylan said. 'What do you think of that, Carrington?'

'Hmm, either it's because you're here and doesn't want to admit things to a guy she barely knows. Or it's all on the D. L.'

'D. L?' he asked.

'Down low,' Aster replied for me as she passed us a mug of coffee each.

'Thanks,' we said.

'How about this, I will share info on Henry if you end it with Kaleb,' Aster said. 'Now.'

My smile turned into a frown. The rectangular device sat face down on the round glass coffee table. It was still pinging from when Aster turned it on before we walked Bianca and Nat out.

'This is a bit excessive isn't it?' Dylan asked.

'He's escalating,' I replied. 'He's lost control.'

Dylan turned the phone over, the screen on. I stared at it, my eyes fixated on the flash flood of notifications. That was until black spots clouded my vision.

Waving his hand in front of my face, Dylan said, 'Earth to McKenna.'

'Hmm?' I replied. 'Huh? Sorry, zoned out.'

*Or more like, feeling like I'm going to pass out.*

'I got you,' I heard Dylan say, his voice muffled as he prevented me from falling forward. 'Is this really what you want, breaking up over text?'

I nodded. 'It's safer.'

A knock at the door made us jump, and Aster went to answer it.

For the umpteenth time, I found myself face-to-face with a police officer donning a blue uniform.

*This can't be happening.*

'You've got to be kidding me,' I groaned and turned to Dylan. 'How long ago did we turn my phone on?'

'About thirty minutes ago, why?' he said.

'Ms Carrington?' The female officer asked.

'That's me,' I replied slowly.

'Sorry to interrupt your evening, my name is Sargent Noella Montee, and my partner, Constable Tom Spady. We're here on a welfare check and possible kidnapping.'

'Kidnapping?!' Aster exclaimed.

I held my hand to silence her. 'Rest assured I'm fine and here on my own volition. These individuals have not kidnapped me, I'm simply hanging out with my friends.'

The officers looked at each other before the constable stepped outside.

I was sobering up quickly.

'He's done this before, where I've been busy and he's blown up my phone and contacted the police,' I explained and pulled my purse towards me taking out the card Constable Langdon gave me when he showed up at my hotel a few weeks ago. 'This is the case file number from an incident in Adelaide.'

Sergeant Montee took the card off me. 'Thank you.'

'We've been out celebrating and now we're here hanging out and sobering up,' Aster chimed in.

'Mind if we take your phone for his correspondence with you?'

I nodded and Dylan brought my still buzzing phone to the officer.

She headed out to the hallway of the apartment complex to confer with her partner and to go through the evidence.

'When I dropped you off?' Dylan asked.

'He called the cops,' I confirmed.

I remained composed, but on the inside, I was fuming. Kaleb's mindset was beyond what I ever could have imagined. It was frightening.

Sergeant Montee came back in. 'Did you file a DVO?'

'No, I was planning to tomorrow, once I had gathered enough evidence and once I broke up with him, which I was about to do before you arrived.'

She nodded and went back to her partner.

My phone was still going off and echoed through the hallway.

The walls of the apartment felt like they were caving in. I wasn't claustrophobic by any means, but this was something else. Even having been inside an MRI machine was less claustrophobic comparatively. Air was struggling to make it into my lungs.

'Breathe, McKenna, you're panicking,' Dylan said.

'W-way. To. S-state. The. Obvious. D-doctor,' I replied, taking deep breaths between each word.

The indistinct murmur of Aster's voice, mixed with the authoritative tones of the officers, made me trip. I couldn't tell if I had tunnel hearing or if they were just that far away.

'Kenz?' Dylan asked, concerned.

He was swift on his feet. I felt weightless as he picked me up and laid me on the couch. Noises mixed as I lay there. I was more alert to the scratchy fabric of the couch and the soft plush blanket that was under my head.

'It's going to be cold for a second,' Dylan said as he leaned over me.

A pink sphere was in my vision and a solid freezing object glided over my forehead. The feeling was easing my wooziness. My eyelids closed, and I hummed in contentedness.

'I could sleep like this,' I muttered.

'I rather you didn't,' Dylan said.

'You doctors are so protective.'

'Alright, did you want to press charges tonight for his behaviour?' Constable Spady asked, passing me my phone.

'I know they're going to argue with me when you leave, but no thank you. I wish to end the relationship first before I press charges,' I said, looking up at the officer from the couch. 'This can be used as further evidence on him though right?'

The officers nodded.

'Well, just so you are aware, he will be charged with making a false report. Here's the case number for when you do make the formal complaint,' Constable Spady said, handing me his card with the case number.

Aster and Dylan followed them out, leaving me alone momentarily. I knew they'd be pissed but I needed to end it, let him stew. Plus I was well and truly wasted, and no good could come of that, I needed to be sober.

My phone was heavy and shaking violently in my hand as I pulled up our conversation.

**Me**: *We're done, I can't do this anymore. This is for the best. I don't deserve the abuse you've put me through. The humiliation. Moving of goalposts. You've put me through hell. All the best, McKenna*

I threw my phone into the cushions of the armchair letting out a sigh of relief. I felt the tension in my body slowly relax.

The officers left.

'He's sure digging himself a nasty hole with these two false reports,' Dylan stated.

'He can keep trying, but I've got plenty of evidence to destroy him,' I replied.

Digging himself deeper was becoming my favourite pastime. Ever since I brought him out from the safety of Snapchat and into the world of texting. It's been so much easier to retrieve evidence and store it without him knowing.

I didn't get into medicine just to piss away what could very well be my only chance on a boy. I didn't suffer over a decade worth of depression, abuse, and suicidal thoughts just to give up either.

'Aster, do you have anything that could take this fucking thing off my neck?' I asked, motioning to the choker.

'Uh, I should have a pair of pliers around here somewhere,' she replied.

She turned me towards Dylan while she got up. The rustle of items echoed through the apartment while she looked. Doors opened, then were slammed shut with a grunt.

'Found it!' she yelled from the bathroom.

She passed the pair of pliers to Dylan, who, without any hesitation, cut into the gold and copper. It fell onto the floor, and we all just stared, not knowing what to do with it.

'Thank you,' I breathed.

Now I truly felt free. Though, the multiple plings sounding through the air said otherwise.

'I'm blocking that fuckwit's number,' Aster said, snatching my phone off the table.

'Wise idea,' Dylan replied.

# 34

# December 2018

*22 Years Old*

The red brick station stood proud in amongst older heritage listed buildings. It was a mere few turns away from where Kaleb and I went for our Valentine's date a couple of years' ago.

'Do you need a minute before we go in?' Aster asked.

I shook my head and pushed myself out of the car.

'Oops, you might need to help me, though. My legs don't want to cooperate,' I said. Dylan immediately sprang into action as he held out his hand to hoist me out of the car.

My heart vibrated in my chest, and my legs were like jelly. The reception desk encroached into the waiting area and hid two large doors that blocked the entrance to the back of the station. Everything was barricaded by bars, hard plastic, and key card pads.

'I'm here to file a complaint for domestic violence,' I said to the officer at the desk.

'ID?' he asked.

I handed over my driver's license and confirmed my details.

'Thank you,' he said, passing me back my license. 'Please take a seat, an officer shouldn't be too long. Also, your friends won't be able to go in with you, they can stay here and wait or there's a great café not too far from here. A little hole in the wall.'

'Okay, I'll let them know,' I replied with a weak smile. 'Thank you.'

I sat on one of the chairs on the other side of the desk, nerves starting to creep in again. The geometric stained fabric reminded me of public transport. It was rough against the back of my knee, which didn't settle the nerves.

*I wish Aster or Dylan could come in.*

The white paint was chipping off the walls in places. A glass cabinet housed dusty awards for the department. The walls started to close in, my leg bounced.

*I can't do this.*

Dylan took my hand in his. I tried to calm down, but I really couldn't, I started to regret my decision to trust Aster.

'You got this,' Aster said, planting a firm hand on my thigh. It was a simple gesture. One that I wouldn't have expected from a friend of only a few months.

We had spent all of last night collating the evidence, not to mention there were two police records too. I was armed and ready. Maybe he thought I would never grow up from the girl I was when we met.

'McKenna?' My name was called, and I immediately got up, he held the door open for me. 'My name is Senior Constable George Button, how are you?'

'As well as you can be when walking into a police station,' I quipped. He laughed, possibly to ease my nerves, but I didn't mind.

'Here we are,' he said, letting me step into the windowless room first.

Paint was chipping off the walls in there too. A long-tattered shelving unit built into the wall, stacked with a disarray of old children's toys.

'So from what my colleague told me, you're here to file a complaint against your ex for domestic violence?' Constable Button asked.

'Yes,' I replied.

'How long ago did you break up with him?'

'Last night.'

'Okay. So here's what's going to happen,' he said. 'This device is going to record and film you. In a moment I'm going to ask you to tell it your full name and date of birth. Then I'll ask you a series of questions. Is that okay?'

'Yes,' I replied.

'I am Constable George Button, it is the 28th December 2018, it is 9.31 am. Can you please state your full name and date of birth?'

I took a deep breath in and sighed, 'McKenna Carrington, 17th of March 1996.'

'Thank you McKenna,' he said. 'Now, what brings you in today?'

I took another deep breath, trying my hardest to steady myself as I replied. 'I have reason to believe I am a victim of emotional abuse.'

'What I'll get you to do now, is to put everything into chronological order. When you met and when the abuse started. If you don't recall, give estimates as best you can. When did you start dating?' he asked.

'Umm, just over three years, roughly twentieth of August Twenty-Fifteen,' I replied.

'When did the abuse start?'

My brain was working hard to try to recall a rough timeline.

'In all honesty, I can't quite recall,' I said. 'I know in the past year it's been bad, but there were moments of emotional abuse. My earliest recollection was around January Twenty-Seventeen, so roughly a year and a bit after we started dating.'

The purple deteriorating shelves took my focus. Talking to the toys put me at a slight ease.

I went into detail about how he used to starve me and lower my weight to forty-five kilograms before I started my placements. It wasn't until I was on a plane ride away, when I was able to gain some weight back.

'The lack of food caused a lack of energy which allowed him to have control. So he was able to make me lose friends. He got jealous of me talking to men on placements, so he started making sure it was known I had a boyfriend,' I explained. 'Any hickey he gave me, I was not allowed to cover it, and I got in trouble by several supervisors. That was how it started. He bought me a collar when he caught me covering up and when I started to take placements that were interstate. The officers saw me wearing it last night, but I had it forcibly removed by my friend Dylan. He claimed it was out of love, but it really wasn't.'

I pulled the piece of jewellery from my purse, handing it to the officer.

'I'll take this for a moment to properly document it,' he said.

I brought up the folder of evidence that housed documentation of the collar on my phone, passing it to him as well. He started swiping through the collection I had made, showcasing that I had worn it for two years.

'Okay, so let's talk about the recent events now. Obviously, there's more than the possessiveness and jealousy?'

'Yes, very much so,' I replied. 'It started in March last year.

'I had help from assignment extensions and a lot of all-nighters. When I was at my parents' so I could do everything I needed to. I did the bare minimum for my OSCEs as well. But he would often ensure that I didn't have my space set up. He'd hide my phone to stop me from using the hotspot to sit any online exams. It was a lot of unnecessary stress. So I kept my phone on me if I left momentarily.'

The emotions started creeping up again. I shifted uncomfortably in my seat.

'There were other things too,' I said. 'He trespassed in Adelaide, a couple of weeks after calling the in a welfare check whilst I was on placement. So I was at the end of my six week placement, and he trespassed on my last full day there. When I got home, he stalked me and sent me the boudoir images I had done for him. He's been using them as blackmail. He's pressured me for sex, and on a couple of occasions, forcibly fingered me.'

I handed him the card of the police officers I had dealt with. As well as full access to every folder on my phone with text messages and photos.

'I know I should've left sooner, but I —'

'It's okay, you're here now. We'll deal with this in the appropriate manner, and make sure you're safe,' Constable Button said. 'I'll take your phone and transfer the evidence to your case file.'

The tears burned my skin as they flowed down my face.

'Lastly, were there any witnesses? Besides these three officers?'

'The lady and man that were with me, not sure if they're still outside,' I replied. 'They're names are Aster and Dylan.'

The officer left to see if Aster and Dylan were still outside.

I watched as they were taken to the separate rooms next door with other officers. Both smiled at me as they walked passed. I knew I was doing the right thing. If I didn't do this, then what kind of woman was I?

Constable Button came back for my phone and the necklace.

'I'll be back in a moment,' he said, and shut the door behind him.

The military-grade recording device was still going.

I stared at the purple toy rack as I waited.

There was something eerie about the toys in the racks. Children were innocent beings, and yet there were some that were not.

*How many children come here in leu of child abuse, being a witness to a crime or their parents' misbehaviour that they need to put toys in here?*

The door creaked open, and Constable Button handed my phone back.

'Now you don't have to press charges, you can withdraw your complaint, and it will sit on his file,' he offered. 'Or you can press charges, and this goes to a full investigation where, pending sufficient evidence, he may be arrested and charged.'

That was a humbling thought. The evidence was overwhelming, and he would get charged with domestic abuse. No doubt about it. He had no way of contacting me, but that wouldn't stop him from going to my parents' place, even if I no longer lived there.

'I want to proceed ahead,' I replied. 'But is there a way to protect my parents? I'm moving down south in a few weeks, but he could still get to them.'

'It wouldn't impact the investigation. We'll still get you a DVO to protect you, and if he troubles your parents, get them to call us and given the investigation we'll be able to further reprimand him.'

The chair suddenly felt as hard as concrete, and the already boxed-in room felt smaller. Maybe this was a mistake. Maybe I'm just supposed to take this to the grave. I wouldn't be able to walk on eggshells for the rest of my life.

*So many women die a year due to partners and exes. Statistics showed that approximately fifty thousand women died this year at the hands of a partner or family member this year alone. Maybe this —*

'McKenna? McKenna?' The officer called my name.

'Sorry, I just ...' I trailed off. 'Are we done here?'

He nodded, and showed me back to the door, separating the back of the station to the waiting area.

'We'll be in touch with the progress of the case.'

'Thank you.' Was all I could manage as I walked out into the humid hair.

Aster and Dylan weren't out yet and given that I was in there for almost two hours, I could be waiting out here for a while. I decided it best to wait at a coffee shop, I was needing my monthly iced tea fix.

**Me:** At *Vinnie's Café. Getting you both your usuals while I wait.*

For the first time in my life, I felt free. Well to an extent.

# 35

# January 2019

*22 Years Old*

My newfound freedom had me sitting my regular hairdresser's black leather chair. Sipping a freshly made flat white coffee while I waited for her to finish up with her previous client. Many say, "never dye your hair after a breakup; always sit on it", but this wasn't any normal situation.

The longer I passed reflective surfaces and saw my blonde hair, the less and less, I saw myself. It was no longer me. More like I was playing into the disgusting trope that my teachers labelled me as, or the blonde fetish of Kaleb's.

'I know that I said I wanted to keep the blonde. But it's not me, I wanna go back to this,' I said to Debbie, my hairdresser, whilst pulling up an image of me back when I was thirteen.

My long brown hair shone in the light. It was one of my favourite photos before I turned into full emo and started to think about suicide. There was the familiar glimmer of innocence that was still in my eyes as I smiled at the camera. Posing happily for Mum.

I had been wanting to dye it back for ages, but Kaleb always forbade me. He'd mention my darkening roots and make a passive aggressive comment about brunettes.

I shook my head.

*How did I stay with him for so long?*

'Oh absolutely! I can ombre it out if you would like? That way, the regrowth after some of the colour fades isn't so harsh,' she replied.

'Yeah, that's fine. Can you also trim my hair? As much as I love the length, I'm starting medical school soon and so my time in the salon won't be as often.'

'Oh, this is a "fuck you, I'm back baby" kind of look?'

'Absolutely Debbie!'

She laughed and grabbed some colour samples from the wall behind. 'I recommend we go slightly darker, so when it fades, it lightens enough to not let a lot of the blonde come through.' She handed me the sample. 'It'll ombre out, like I said.'

'Sounds perfect. Let's do it!'

I'd been going to Debbie since I started university, no longer trusting Mum with the box blonde hair dye. My hair had gone from feeling like straw to feeling healthier and more had a shiny glow to it.

In mere hours, I'll be really back.

To commemorate the moment, I even hunted for my copy of *Sense and Sensibility*. My favourite novel from back then. Jane Austen had a special place in my heart. Mum used to read them to me growing up. I always thought of myself to be a bit like Marianne, but with each day I matured, the more I saw myself as Elinor: reserved.

'Oh, that takes me back. I wish I could read it for the first time all over again,' Debbie cried when she came back with the colour.

'I found the trick. You wait about ten years, then, thanks to other books, movies, and reality, you forget all about the book,' I replied.

'Genius!'

I paused from my book and watched in the mirror as my head got lathered up with the cold dye. I could feel the confidence start to slowly creep back in. A smile forced its way on my face and became a permanent fixture.

I turned back to my book as Debbie turned on the timer. Half an hour then I get to see who I used to be again. My inner child healing by the minute.

*If the bullying and abuse never occurred, where would I have ended up? Would I be already in medical school?*

But no use dwelling on the past, who I was now and who I was becoming was what mattered. There was a strong resilience that would take others well into adulthood, to develop. I felt unstoppable.

'Ready to wash out?' Debbie asked.

'Absolutely,' I remarked and followed her to the basins.

As water trickled along my scalp, my thickening mop started to weigh me further down. My neck started to ache as I struggled to get into a comfortable position.

'Sorry, thick hair troubles, anyway we can lessen the weight on my neck?' I asked.

'I'll try a pillow, if at any point you need a break we can sit you up for a little bit,' Debbie suggested.

'Sounds good,' I replied.

She adjusted me with a pillow and extra towel for support, and I felt less pull on my neck. Debbie's fingertips worked their way into my scalp. My eyes fluttered shut, and just as I was about to doze off to sleep, lukewarm water ran along my skin. Her fingers still massaging me, helping the product leave my thick mop.

'Ready to go?' Debbie asked as she wrung the excess water out of my hair.

'Yep.'

I bounced out of the basin chair and headed for the other seat, eager to see myself in the mirror.

Though it was still wet, I was beaming.

'I love it,' I stated.

'Hold on, let me blow dry it and then you can tell me how much you really, *really* love it,' Debbie joked.

I usually hated this part. Hair blowing in my face, hot air drying out my eyes. But today, I was more excited for the end product.

'Oh. My. God!' My hand rested above my heart as I stared in the mirror. 'This is fabulous!'

'There's a positive shift in energy here, Soon-to-be-Doctor Carrington.'

'I feel like myself,' I muttered. 'Thank you Debbie, for everything. Next visit I have with the folks, I'll be sure to visit the salon, even if it is just for a wash.'

I paid with an under the table tip and left the salon beaming brighter than I ever had.

# 36

# February 2019

*22 Years Old*

Adelaide airport was abustle. Shopfronts packed with elderly people and businessmen took over most of the cafes. My carry-on suitcase hummed softly behind me as I headed towards baggage claim. Reality slowly setting in that my new life was now in order.

My parents went with Will to Brisbane where they then drove down to the Gold Coast.

'McKenna!' I heard my name being called from a distance. 'To your right!' It called again.

I slowed my pace to find my bearings. It didn't take long before I spotted a familiar man in a pair of bright teal scrubs — Dylan's favourite pair.

'Oh my god!' I exclaimed as I bolted over to him. 'I wasn't expecting this.' I threw my arms around him. 'Last time I saw you I was —'

'It's okay, you're safe and here, where you have me.' He gestured to himself. 'Oh and of course the girls too.'

'Can't forget them,' I laughed.

He took my suitcase off me and led me down towards baggage claim for the rest of my suitcases.

'We're in the same building,' he blurted to break the awkward silence. I raised my eyebrows, confused why he brought it up.

It dawned on me in a few seconds. 'Oh right, forgot I sent my address.' I face-palmed myself, he had told me many times where he lived, and I never fully put two and two together.

The first two of three bags came swinging out and I ran towards them, escaping the awkward situation. He was hotter than I remembered. The sleeves of his scrubs were tight around his biceps, and his dark curly brown hair slightly shorter accentuating his sharp jawline.

*Has he been working out?*

'Crap,' I muttered as I watched my final teal bag zoom past out of my peripheral vision.

*Pull yourself together, dammit.*

It wasn't only him though. Aster noticed me checking out guys while we were at lunch. She claimed it was normal, but nothing about any of what I had gone through was normal. It was far too soon, but then again, maybe that I was no longer tied into an abusive relationship, my body craved human touch.

As I walked back towards where I had left Dylan, I felt a hand on the middle of my back. My muscles tensed at the touch.

I felt his warm breath against my ear, 'Ready?'

*Oh dear. It's nothing.*

'Yep.' I handed over the largest suitcase to him.

With two suitcases each in tow, we headed out to his vehicle, hidden behind the surrounding big SUVs and 4x4s. It looked cute, almost like it had its own bodyguards.

'Will they fit?' I asked. A little concerned that my biggest suitcase wouldn't have room in the boot of his black 2010 MX-5 next to the other three.

'Just means you'll have a bag or two at your feet.' He shrugged.

The largest, plus my carry-on fit in the boot perfectly, the other two got to ride in the cab with me. I laid both down horizontally, giving me some leg room left over. Squishy was being kind.

'Ugh,' I groaned trying to get comfortable. Dylan was laughing, able to stretch his non-driving leg all he wanted. I playfully slapped his arm. 'Shush, Dyl.'

'We'll be at the complex in no time.' He turned the key in the ignition.

'Yes, and I can't wait.'

As I pushed open the thick wooden door, I was greeted by the new apartment smell, combined with woody, musky scent of the cardboard boxes that were scattered across the apartment.

It was surreal.

My fingers danced along the tops of the boxes, collecting a thin layer of dust as I walked towards the balcony door off the living room.

'This is all mine?' I exclaimed, drawing back the sheer rough linen curtains, exposing the clear view of the city. 'Holy crap, look at the view!' I dashed out to the balcony.

I could hear Dylan laugh behind me, but I didn't care. This was home. My home.

'Wait until you start university.' He leaned against the black aluminium doorframe.

'Way to kill the mood, Dr Atwood.' I said walking past him and started to open up one of the boxes.

'Just making sure you remember why you're here.'

I rolled my eyes. 'You going to help me or what? I kinda need your muscles.'

'You owe me a beer though.'

I ignored his comment. 'We'll start with the bed then the couch.'

Two doors stood closed next to the television that was already fitted to the wall. Only one had the view of the city, through the door on the right I went. The timber bed-frame laid against the furthest wall of the bedroom. Except I was eyeing the distance between the wall looking at the balcony entrance. It would fit my queen bed with plenty of space between the foot and the balcony entrance.

'Can we move this, so the bed faces the balcony entrance?' I asked.

'You're kidding right?'

'You said I owe you beer!'

For a solid timber bed head, it was surprisingly light. Dylan, on the other hand, was struggling.

'Aren't you trying to get the ortho Fellowship?' I teased.

'It's the grip I have on it.'

I exaggerated an eyeroll ending with a wink as I continued to take baby steps backwards to where I wanted the bed to sit. Perfectly aligned with the middle of the door. Now all I needed were my blinds on a control panel so I could open them without leaving my bed. To wake up to a view like that was a dream, and I was living in it.

We grabbed the other pieces of the bed-frame and started to work together to fit the bed together.

'I'm actually jealous,' he said as he held the arm out so I could screw it to the headboard. 'You have a better view than me.'

'Oh do I? What do you look out to?'

'My roommate's bedroom.'

I started laughing.

'You mean your cute dachshund? That's the best view! I'm jealous.'

'Nothing beats the city.'

'Ferni does. Can I see him? I'm sure he'll be happier here than alone on the balcony.'

His mum bought him Ferni a few weeks ago, thinking her son was lonely. Instead of doing the motherly thing of mentioning online dating or suggesting heading to a bar, she got him a dog as a late Christmas gift.

Dylan rolled his eyes but my pleading puppy dog eyes prevailed. He got up, leaving me with the bed-frame. It didn't bother me. I got started on the other side, contorting my body to be able to hold the arm up steady to fasten it to the bed head.

By the time he came back with Ferni, I had completed it on my own.

'Ferni!' I exclaimed as the small black furred dog came running as fast as he could into my arms.

His tail whacked my legs as he bounced up and down trying to kiss my face. I picked him up, cuddling the tiny animal. His warm wet tongue tickled my cheek.

'Oh I'm happy to finally see you in person too, Ferni,' I said, putting him back on the ground, rubbing his tummy. I turned my head to wipe the slobber off my cheek with my sleeve.

Dylan placed the planks down into the frame for the mattress, while I watched on. Ferni in my arms now he was trying to actively bite my hand. His teeth scratched my skin, causing me to put him down. He scampered off to my couch, using the boxes nearby as steps.

'You okay?' Dylan asked. 'He didn't hurt you did he?'

He brought my hand to eye level to investigate, only to see a couple of scratch marks.

'Oh my god, I am —'

'Don't apologise,' I interjected. 'It happens. Remember, I had a puppy once, you've seen the photos and videos of Cocoa. She was a little mischievous thing. Used to do the same thing when she was a puppy. Just teach him the word "gentle" and hopefully he'll learn,' I said. 'He didn't draw blood, just scratched my hand with his teeth.'

'I'm so—'

'Again, no apology needed. He's a puppy. They're either an angel or a gremlin with nothing in between.'

I headed to the hallway to drag in the mattress.

'Wow, this is a decent plush mattress, expensive too,' Dylan said.

'My parents said that I am to have good furniture to maintain perfect ergonomics,' I replied. 'So they see it as a benefit to not only my education, but my career.'

'Ah well, they're not wrong.' Dylan moved around the bed, helping me guide the heavy mattress onto the frame. 'Maybe I should move in, could take the bed in shifts.'

It was an obvious joke, and I laughed. But deep down, a part of me wished it wasn't a joke. The thought of living with someone and starting a life together was something I longed for. Whether I would have that was another story.

Kaleb was an amazing guy at first, it was easy to love him. In the end, he became someone unrecognisable. He wanted full control over me, when he knew he couldn't.

Dylan, or any man for that matter, for all I knew, could put up a front. Kaleb was sweet at first, kind, compassionate, the list went on. Then again, he was far more caring and intuitive than Kaleb was in the beginning.

*Maybe my initial thoughts were correct, this is what a boyfriend should be like.*

After all, his friends thought the world of him, both the boys and the girls. Kaleb didn't have any female friends of his own, only taking my high school friend group when it suited him. Now that I thought about it, not having female friends wasn't a complete red flag. It was more the fact that he hardly had any friends that raised several issues regarding his personality and ability to have healthy long-term friendships. Not just with women but with men too.

'You okay?' Dylan asked. 'You kinda spaced out there.'

'Huh? Oh yeah, I'm fine,' I replied. 'Let's get a wriggle on with the study. Pull out is already in there, just need to set up my desk and note wall.'

The two of us powered through the rest of the furniture. It was pretty easy given that most of it was already assembled.

We moved the dining room table behind the island bench. Dylan sighed and said, 'There's this amazing Thai restaurant you'll like. You stay here, I'll be right back.'

'Oh, okay. Sounds good. I'll start unpacking some of the boxes and my suitcases,' I replied.

Dylan headed out the door, leaving Ferni and I to ourselves.

'Want a box to play with, Ferni?' I asked the tiny dog.

I tipped the contents onto the island bench, and disassembled the box, ensuring that he couldn't injure himself.

'Keep yourself occupied with that,' I said.

I walked around the apartment putting clothes, books, and study materials away. The only things left were my kitchenware, which I swiftly put into the dishwasher.

*Hopefully that's done by the time he gets back.*

As a housewarming gift, my parents bought me alcohol and a shelving unit for all said alcohol, and Will bought me a gin distilling kit. Boxes of all my unopened bottles of gin, vodka, rum, whiskey, and wine sat at the base of it.

Now the fun could begin. I had always wanted to have a gorgeous alcohol shelf. Even though I was not a massive drinker, I had a somewhat expensively eclectic taste. I sorted through the bottles and placed them like how bars showcase their alcohol. Cheap stuff within reach, the more expensive bottles, on the upper shelves.

There was a knock at the door, and I let him in.

'Dinner, and the muscles, have arrived,' Dylan said.

As I followed him past the kitchen island, he saw the cardboard littered floor.

'Oh my, you've been busy Ferni,' Dylan said as his puppy ran towards him.

'Yes, yes he has. And he's enjoyed every second of it,' I replied.

'Now, here's the dinner, as promised,' Dylan said. 'I got a bit of everything, and if we don't finish it, it'll be our dinner for tomorrow night.'

'Inviting yourself over Doctor Atwood?' I cocked an eyebrow as I grabbed cutlery from the drying rack.

'Well, if you'd be so kind, I did do some heavy lifting for you today.'

'What, the bed-frame and *maybe* two boxes?' I scoffed.

'I moved four boxes, two of them were your textbooks, that weighed way more than the headboard.'

I rolled my eyes. 'Oh okay, Hulk, would you like a trophy or spring roll for your kindness?'

He started laughing and I couldn't help myself either. My eyes started to water.

Then it died down, and he looked at me with a look in his eyes that I couldn't quite describe. I searched for a tell, a slight move of a muscle, dilation of a pupil; nothing.

I blinked and stood up. 'Want some wine? Gin and tonic?'

Dylan cleared his throat. 'No. No, thank you. I'll just get some plates.'

I nodded and the two of us headed towards the kitchen but remained at an arm's length. The only sound emanating was Ferni's gnawing on empty cardboard boxes.

# 37

## February 2019

*22 Years Old*

I pushed open the frosted glass door and into the small cold waiting room. Never thought I'd see the day I'd describe a psychology clinic's waiting room as cold and dreary. All that my eye could see was white walls and uncomfortable black seats.

*Isn't a psychologist's office supposed to be welcoming?*

'McKenna Carrington, nine o'clock with Xenia,' I said to the receptionist.

I made a promise to myself, Aster, and Dylan that I would seek a psychologist the minute I moved to Adelaide. After years of neglecting my mental health, I needed to end the cycle of self-neglect. My internalised victimisation was a beacon of detrimental situations. And I was not about to let it impact medical school.

'Take a seat,' she said coldly.

I took a seat in one of the hard plastic black chairs by the clinic's entrance and stared at the bare white wall in front of me. It was quiet, too quiet, aside from the receptionist banging her keyboard loudly.

'McKenna?' I snapped my head towards the voice and saw Xenia. A tall young woman with bright pink hair stood at the end of the reception desk. She was dressed in a short-sleeved chocolate button up shirt, tucked into a pair of cream colour linen pants.

'Hi.' I followed her down the hall to her office. It smelt like the woody scent of juniper berries, oranges and basil. It was the tri-factor of childhood bliss. The nod to the coastal vibes of relaxation.

*Heavenly.*

I melted into the soft cushions of the beige linen sofa. My purse dropped to the floor, and I crossed my legs, letting myself find comfort in the deep pillows.

Xenia sat across from me in the matching beige armchair, armed with her notepad and pen.

*Here I am safe.*

'So I've read over your forms you filled out, can you tell me a bit more as to why you're here?' she asked.

'Absolutely,' I replied. 'Where do you want me to begin?'

'Anywhere you'd like.'

I started at the beginning.

That fateful day back in two-thousand-and-six. Mrs McConnell and the humiliation. To me it was the catalyst for everything in my life going up in flames. Sure it built resilience, but it had also led me down a dark path.

Depression had become my baseline emotion, I had no idea what normal was anymore. Happiness was nothing. It was a mere temporary emotion, that was overshadowed by dark clouds known as depression. Anxiety looming in the background always waiting to pounce.

The irony was, I had dreamed of running away to Adelaide and starting a life. Here I was embarking on a new life with new friends. Meanwhile my two loving parents remained on the northeast coast of Australia.

'How does that make you feel, being here and away from your parents?' she prompted.

'It feels okay.' I shifted on the couch. The weight on my chest altered, still there, still heavy. 'I don't know. There's part imposter syndrome, part glad that I could leave my old life behind. I've finally gotten myself to a point where I don't want to die. I just don't want to exist. I want to create a new identity and run. "McKenna Carrington", the name, dies, but I live on. If that makes sense.'

'It does.' She flashed her ocean blue eyes at me, urging me to continue.

'To make matters worse, I think everything I've gone through — I think I've victimised myself internally.'

'What do you mean? How would you have done that?'

'I don't know. I just seem to attract bad people. I've been bullied probably from the ages of five or six to seventeen, abused by various teachers, and I've been in an abusive relationship for three years.' I repositioned myself, letting myself sink into the couch as I spoke. 'I'm meek. Easy prey.'

I knew that my words were fighting words. Xenia was looking concerned as she wrote away in her notepad. I watched as she glanced at her previous notes.

'I'm curious, you say that you're "meek", "easy prey", and you "attract bad people", so why medicine? I don't know much, but I know I considered it for psychiatry. It isn't exactly an easy road, it's cutthroat and I'm sure as a nurse, you've met some pretty nasty doctors.'

'I did,' I confirmed. 'Got yelled at by one for not dressing a wound the way he liked it. But it's more than that.'

I recalled my first encounter with Dylan. How he confused me for a medical student because of how in-tune I was than any of the actual interns in the room. Both Dylan and that patient convinced me that nursing wasn't my future, medicine was. My lips twitched upward to a tight smile.

'Being made to feel like I was smarter than three interns ... It was pretty special,' I replied. 'Boosted the ego a little bit. But it gave me the motivation I needed.'

'Based on what you're saying, I am gathering you're a very selfless person despite the abuse and bullying you've copped.'

'That's correct.'

'Does anyone help you?' I shake my head. 'So what do you do when you need a little attention? Do you do a spa day? Go for a run? What do you do?'

*When was the last time I looked after myself? Never?*

'I've lost touch since Kaleb. I'm not blaming him, but I think just that relationship in general — I'm realising how much of a toll that took on me.'

I haven't looked after myself in so long. Running I barely did on account of how skinny I was due to lack of food. Even though I spent some days at my parents' house, I still barely ate.

'I miss running. Last time I ran, it was because Kaleb stalked me and I didn't know what else to do, I wanted to clear my head. So I went for a run, only I saw him watching me, so I bolted back, only to collapse and puke when I got home.'

'What did your parents say?' she asked.

*Dammit. She had to go there.*

'They support me, I know they do, but I couldn't even tell them about the emotional abuse I faced as a child. Mind you, emotional abuse wasn't even classed as child abuse back then, I don't think it is now, still. Only physical and sexual ...'

I reached for the tissues on the light birch table beside the couch.

'If I told them, I think they would've gotten me help but ...' I trailed off, touching the soft tissues to my nose, letting myself room to breathe. 'I couldn't. Telling them about Kaleb is just as scary. It's embarrassing. I mean, how does this happen? Why did I stay? I'm not some helpless woman ... am I?'

'No of course not,' Xenia said. 'But to use your words again, you claim you're a "beacon".'

Oh.

'You have internalised victimisation, but you also have externalised victimisation. Being left out, singled out, or being called a troublemaker when you aren't,' she continued. 'There isn't anything wrong with you. Abusers need to use others to assert themselves, so they feel bigger than they truly are.'

'So why me then?'

'We may never get an answer, bullies bully for different reasons, just like abusers. It could also be a power trip.' Xenia gave me a comforting smile, before it dropped as she continued. 'As for teachers, it's easier to single out one child than three or four. Some even play favourites and won't call them out.'

'What do I do then? I'll be faced with doctors on power trips all the time.'

'Well, firstly, seeking help is the right step.' She flicked her wrist over. 'Next step is homework as we have run out of time.'

'Damn,' I joked, I was really comfortable. The ten million bowling balls on my chest were slowly lifting.

'All good, we'll make a booking for next week. In the meantime, I'll get you to focus on finding some daily, weekly, and monthly goals. And sorting a "self-care" schedule that will make you focus on you. I also want you to start setting healthy habits, make small smart goals to reach the bigger habits if you need to. Sound okay?'

'Sounds great,' I replied.

'Awesome, so let's book you in. Same time next week?'

I whipped out my phone and checked my calendar. 'Yes, that works for me.' I replied.

She led me out of the office and to the front desk.

'See you next week,' she said as she left me with the receptionist.

'See you then.'

As soon as I got to my car, I burst.

Nothing was more powerful than the validation I've desired for more than a decade. The tears flowed down my cheeks as I whispered to myself, 'It was never my fault. It was *never* my fault.'

# 38

# February 2019

*22 Years Old*

I wasn't sure if it was the coffee, nerves, or the cold air in the lecture hall that were making me jittery. My leg bounced like it had a mind of its own. First day of postgraduate medicine and I had back-to-back classes all day; talk about full on. This was either about to be fun or my worst nightmare. I guess time would tell.

'Hi.' A female voice came from my left. 'Mind if I sit here?'

'No, not at all, please, sit,' I replied, moving my bag over with my foot so she had room. 'I'm McKenna.'

'Louise,' she replied as her long golden hair dropped over her shoulder onto the skintight pink t-shirt. 'Nervous?'

'More than I thought I would be. You?'

'Same.'

Thanks to nursing, I was able to take most of the basic classes off my schedule. I didn't mind, it only meant that I was going straight into the lion's den with no protection. It was an exciting thrill but terrifying all at the same time.

'Let me guess, your previous degree was nursing?' Louise asked, eyeballing me up and down.

*That's a little presumptuous and judgemental.*

'That obvious?' I retorted with a chuckle, going along with her "game".

'Yeah.'

Everyone looked different. Many dressed in shorts and a t-shirt, some in office casual. I couldn't even begin to guess anyone's previous degree. She wore black pants, and a tight pink t-shirt tucked into it, with a pair of black joggers.

'This seat taken?' A man in jeans and a basic white t-shirt.

'No, no,' I replied to the guy.

'I'm Jonathan,' he said, holding his hand out for me to shake.

'McKenna,' I replied.

Louise reached over to introduce herself too.

'Think this is the start of a grand friendship,' she said.

The clock was ticking down.

Only a few minutes until the lecturer would make their appearance and start class. I had already gone through the material, but this was beyond anything I had ever done before. It was far more intense than I predicted, and my nerves were shooting through the roof as we waited.

And waited.

I gently tapped my Apple Pencil against the screen of my iPad.

Out of the corner of my eye, a short woman with short black hair and donning a white coat and black pants made her way down the stairs.

'Hope you all are ready, my name's Doctor Teagan Welner. Today we're starting hot and heavy, so hope you're all caffeinated,' she announced as she got to the podium to set up the lesson. 'I'm not usually late, however, I had a meeting so this will be a one off.

'I will also say that in this course, you will learn faster if you come to class having done the readings prior. I know medical school can be ruthless, that's why I give tips throughout my lessons on how to pass my course. Don't show up, you don't get those tips. Don't do the weekly readings, you will struggle.'

That was a scary introduction, but I could understand why. Not only was this a postgraduate program, but it was also one of the toughest degrees out there. We were all barrelling towards a ruthless career that took no prisoners.

Human anatomy and physiology weren't easy subjects, and we only scraped the surface in nursing school. I mean, I did do a subject called "Human Anatomy & Physiology 1". What was in number two? I was probably about to find out in this lecture.

Doctor Welner seemed friendly but very blunt on her expertise in the field. It was refreshing to have that. Considering most of my previous lecturers up-played how great nursing was. When in reality, so many nursing departments overworked what staff they did have due to understaffing. Medicine was about to become a whole other ball game, and my mental health could not take a dive.

As Dr Welner continued to set herself up. I jotted down ways to maintain my sanity over the next four years. There was no way in hell I was going to let my past start to slip through the cracks that I was slowly patching up.

'Do you two have your specialties picked out already?' Louise asked quietly. 'I'm going for neurosurgery.'

I wrote down "paediatric surgeon/general practitioner" on my iPad, turning it towards her and Jonathan. Jonathan wrote down "pathology/forensic medicine" on his note pad, turning it over to us.

There was a high chance that the three of us would eventually change our specialties as we continued to push through medical school. But there was the other possibility that we may end up solidifying our desired goal.

Doctor Welner had switched the screen to the tutorial questions. I already had them up on my iPad and filled in from last night's pre-reading session.

'Alright, here's how this will play out, I go through questions, and you may respond with a raised hand,' Dr Welner said. 'As there may be a number of you who don't understand, I'll explain why the answer is the way that it is, or you may discuss it.'

I also knew better than to continuously raise my hand. Picking and choosing what question I raised my hand for was golden. As she explained and taught, I wrote down her tips on where to focus our studies on, in relation to our textbooks.

For the first time, I felt like I was right where I belonged. Dylan was right, and most importantly, I was right. With each question asked, I was getting almost everyone correct. It was the first time, for a while, where I felt like I was confident enough to ask and answer questions.

Maybe that was Dylan's doing, letting me answer or ask him questions while he and I worked. He was by far the best doctor I met. I had met other great ones, but none that nurtured my curious mind.

Doctor Welner hit the next screen, with the question: "*What are the four major biomolecules in the human body?*"

'A four-mark bonus will be added at the end of the semester for the student who can also give me one type each,' she said.

Almost every hand raised. But just as I was about to enter myself in the sea of hands, a message popped up on the screen

**Dylan:** *I know class is almost over, but I hope your first day went really well xx*

I smiled at my screen and proceeded to raise my hand.

'Yes, McKenna?' Dr Welner called out.

'Lipids; triglycerides,' I listed. 'Proteins; Haemoglobin. Carbohydrates; polysaccharides. And Nucleic Acid; DNA.'

'Those are correct,' Dr Welner said. 'That's all for today folks. See you on Friday for the first quiz. Remember these are every week and count for two percent of your grade.'

As we started to load our belongings into our bags, Jonathon piped up, 'Hey do you guys want to head to the library to study?'

'I can't, have work,' Louise replied. 'Rain check though.'

'That's okay,' he replied. 'McKenna?'

'Yeah sure, I'm in,' I replied.

**Me:** *Thank you so much for your vote of encouragement. I scored 4 bonus marks to my end of semester grades. You da best xx*

# 39

# February 2019

*22 years Old*

By the time I got home, I was exhausted, mentally and physically. It was back to the same old university exhaustion. Stress was already starting bubble away in the deep pits of my stomach. Waiting to wear me down to nothing until I caved into the inevitable mental breakdown. First day and first week of the term set the pace.

*Not today bastards.*

My stomach rumbled, and I pushed myself off the sofa, heading over to the kitchen to start cooking. I had a list of meals that didn't take long to prep or cook after working with a dietitian.

I was eager to set up a schedule, that also included planned calls with my family. I wasn't prepared to fall back into my negative study habits that I had during high school or nursing, such as forgetting basic human requirements, like eating and drinking. Almost as if I had to still prove to myself, to my old teachers, that I had what it took to achieve high grades.

*If only they nurtured my eagerness to learn like my university professors did.*

Healing was never going to be easy, but it was a battle when combining university into the mix. It was why Dylan, Bianca, and Natalie made it their life mission to try to help me as best they could. I didn't deserve friends like them. They had made plans to help me out for the first couple of weeks of uni to ensure I was stuck in the routine.

It was a little overwhelming. Overbearing. Suffocating. But considering everything I had gone through, one little slip and I'd be six feet under; unrecoverable.

There was a knock at my door, followed by Dylan calling out my name. 'Ugh, who am I getting tonight, Dr Atwood, or my best friend?' I called back as I answered the door.

'Depends,' he replied. My question dissipated in the air. 'Oh, this smells amazing.'

'Oh, that's my pasta alle vodka,' I replied.

He was right, it smelled amazing in here. It was one of the great beauties of homemade meals, other than nourishment. Cooking wasn't something I could leave off my "health habits" list. I was actually gaining weight. Albeit slowly. It was progress in the right direction and soon I would be able to start weights and go for runs again.

As he rounded the corner, Dylan spotted my updated schedule board next to the kitchen island.

'What's this?' Dylan asked.

'That is how I'm going to survive med school,' I said to him. 'By the way, Natalie said she couldn't make it. A double shift came up.'

'Damn, poor thing, oh well more pasta for me then.'

He wasn't wrong. It made me feel like I never truly left home. Considering Dad and Will would pig out on the home cooked meals, whether Mum made them, or on the off-chance, I cooked.

I missed them enormously, but Facetime existed for a reason. Once a week; every Friday night at 7pm, were our Facetime calls.

That was the deal. Though Mum and I had our own private agreement on texting during our favourite shows to gossip. It became a tradition we didn't want to lose.

'You gotta let me be alone one of these days,' I said to him as I piled pasta onto my plate.

'Maybe I'm just here to hear about your day and eat your delicious food.' Dylan sat down at my island bench, his plate full of at least two helpings of my pasta. 'So, do tell me. How was the first day?'

'Full on,' I replied. 'How did you do it? I'm already one day in and I'm stressed.'

'Lots of coffee, tutoring, and group study sessions.' He took a bite of my Penne alle Vodka. 'Mmm, how'd you make this?!'

'A chef never reveals their secret.' I smirked.

'I tutor you in med, and you teach me how to cook? Sounds like a win-win for me?'

'You got a deal.'

His grip was firm as he shook my hand. Only there was an undeniable jolt of electricity. We stopped. Our eyes locked. Our hands still grasped. The warmth emanating off his hand was comforting and yet scary. It shouldn't be. It should've been a normal handshake, but judging by the surprised look in his eyes, he felt it too.

I immediately pulled away, not wanting to remain close to the flame. Only we both reached for the bottle of Baressie's white non-alcoholic wine. Another zap of electricity and burn ran through my fingers as our hands collided. We both pulled back.

'Seriously, this is so freaking good!' He proceeded to take another mouthful, trying to ignore the rapidly growing elephant in the room.

'There'll be leftovers, feel free to take some. I don't mind,' I replied, pouring us a glass of the wine.

'I shall.'

As we ate in silence, my mind went back to Kaleb. The love I shared with him was the kind of love that behaved in a similar way to a cyclone. It was the calm before the storm. When it hit, you had no idea what sort of path of destruction it was going to leave behind in its wake.

The friendship I had developed with Aster, Bianca, and Natalie was more powerful than I ever could have imagined. My support and kindness is reciprocated back at the same level. I never had to hide parts of my personality because they didn't like it. We all were unique and it made for the best girls' nights.

Dylan, on the other hand. He was different. While he was my best friend, he not only matched my support, kindness, and enthusiasm, he went above and beyond. When I felt down, he was there, shining a light that drove the darkness away. Yet, I was still waiting for his light to become a storm. Strike me down with a bolt of lightning. Drown me with rivers of flash flooding.

'Oh, did I tell you? I made a couple of friends today,' I said, breaking the silence. 'A Paramedic grad who's wanting to do Neurosurgery, and a Forensic Science grad hoping to become a Forensic Pathologist.'

'That's amazing!' Dylan replied.

'Yeah, we've created a small study group.'

'That's even more wondrous.'

'It is. It feels great.' I stood up to take the dirty plates and cutlery to the kitchen. I paused before I bent down to load the dishwasher. 'I just want to say, Dylan, thank you.'

'For what?' he asked.

'For indirectly saying you believed in me. Words have an impact. Until we met in the ICU, I was locked in on believing this, med school, was impossible.'

# 40

# September 2014

*16 Years Old*

It was the day I had been waiting for: Dissection Day. My hands shook in anticipation as I took my usual sport right in front of Mr Domelio's desk.

'McKenna, Harry, Lucille, and Jack,' Mr Domelio called. 'You're in a group, here's your rat and utensils.'

Lucille grabbed the rat and utensils off Mr Domelio while we set up at our usual table, closest to the teacher's desk and entry to the science lab. She placed the rat on the bench, and I immediately went back to grade eight. I opted out of the dissection back then, unable to fathom how anyone could cut open an animal to get a visual of the body's organs.

My hands still shook, only now I couldn't tell the difference between anxiety or an adrenaline rush. Only thing stopping me from taking a position against the hallway wall outside, was the fact that I regretted not doing this back in grade eight.

*If I want to be a doctor, this is the way to know if it's a step in the right direction.*

I hung back, letting one of the other group members take the rat. It was already prepped for its dissection, its paws pinned to the board. I felt myself cringe at the sight, as I made my way to our designated experiment bench.

'Kenz, wanna help peel the skin from the muscle?' Lucille asked.

Regret was a nagging thought in my head, but if I did it, I would be proud of myself. If I didn't do it, what was the probability of me regretting my decision? Highly probable.

'Alright,' I said, rolling my shoulders back, stretching my upper body. 'Tweezers and scalpel.' I held my hands out like a surgeon and took the tools off Harry. 'Thanks.'

Carefully, I peeled the skin away from the muscle. A weird feeling washed over me with each passing millisecond.

*Am I enjoying myself? Is that what this is?*

Images of my future self-started to float around in my mind. The white coat, the scrubs, me standing over my patients wielding the tools that would give me the power to save their lives.

It was the ultimate dream. This is what I wanted for my life. I wanted to save lives, I wanted to find the "why" and the "how". I wanted to look after patients either as a Paediatric Surgeon, or General Practitioner with special interests in paediatrics and women's health.

The only downside was that no matter how hard I worked, my efforts were met with contradictions and put downs by the very people who are supposed to teach me.

*How can I explain this to my parents in a way that will help them understand?*

'Aww look at all the babies!' One girl cried excitedly from two benches down from where my group was.

'There was only one female, so if any of you want to see, come over,' Mr Domelio said.

I hung back.

Exciting as it was to get a hands-on learning experience, it was already upsetting enough that I was dissecting an animal. Seeing a female rat and its babies was not something I braced myself with. Yet, I looked over from my position. Only as I did, my eye caught a glimpse of the six little sacs housing six kidney bean-sized fetuses through the gap made by my peers.

'When you go back to your table, you can either opt to finish up or you can take out a kidney,' Mr Domelio said.

*Oh boy!*

My hands started to vibrate again as I waited for the group to come back to the table.

*I want to take the kidney out.*

'McKenna, you okay?' Harry asked.

'Oh, yeah, just didn't feel like seeing the tiny things,' she replied. 'I know that they're bred for science, but it's still sad. Ya know?'

'Oh I totally get it, but it's great to learn too,' Lucille said.

'Exactly right,' Harry chimed. 'Now, shall we take out a kidney? Kenna?'

'Sure,' I said, as I picked back up the scalpel and tweezers.

With a firm grip on the right kidney, I cut it away from the tissue. It was quick and easy with perfect technique. Not once did I accidentally knick something I wasn't meant to. According to my research, I had performed a perfect Nephrectomy in about four minutes; the margins were clean, and the kidney wasn't cut.

'If you want to, you can cut it open and have a look inside it,' Mr Domelio offered, seeing that the kidney was removed and lying next to its deceased owner.

I couldn't help myself. None of the other members of my group wanted to, so I did it.

As per the class lectures and textbook, I sliced the sharp tool down the coronal plane, separating the front and back portions of the kidney. There was nothing much besides wiggly lines along the walls. Mr Domelio allowed us to run out gloved fingers along the inside wall of the kidney. It was surreal.

'Alright, what I want you all to do is leave everything where it is, remove your PPE, wash your hands and sit back at your desks.'

*Best biology class ever!*

Once I had tidied up, I sat back at the desk but couldn't focus on my teacher. Cloud-nine was a great yet dangerous place for me to be. After everything that had happened, I couldn't trust myself being happy.

Holding that scalpel was something else. I could see myself as a doctor.

The bell rang, and I headed down to the student reception to sign out for my double study period. As soon as I typed in my student number and clicked the sign out button, I rang my dad.

'Hey, everything okay kiddo?' Dad asked.

'Yeah. I've just signed out and heading to the bus stop,' I said into the phone.

'Oh, excellent,' he replied. 'How was it?'

'So amazing!' I gushed. 'You should've seen me with the scalpel!'

'Does that mean that I'm talking to a future doctor?'

'Possibly. I'm going to do nursing first to boost my grades, 'cause let's face it ... But I really wanna try for the UCAT.'

'That's amazing sweetie, I'm so glad that you had a good day.'

I could still feel the weight of the scalpel in my hand. It felt right, like it truly fit. Was what everyone was feeding me correct? It felt more like a glimpse of what was at the end of the tunnel if I could push through.

*Dr McKenna Carrington has a good ring to it.*

# 41

# March 2019

*23 Years Old*

My birthday came around, and I was surprised with tickets and accommodation to Melbourne from my parents a couple of days ago. The excuse being "just because it's your birthday". I didn't buy it. It wasn't just for me but for four of my friends as well. We flew in on Friday night, and spent the full Saturday walking around the city, shopping and seeing the sights. Today, they had a surprise that Dylan had supposedly organised.

My brain was full of medical knowledge, and stress, but this was exactly what I needed.

As I sat at the marble stone dining table, I waited for my parents to answer my Facetime.

'Happy birthday, our gorgeous girl!' dad yelled as the two of them popped up on my iPad.

'Thank you,' I sang.

'How's Melbourne?' mum asked.

'Really nice. The hotel is amazing.' I rambled on hundred kilometres a minute. 'Massive rooms – Dylan took the couch so the four of us could have the beds. Bathrooms are just … I gotta send you photos. We got an insane upgrade to the room you had originally booked. And we're going for a surprise outing in about an hour to celebrate.'

'Is that a marble countertop?' mum asked. I nodded 'Do a pan?'

I rotated the iPad slowly around the room, showing the view that I was facing.

'Oh wow, is that the penthouse?' dad asked.

'Yep.' I placed my iPad back down on the table. 'Like I said, we got an upgrade like you wouldn't believe.'

'Seen anyone famous yet?' mum asked.

'Uh, no, why would I?' I replied

'Heard from your brother yet?' dad asked.

'Nah, he's got tutoring jobs all day, so I'm expecting either a text or voicemail later,' I said. 'It's all good, we're both living the busy lives at the moment.'

'That you are honey,' mum said. 'We better go. We miss you…'

'So very much,' dad finished.

'I miss you both too and thank you. Love you.'

'Love you too,' they replied in unison.

It was the issue with moving so far away. I loved the autonomy and living my adult life the way I wanted, but I missed my parents. It was days like today that made me miss them more.

The thoughts were drowned out by Aster, Bianca and Natalie walking into the living room.

'I'm surprised you haven't clocked on yet.' Bianca sat down beside me.

'What's that?' I replied.

'Didn't you say, last night, that you thought you saw Sebastian Vettel?' Natalie piped up. 'You know. Famous Formula One driver…'

I stared blankly at Natalie.

*What is this weekend? It's just my birthday.*

'Guys, my brain is fried,' I said. 'If it isn't to do with the brachial plexus bundle or remembering the ten cranial nerves and what they do, I got nothin'.'

'You of all people should know what this weekend is,' Aster said.

I blinked.

'Um, should I?' I replied. 'Seriously, I'm fried. Help me, please?'

'We're taking you to Albert Park,' Dylan said, holding up a brand-new Red Bull jersey and my very worn Mercedes cap.

I moved towards him, reaching out to the jersey. The feel of the soft fabric between my fingers was almost too much.

*They didn't. Surely they didn't get me tickets to see the Formula One. No. No. They're pulling my leg.*

'Seeing it live was always —' Bianca said.

*Yes they did. Otherwise, this was some cruel joke.*

'The dream,' I finished, still holding the jersey between my fingers. 'Yeah, I was saving up to go.'

*I seriously have the best of friends.*

'Happy birthday,' Dylan said.

I pulled my hands back and turned my head between the four of them. 'Oh my God! Really?' My voice jumped an octave.

'Yes,' Natalie said.

I ran between the lot of them squeezing them into a hug. 'Thank you, thank you, thank you, thank you!'

I took the jersey off Dylan and shut the door to one of the bedrooms. Off went my black tank, and on went the Red Bull jersey. I tucked the shirt into my denim shorts and pulled my ponytail through the hole of my Mercedes cap.

'That just looks all kinds of wrong,' Aster joked as I walked out of the room. 'Mercedes and RB …'

'What, a girl can be a supporter of two teams,' I replied.

'Don't worry hon, you won't be alone in the double team support,' Bianca said. 'I'm going to change.'

A few minutes later, Bianca walked out in a Ferrari jersey and McLaren cap.

'Hell yeah!' I exclaimed, giving her a double high-five.

# 42

# March 2019

*23 Years Old*

The atmosphere was orgasmic.

There was nothing greater than smell of the unleaded fuel and listening to the dulcet sounds of Formula Three cars zipping around Albert Park.

As we walked through the gates, the park was buzzing with a flurry of team merchandise and people yelling to be heard over the sound of the cars.

'How are you feeling?' Natalie asked.

'Like this is the best birthday gift a girl could've asked for,' I replied. 'Seriously, I can't thank you all enough.'

'You've thanked us enough. You don't need to thank us for any presents we give you for the next twenty years,' Bianca said.

My feet sunk into the soft spots on the dirt path to one of the main food courts around the park. The dirt felt rough against my skin as some particles settled on around my socks. This was what I lived for. A whole experience like no other.

The sun was out. We were lathered up with sunscreen, ready for the day to be spent track side nor without shade.

'Top of 25 today apparently,' Bianca said.

'Perfect weather,' I replied. 'Can be in denim shorts without chaffing.'

The girls laughed and agreed.

'Who'd you reckon will win?' Dylan asked.

'Oh, Hamilton for sure, though one of the Ferrari's may give him a run for his money,' Aster said.

It ended up leading to a massive debate between the lot of us. Dylan, more so, trying to wrap his head around the whole sport in general.

'We turning you into an F1 fan yet?' I bumped his shoulder with mine, gazing into his blue eyes.

'Guess we'll see when the race begins, won't we?' he replied. 'Speaking of, didn't you ladies want to watch the F2 race before the main event? It's about to start in twenty minutes and we have no clue where our grandstand is.'

We quickly grabbed our belongings from the table and tried to navigate the vicinity.

'Are we on the inside of the track or outside?' I asked.

'No, we're along the pit straight,' Bianca said. 'So judging by the map ... we gotta head back towards Gate 5?'

The rest of us looked at the map before I quickly caught on. 'We're here already.' I pointed to where we were previously sitting. 'See there's turn one, and up there is the next lot of grandstands.'

'Oh perfect!' Dylan exclaimed. 'My feet are already killing me.'

'Aren't you on your feet all day? You just started your Ortho Residency,' Natalie stated.

'Oh hush,' Dylan joked.

We figured that we could hang out a little more in the shade of the trees. Only downside was sitting in the sparse grass and compact dirt. Not totally comfortable but sufficed for the twenty minutes as we waited.

There was nothing sweeter than friendship. Though we all had different schedules, or lived a few hundred kilometres away, our friendship remained strong.

'So, do those hot girls do the whole like flag drop thing?' Dylan tried to hide his chuckle.

In response to his joking remark, we gave him light whacks to the arm.

'Only hormonal sexist men,' Aster laughed.

'I don't know what you're talking about.' Dylan looked away.

'Oh come on, as if you don't know.' Bianca snorted. 'When was the last time for you?'

'How many Canadian Clubs have you had?' Dylan replied.

'None,' she said. 'Been with all of you this whole time. So what gives?'

'Nope, we're not doing this.' Dylan got up from the ground. 'Coming? Formula Two is about to start.'

'This isn't over Atwood,' I remarked.

Dylan all but rolled his eyes as he made his way to the stairs.

I made it halfway before my palm collided with the metal handrail, my skin sizzled for a second.

'Ouch,' I yelped, shaking my hand.

Dylan, being the keeper of tickets, handed them to the ticket inspector, dressed in black. He led us up to our seats, halfway up the grandstand, with a crystal-clear view into turn one and almost the full grid.

My jaw dropped.

'You can thank Dylan for the seats,' Bianca said, passing me. 'He wanted us to have the best view in the place.'

*These seats weren't cheap; how selfless of him.*

Dylan took the isle, leaving me to take the seat between him and Aster. His head turned towards the sun, squinting to look up the grid. I gently tapped his denim clad leg.

'Thank you,' I said, kissing the soft skin of his cheek. 'Best view in the house.'

'You're welcome,' he replied with a smirk and a wink. Both sending a kaleidoscope of butterflies mad in my stomach. He patted my leg, only to rest his hand on my knee like it was meant to be there.

'Should we get a photo?' Aster asked.

'Yeah,' we said.

With not many people coming, the ticket inspector agreed to take one for us – the track and F2 cars right behind us.

As soon as we sat back down, Dylan's hand was back on my knee. He wasn't overtly affectionate. Sure hugs were a common thing between us, but we weren't touchy like I was with the girls. But this was comfortable.

'Oh, they're starting the formation lap!' Bianca announced to us.

The sound of the cars filled the air. Many of the seats were still empty.

'So this is Formula Two?' Dylan asked.

I leaned over, hovering my lips next to his ear, 'Yeah.'

A couple of hours later, we were watching the main event circle around the track to their grid boxes. The last of the seats in our grandstand filled up. It was a gradual build-up of suffocating body heat and a combination of the smells of burnt rubber, fuel, body odour, and dozens of deodorants, perfumes and colognes.

'Excited?' Dylan asked me, his breath warm against my cheek.

'Nah,' I replied dryly. 'Not really.'

'Nice try,' he replied. 'Should know by now that you can't do sarcasm.'

'Dammit.'

'How much longer until lights out?' Aster asked.

'Five minutes,' Dylan said.

Time slowed down as our gazes focused on the cars and people below.

The feel of everyone's body heat suddenly overwhelmed me beyond belief. Dylan pulled out the map of Melbourne we got from the tourist centre two days ago and started fanning himself and me.

'You feeling it?' Dylan asked as he leaned closer to me.

'Yeah, thanks,' I replied.

The mechanics proceeded to move off the track, and the drivers started to make their way around Albert Park for the Formation Lap, letting the Track Marshalls clean the track and remaining personnel to exit.

'Oh my God, they're starting,' Aster whispered excitedly in my ear, like a kid in an amusement park.

I chuckled and we moved with the crowd. Sitting on the edge of our seats as we watched the first of the cars enter the main straight to their grid box. My heart began to thump harder now.

'I think he likes you,' Aster whispered.

'No, he doesn't,' I replied.

'Hmm, I don't know, that's not a friendly hand on the leg.'

I looked down at Dylan's hand, it was just above my knee, curled in towards my inner leg. Most of his forearm resting comfortably on my thigh.

'Just saying hon, if you don't like him, you might want to move that hand away,' she said.

*I could either focus on whatever this is for the next two hours, or I focus on the race.*

Next thing we knew it's light's out and the cars are off. The entire grandstand was on the edge of their seats as we watched the cars enter into Turn One.

Dylan's hand moved with me as I shifted in my seat trying to get a clear view of the action. Most of the cars came out unscathed besides a lock-up from a Renault.

His hand was keeping me grounded, refusing to let me get too carried away in the Formula One stratosphere.

'Thank you again, Dylan,' I said as close as I could to his ear.

He removed his hand from my thigh, placing his arm on the back of the chair instead.

'You're welcome,' he said leaning into me.

*Now this is incredibly intimate. Are you sure you're just friends?*

The cars came back around to start lap two of the race, and my focus was back on the cars and the radio. Except I couldn't, his weight and presence pulled my mind away.

*He was the one that suggested getting tickets. He got my parents on board.*

As the race went on, the more and more I thought.

Kaleb would never have done this for me, let alone any of my high school friends. They were so self-engrossed that they never once thought of those who they deemed "lesser" than them. I was a nobody; a somebody who was desperate to fit in.

*Dylan though. Is he just being kind or is Aster right?*

I couldn't keep up with my thoughts anymore, I hadn't even been able to enjoy the race. This was such a thoughtful gift, and I felt like I was squandering it by focusing on a "does he, does he not" situation.

Especially when he not so subtly moved his hand to my left arm. His thumb rubbing small circles on my soft skin under the sleeve of the Red Bull jersey. As much as I felt like it was wrong, it felt right. But it was too soon, wasn't it?

*Maybe Aster was right, maybe I should cons—* No, *girl stop, focus on the race. Enjoy the gift and the view.*

By the time I looked back at the score board, we were twenty-nine laps down from the fifty-eight-lap race. Three cars were already out, I couldn't quite see who.

'Who's out?' I asked Aster.

'Not sure, but I do know it's a Renault, a McLaren, and a Haas,' she said. 'Not paying attention?'

'Kinda hard not to.'

She grabbed my left hand, signalling me to my feet, and told the group that we were heading to the bathroom. Instead she took me to a tree.

'Is he usually this touchy feely?' she asked.

'No, but then again, we have a ... *flirtatious* friendship.'

'The signs are there, just a matter of you deciding if this is what you want. In all honesty bro, should go for it. If *this—*' she pointed at the surroundings '— is anything to go by.'

'Okay firstly, he doesn't like me that way, and secondly, even if he did. I've barely been out of a relationship.'

There was also the possibility of him also treating me like Kaleb. Considering Kaleb was just as charismatic as Dylan when we first met. It was exactly why I felt like I needed to heal before I fully swore off dating.

'So? He'd be good for you. It wouldn't be a rebound,' Aster said.

'Yeah, nah.' I started to turn back towards the steps of the grandstand. 'Can we go back to watch the last bit of the race?'

She nodded and I headed up first, taking Aster's spot next to Bianca. With the race in the closing stages, I wanted to focus on the last laps rather than whether or not Dylan liked me, and whether I liked him.

*Sure it was a crush, and we flirted, but crushes mean nothing. It'll pass.*

The sound of cars coming out of the last corner stopped my thoughts in their tracks. I watched as the cars came in broken lots. First were the top few separated by mere tenths of a second with lapped cars in tow, followed by the rest of the evenly spaced midfield. I watched as battles happened before my very eyes and Bianca, and I cheered on. My cheeks ached as I smiled.

As the race drew to a close, the two Mercedes drivers came down the main straight and the chequered flag waved below. As soon as the both of them crossed the line, I, along with half the grandstand, stood up, cheering.

# 43

# April 2019

*23 Years Old*

Trays of mocktails and finger food decorated my kitchen bench and coffee table. My television hosted several PowerPoints of funny games associated with medicine. We found it beneficial as we were all blitzing the exams compared to quite a number of our peers.

Dylan, Bianca, and Natalie, even joined on the odd occasion. Dylan had managed to burst his own ego with forgetting key concepts.

'I don't get it, why am I so bad at this?' Dylan exclaimed.

'Maybe because you haven't needed to use half of this since you graduated?' I poked my index finger into his shoulder.

'Or maybe I'm just stupid,' he retorted.

'I wasn't going to say anything.'

He was quick to look at me, his blue eyes darkened. For a split second, I thought I pushed the banter too far, until a cunning smirk grew on his face. Before I knew it his fingers dug into my sides, tickling me.

'Dylan,' I yelped. 'Stop it.'

'Not until you apologise, missy.'

'I'm sorry.' He stopped. 'I'm sorry.'

'And so you should be,' he laughed.

My new medical school friends and I decided to have a games night as a way to study. Making it was the only way we found ourselves keeping up and enjoying the heavy content.

Every Friday night we were over at someone's place with a new PowerPoint on new and old content. We were constantly trying to stump each other and prove that the maker of the quiz was smarter. Only thing was, we were all pretty much equal.

Nobody wanted to be humiliated, and that wasn't who we were. We were supportive and helped each other. Nobody was going to flunk out if any of us could help it, even if it was early days. We worked hard to get into medicine.

'No!' We all exclaimed, as we collectively got a question wrong.

'Youse are going to fail,' Dylan laughed as he tried to mimic the Australian accent, but his British accent was still thick.

'Shut up, we are not,' I replied, shoving his shoulder. 'Have some faith. Besides, you got it wrong too, and you're qualified.'

'Ouch. You've gotten sassy tonight Dr Carrington,' Dylan replied, shoving my shoulder.

'You guys are too cute,' Louise said.

Dylan pulled me closer and chuckled, 'We are, aren't we?'

'Totally,' I replied.

Dylan scooted away from me, and the loss of his immediate presence caused my heart to skip a beat, longing for his touch again. All because his hip bone was no longer touching mine.

'You two are such teasers,' Sam said.

*How did I not realise how close we were sitting?*

'Oh come on, there's something clearly going on,' Natalie said.

Dylan stayed quiet, opting to dive into a conversation with one of my new friends, Sam.

'I'm turning this into a cocktail, anyone else?' I asked, getting up from the sofa, full cup of apple juice in my hand. Nobody responded. 'No? Okay.'

I felt Dylan's gaze on me as I walked to my liquor cabinet. Jonathon and Louise chuckled as I walked past.

'So naïve, hon,' Louise whispered.

I cowered away to take a discrete swig from my Eiko Vodka bottle before pouring a shot of it into my mock-appletini.

Natalie walked up to me, her hand between my shoulder blades. 'Kenz, can I talk to you for a sec?'

I nodded and followed her to my office. She sat down on the pull-out couch, motioning me to join her.

'You should go for it,' she said.

'What do you mean?' I asked.

'Dylan.'

Oh.

'Dude, no. I — I'm not …' I pursed my lips together and breathed out heavily through my nose. 'He's great and all, but no. Besides, even if I did like him, I'm not ready.'

'I know I'm not Aster, but you can talk to me. I'm here.'

I knew she and Bianca were there. We were the unstoppable Paediatric Nursing Trio. A sisterhood.

'I just feel like it's too soon. I just broke up with Kaleb four months ago,' I said. 'But—I don't know. I feel like I'm ready, yet I feel like it's too soon all at once.'

'I get it. You're working on yourself.' She stood up to adjust her pants that had twisted. 'I was in your shoes once. When I left my toxic relationship, I started to mend myself.' She continued as she sat back down. 'I got into nursing, started working as an assistant nurse, and rekindled with my old friend group. Somewhere along the way I met Robbie. I was scared, roughly seven months out, but he was exactly what I wanted in life. Life doesn't stop Kenz. You are as powerful as you let yourself be — a force to be reckoned with. You wouldn't have fought for medical school if you didn't want to let your life be guided by your past.'

She was so right. I didn't want to go backwards. Making friends and hanging out with them was me stepping outside my comfort zone. Maybe it wasn't so far-fetched to start really letting myself embrace this new life I had. I could do whatever I pleased without having to factor in another person. If I got into medicine, the world was now my oyster.

'Thanks Nat,' I said.

'You're welcome.'

I headed out the door and back out to reclaim my spot on the couch.

'We're going to go Kenz,' Jonathan said, leaning down to hug me, the girls, and Robbie, Michael, and Sam trailing behind him.

'Oh, okay,' I replied, reciprocating their hugs. 'See you tomorrow.'

I once again left the couch, only momentarily to see the group out the door, each taking their trays of mostly eaten food and empty cups. Dylan was still in my apartment though.

'You heading off too?' I asked as he lingered at the corner of the island.

'I can if you want me to, but I was actually opting to help clean,' he replied.

'Oh, by all means, stay.'

There wasn't much to clean up, considering my friends had taken their rubbish along with them. Though, that didn't stop Dylan from wiping down my bench.

It was highly domesticated, and my brain couldn't quite comprehend it. While I knew that this was normal, it wasn't for me. Kaleb hated cleaning. My old friends would piss off when given the chance.

But Dylan wasn't like them, so why did I keep going back to the abnormal behaviour of my old life?

'Where do you keep your rubbish bags?' he asked.

'Under the sink.' I pointed to the cupboard.

'Bench is wiped. Put down those cups, I'll do that.'

'Oh come on, it's fine.'

'No, please, allow me.'

I placed the empty plastic cups back on the bench and raised my hands up. Instead, I started to put the alcohol back on the shelves, and the juice and soft drink in the fridge.

What he was doing was proving to my brain that I deserved an equal or someone who would worship the ground that I walked on.

Dylan put one of my pot plants in front of the door to keep it open while he carried the two large rubbish bags out to the trash chute.

Maybe, just maybe, Natalie had a point. I'm happy and have remained happy for a few months now and that was during my first term as a medical student. It had been a ridiculously hard term and yet, I have not faltered on my healthy habits and self-care.

*If anything were to happen, I'd let it.*

'What else needs doing?' Dylan asked when he came back in.

'You can help me rinse if you'd like?' I replied.

'Sounds good.' He stood beside me, ready to start rinsing and drying the dishes. 'Can I ask.'

'Hmm,' I replied.

'You doing okay? You seem to have mellowed out a bit.'

'You know, for the first time in my life, I'm not stressed.' I replied, passing him a soapy cup.

'It looks good on you. Happiness and health.'

'Oh does it?'

'Yeah.'

I could sense the tension becoming awkward, so I flicked him with water.

'You did not just do that Doctor Carrington,' Dylan laughed.

'Oh but I just did, Doctor Atwood. What are you going to do about it?'

He grabbed the tea towel from beside the drying rack, twirling it around. A loud crack echoed in the air as the tip landed connected on the corner of my kitchen bench, narrowly missing the top of my butt.

'Oh,' I laughed. 'So that's how you wanna play?'

I grabbed the towel from the oven handle behind me, twirling it. I aimed for his calf, flicking my wrist quickly.

'Ouch, McKenna!' he yelped. 'Damn, you're good, but not good enough.'

He flicked his wrist, but I couldn't move out of the way fast enough. The sound of the tip connecting with the fabric that covered my ass echoed through the air.

'Ow, dammit, Atwood,' I laughed.

'Shit, sorry.' He gravitated back towards me, his hand on my lower back. 'You okay? I didn't mean to –'

I laughed. 'It's fine, Dyl. I did attack your calf. It's all in the game.'

His hand lingered on the small of my back for a second before we continued to wash and rinse the dishes. Our fingers occasionally brushing together, only to immediately pull away. Electricity ran through me urging me to move slightly more to the right, keeping myself away from him. Yet, I still gravitated, operating with him just mere millimetres away. I could feel the warmth emanating off his body, the sound his shirt made as it shifted with every muscle that tensed to rinse and dry the crockery and cups.

'When you pass your final exams for the term,' he said, breaking the silence. His gaze still trained on the items he was drying. 'Wanna celebrate? Just — Just the two of us?'

I looked at him, trying to decipher what he was non-verbally saying, but I came up empty handed.

'Oh, uh, yeah. Sure,' I said.

# 44

# June 2019

*23 Years Old*

Xenia had added new furnishings to the space. It felt more like a cabin in the woods than a psychologist office, with its deep greens and dark timber accents. It was far more peaceful. New mixed modes of art hung on the walls, wooden knickknacks sat on the shelves and tables, and a large brown shaggy rug sat between the patient's sofa and her chair.

'How was your month?' she asked.

'Can we please skip the pleasantries today?' I asked, as I got comfortable on the beige sofa. "Cause it's been pretty shit.'

'Oh? I'm sorry to hear,' she replied. 'Tell me more.'

The fabric of the couch felt rough against my fingertips as I ran my hands over it. Trying to smooth out the ripples I made upon sitting.

'My exams went well, but ... I don't know. It appears as though I have no backbone,' I said, my eyes trained on the shaggy white rug. 'I know that I'm feeling like I'm very obviously in a depressed state, and I feel like I've been taken back to high school. If you took one look at me, I'm an easy low risk victim as you know I won't fight back. I don't know.'

'Okay, we haven't spoken about high school since our first appointment, so why don't we go deeper about what happened back then?'

*That's because the entire point was to sort out my issues with Kaleb, not about my past ... Yet, here we are.*

'I was told by a teacher that I would never get higher than a C-minus. Same teacher then proceeded to say that university wasn't the right fit for me,' I said bluntly.

'That's an awful thing to say,' she clarified for me.

'Yeah, she was a real ... *treat*,' I mumbled.

'How did that affect you at the time?'

'Well, I was in year, I wanna say eleven at the time, and so it was a tough pill to swallow. I took it at face value because that's what I was taught. I mean ...' I let out an angry chuckle. 'I was forced into a box of mediocrity probably since grade three, maybe even grade six. So if she didn't think that university was for me ... I accepted it.' Before she could chime in, I continued, 'Like, I asked for fucking help, and they gave me nothing. It was a slap to the face. They may as well have said: "Hey McKenna, you're barely passing and you're asking for help. Sorry, I don't help average-grade students." What the fuck?'

I snatched a couple of tissues from the box that had been haphazardly tossed to the side.

Xenia was ferociously writing, 'So why do you think that it's taken this long to feel something similar? I mean, you stated that you graduated top of your class in nursing.'

'Oh, I don't doubt my intelligence. I just ... I'm in with super smart people. I'm glad I'm passing, it isn't easy, but no matter how hard I study, I'm not like my friends.'

*There wasn't any reason for me to feel the way that I did, yet I did.*

'Did your high school ever help you?'

'If you mean if I saw their counsellor, then yes.'

'And what did they do?'

I kicked my right leg out and crossed it over the left dramatically. 'Kept me in the classes with teachers who neglected me during a time of severe bullying from my peers. Not only did I sit alone, but I also had rocks thrown at me in the change rooms or out in the school yard. There was no reprimanding of students.' I started laughing. 'I-I even told the counsellor that I was suicidal, but nothing was passed on to my parents, no duty of care followed. I was left.'

'Suicidal?' she prompted.

'I thought about it. Never attempted,' I stated. 'I never walked in with my arms covered in self-harm scars. Maybe if I did, maybe it would've prompted urgent action. Instead I used masturbation as punishment.' I choked back saliva that pooled into my mouth. 'An orgasm should be celebrated, instead for me I saw it as a reward that I didn't deserve. So from fourteen to eighteen, I nev—'

I sobbed into the soft tissues, pulling more as the tears kept coming. There was not a single care from my high school. For years I carried the burden, thinking that how I felt didn't matter.

'You asked last session "why did I stay with Kaleb for so long?"' Xenia said slowly. 'He treated you the way you had been treating yourself. He fed into your dark thoughts, aiding in lowering your self-esteem to a point where your achievements didn't feel like achievements.'

My bony elbows dug into my knees, supporting my weight as I leaned forward. It was like I was on a sinking ship with no lifeboats. My awards felt like how orgasms did, empty and painful.

'Nobody cared then, nobody cares now,' I whispered, thinking she wouldn't be able to hear.

'Thought you had friends?'

'I do, but I guess it's this irrational fear of not being enough?'

'I'm going to challenge you a little bit here. The notes from the previous session.' She paused for a moment. 'It makes me believe that it isn't true. If you, to quote yourself, "weren't enough", I don't think they would've taken you to Albert Park. The likely cause is because it's what your mind is used to, but with Kaleb, something tells me that it goes well beyond that.'

*It does. High school?*

I looked out through the window beside her that opened up to the cityscape, with the River Torrens right outside. 'My high school friends often left me behind while they gallivanted overseas, holidays in luxury resorts, or cruises,' I said, turning back to face her. 'It wasn't like we weren't rich or my parents were likely to say no if I asked to go with them. Then when Kaleb came into the picture, they were quick to take his side despite me being the group "psychologist". I stayed friends with them, even when they ditched me again as university students.'

'You didn't broadcast your wealth, so they excluded you?'

'I think so, or because I wasn't a high achiever like they were. There's a long, long list of possibilities, and I doubt I'll ever know why.'

Xenia thought for a moment, glancing at her notes momentarily. 'So then if we look at the present for a moment, has something happened that has led to this "irrational fear" to come out?'

'I'm honestly not sure,' I said. 'I think that for once it's a positive experience. The whole trip to Melbourne, for example, was amazing. And how the four of them supported me with the police.' As I spoke I came to the sudden realisation. 'This isn't my normal, but it should be.'

'Exactly right,' Xenia exclaimed. 'You beat me to it.'

I gave her a slight chuckle.

'What you have is support outside of family,' she continued. 'And it is very important especially as you live quite far from yours.'

'Yeah, the group try to come over once a week, or Nat, Bianca, and I go to the pub for dinner after our shifts on Saturday nights.'

'And Aster?'

'We text, call or facetime almost daily.'

'What about Dylan? Do you have something that is just the two of you?'

'We made a deal on the first day of school, I teach him to cook, and he tutors me. Once a week we have a tutoring night, roughly an hour each.'

'Nothing going on there?' she asked. 'You softened your voice, and it raised in pitch slightly, so I could only assume.'

I held my head in my hands as I thought.

'Maybe,' I said. 'We've had a *flirtatious* friendship since I moved here. But that weekend at Albert Park, then again several weeks ago, back in April ... There were non-sexual touches. Taps on the leg, hand on the back, that sort of thing, and I didn't flinch. Usually any sort of touch like that would make me flinch, jump, or react in some other way.'

'And why would you flinch?'

'Because every time Kaleb did, it was because he wanted something, usually sex. Dylan's is —' I searched my brain for the right word, but nothing came to light.

'Affection? Is that the word you're looking for?'

I hit my fist on my knee. 'Yes. Like, even Natalie and Aster made a comment saying I should go for it, but is it too soon? Wouldn't Dylan be a rebound? I'm not sure what to do. I like him, but given everything, shouldn't I heal first?'

'Healing doesn't happen overnight, McKenna,' Xenia said. 'Healing is a long journey, especially with complex trauma like yours. There are highs and lows in the process, good days, bad days, maybe weeks.'

I nodded.

'As for Dylan,' she continued. 'It's a personal choice, so I can't say whether you should or shouldn't date him. What I can say is that a supportive partner will respect the boundaries that you set. Rebounds are more if you are still hyper-focused on Kaleb, and from what I can see, you are not. Things may trigger you, so if you aren't ready, you aren't ready. But if you are, I'm sure Dylan will understand if you need to move at a more comfortable pace.'

'How do I navigate these triggers? I don't know what sets me off.'

'Repressed memories are something we do to protect ourselves. So what we can do is something called Eye Movement Desensitisation and Reprocessing, or EMDR for short. You will focus on a specific memory, this could be one or if you have many small, targeted memories, we could go through most of them in one session. I will guide you through it.'

'Might help me understand my triggers too?' I asked.

'Yes, it helps in the reduction of intensity, so processing will help ease your emotions when faced with a particular trigger. It is a therapy that is used for post-traumatic stress and other types of traumas and phobias, so hopefully this will help in finding what may trigger you from each moment in your life.'

'Okay.'

'It's an intense process, so we can do it only if you're ready.'

I thought about it for a minute.

'Yeah, sure, sounds good,' I said.

# 45

# July 2019

*23 Years Old*

My phone was set up on the other side of my bedroom with Aster on Facetime while I almost pulled out my entire wardrobe.

'What do you mean he asked you out?' Aster's voice asked through my AirPods.

'He didn't ask me out. He's just taking me out to celebrate finishing my first term of med school. Nothing special. We planned it like two months ago, at the games night,' I replied.

'So, is that why you're panicking right now?' she asked.

'I'm not panicking. Bastard didn't tell me what I should wear.' I rifled through the pile of clothes. 'Obviously I want to be warm, but like, do I need something I can walk in?'

Sure we've been alone plenty of times, cooking and studying together. But this was the first time we've hung out outside of work and our apartments. To make it worse, he's wanted whatever he was planning to be a surprise.

'Mate. It's a bloody date. So that's a negative on jeans, unless you have a skinny pair?'

I dug through my wardrobe and pulled out my favourite jeans. They weren't super skinny anymore and sagged slightly where the crotch met the thigh.

'Perfect shade for your grey coat!' Aster screamed.

I pulled out one of my new white tops that would go well with my favourite pink scarf and boots. Throwing it all on one hanger, I held it up to my phone and Aster squealed.

'Babe. You are going to look drop dead gorgeous!' I laughed. 'Wear a g-string too.'

'Oh my god, Aster! It's not a fucking date!'

'Sure it isn't,' she sang. 'Still, shave, just in case.'

I chuckled and moved aside so I could change out of frame. Aster was still going on about how it was a date and how handsome he was. Yet, despite the conversation with Xenia, there was still that nagging thought that dating would be too soon.

'I got into your head, didn't I? You've migrated into the frame, love.'

'You didn't get into my head.'

'Mmm sure, that's why you're running your hands over your legs.' I immediately stopped feeling for any stubborn, lonesome prickles.

I quickly stepped out of frame and shimmied on my jeans. 'Hon, really quick, before I hang up. Red or nude lippie?'

'Red, the matte one, less chance for it to move. Oh, and your *Black Opium* perfume.'

'Aye, aye cap'in.'

I ended the call and proceeded into the bathroom, keeping my makeup basic. Mascara, eyebrows, and, of course, the red matte lipstick.

**Me:** *Are jeans okay?*

**Dylan:** *Maybe pants. We'll be doing a lot of walking*

**Me:** *Seriously? You know I'm lazy ~insert eyeroll here~*

**Dylan:** *Better get used to it if you want to be a doctor ;)*

Keeping my white top on, I changed into my grey pin-striped pants and shrugged on my grey coat before spraying on a few puffs of the Black Opium.

There was still the nagging thought of Dylan's plans. He and I were friends, and I didn't want anything to ruin that. Never mind the feelings I had for him. Crushes pass but dating poses an element of uncertainty and bestows unnecessary fear. Kaleb did a lot of damage to my psyche. Gambling on my feelings for Dylan could either benefit me or cause me more pain.

*Do I really want to do this?*

There was a knock at my door.

*No point backing out now.*

'Hey,' I said, letting Dylan into my apartment.

He was dressed in navy slacks and a long-sleeved, white button up with a tan coat. He looked far more business casual than I did. Compared to him, I feared that I was too business for the day he had planned. My denim jacket was hanging on a hook by the door, while I could've swapped it, but I doubted I'd be warm enough.

'Holy shit,' he replied. 'You look amazing.'

Heat rushed to my cheeks, and I smiled at the ground. 'So do you. Navy suits you.'

I grabbed my purse off the kitchen bench and led him out of my apartment, locking the door behind me.

'Oh, I should warn you, the AC isn't working,' he said

'Of course it isn't. Wanna take mine instead? Mine has a functioning everything.'

He laughed but proceeded to lead me out of the building towards his car.

'We are a good way away from our first destination. Think you can last an hour's trip with me?' he asked.

'Are you taking me to my death? In which case I'd like to very much say "no",' I replied, and he laughed, shaking his head. 'Where on earth are you taking me, sir?'

'I know how much you love wine, so I've booked us a wine tasting session at Baressie.'

My eyes widened. It isn't right, calling him my "friend". This isn't a friend outing. Maybe if it was with Aster or Natalie.

*This is a date.*

A date with a man who actually listened to what I like and has decided for a date to last more than an hour. This was downright insane. I thought I knew what love was, but now I wasn't sure. This feeling was beyond anything I had ever felt for a guy.

'Oh my god.' Was all I could say.

Beautiful rich green trees lined the road entrance and the car park. It was exactly like the images online. Gorgeous and lively. Even though it was freezing cold outside, I couldn't wait to get out of the vehicle.

'You okay there?' Dylan asked.

'I'm in absolute awe,' I replied. 'How'd you know?'

'You have a pretty extensive wine and gin collection in your apartment. I know you occasionally make your own gin, but you don't make your own wine.'

*I need to stop being in my head so much, Aster and Xenia are right, I like him, he clearly likes me. This is right.*

'You're amazing.' That wasn't a lie. So far from it. Truth be told, I think I was falling in love.

Dylan walked around to open my door for me and helped me out.

'Ah, the gentleman's treatment. So chivalry isn't dead?'

'Definitely not.'

He took my hand and led us into the precinct.

The crunch of the gravel beneath our feet echoed off the two rich red acid-washed brick buildings. Strings of twinkling lights dangled over the main thoroughfare, between the two dwellings. Southern Magnolias lined the walls and were nestled in a bed of rich purple Native Lilacs.

There was no way that this was real; surely this was a dream. A cruel dream. One that I would wake up from any minute.

The inside of the reception was like a romantic ski cabin getaway. Warm stained timber flooring and matching timber accents stood out against the white painted walls. Several dark empty wine barrels and black stained timber bar stools stood proud around the small waiting area.

'Hi, Dylan, party of two for the estate picnic, and tasting at 11.30. We are a bit early,' Dylan said to the receptionist.

There were no words to describe how I was feeling, only that electricity was running through my veins. I stood beside him in a daze and followed them to the waiting area.

'What's going through your mind?' Dylan asked.

'Just taking in the royal treatment,' I said.

'Well, a queen deserves to have only the best,' he winked.

It was like the Formula One all over again. He paid attention to me in a way that Kaleb never did. This was the date of my dreams, wine tasting and a meal at one of the most romantic places.

'Dylan, party of two?' A middle-aged woman, dressed in black pants and shirt, asked, as she entered through the doorway.

'That's us,' Dylan said, as we both stood up and walked over to her.

'I'm Kathleen and I'll be looking after you for the tasting,' she said.

'I'm Dylan, and this is my *girlfriend*, McKenna.'

I tried to not visibly show my shock at his choice of words. It rolled off his tongue, and he didn't bat an eyelid.

*That's sudden.*

'I have some forms for you to fill out. It's to get an understanding of your personal tastes. We like to create a more individualised tasting for you after the tour,' Kathleen said.

She handed us a clipboard each, but before I could even fill it out, Kathleen asked for my ID.

'I look younger than 18?!' I gasped as I reached into my handbag for my wallet. 'I'm touched.'

Dylan chuckled beside me as he filled out his form. I shoved him lightly.

'Thank you, dear,' she said, passing my driver's license.

I put it back and quickly filled in my form, since Dylan had already finished. I glanced over to look at his handwriting.

*My goodness, stereotypical doctor's chook scratch; but I can't talk.*

My handwriting somehow went from neat, to chook scratch itself in a matter of months.

'Alright, please follow me,' Kathleen said.

Dylan intertwined our fingers as we followed our tour guide out to the gardens. The sun shone brightly illuminating the gorgeous green leaves of the plants that lined the paths. Each one darting off in multiple directions to the eating areas and various barns full of wine.

'We usually do our tastings in the barns. But as requested, and since it's a beautiful day out, I've set up a station in one of our private gardens,' Kathleen said.

The grounds were gorgeous; the paths were made up of neatly laid sandstone pavers. Flowers and rich green grass lined the edges. We rounded the corner to a private garden.

'Alright, here we are,' Kathleen announced leading us through an opening between tall, bushy hedges that lined the perimeter of the garden. Flowers scattered around to add a pop of colour and soft scent that floated in the breeze. I had never seen such a lively garden in the cooler months. 'I've organised two non-alcoholic whites, chardonnay and pinot grigio, as well as one of our most popular vegan Shiraz.'

We took our seats at the barrel and looked at the six pairs of glasses before us. A neatly laid charcuterie board of meats, cheese and crackers, and a jug of water was put on a smaller barrel within arm's reach.

'Before we start, can we get a photo?' Dylan asked, pulling his phone out of his pocket.

'Absolutely,' Kathleen replied, taking his phone.

I wasn't going to lie. This was slightly overwhelming, but yet I couldn't stop smiling and embracing this unknown feeling. The feeling of Dylan's hand in mine and another wrapped around my waist was sending me into a tailspin of glee. His touch lingered as he moved away to take his phone back from Kathleen.

It felt right. Like this was what my life was missing. I was finally happy and looking after myself. The universe rewarded me with a guy who was respectful, supportive, and wants me to succeed *my* way, not his.

'Alright, shall we begin?' Kathleen asked.

All too enthusiastically, I responded, 'Absolutely!'

Dylan laughed beside me and rested his hand comfortably on my thigh.

Our tour guide left us alone for lunch once she took us to a picnic table up on a hill, overlooking the vineyard. I was tipsy on enough wine to start bursting out the opening scene to the *Sound of Music*.

The blue sky and beaming sun and the aromas of our pasta meals, made up for the frigid breeze.

'Everything okay?' Dylan asked.

'Yeah,' I replied.

'You went quiet after I accidentally called you my "girlfriend".'

'Just took me by surprise,' I said, taking a sip of the non-alcoholic white wine.

'McKenna,' he said, reaching for my hands. 'Talk to me.' I released one of my hands, taking the glass of wine for another sip. Savouring the liquid's sweet fruity flavour. 'Kenz, if this is too much —'

'Dylan, no, absolutely not — how can I say this?' I stopped for a second. 'Today's been wonderful. Honestly, you've rekindled my faith in humanity. I like you, and I — This is — It isn't that it's too soon, it's more of the fact that I fear that I'm extremely ... damaged.'

'McKenna,' he said quietly. 'You're not damaged. I like you too, probably since the day we met in that ICU room. You were an absolute legend. I know, Kaleb didn't treat you well. He's an absolute dickhead, sorry, I know you hate using profanity to label him. But he — he is, because you are amazing and honestly, worth so much more. I will respect your boundaries, if we need to move slow, so be it. I'm with you.'

'Slow is definitely for the best, at least for now,' I confirmed.

'Got it,' he replied.

I looked down to my half-eaten Fettuccine Alfredo, twirling my fork around. 'And, um, if you wanted to refer to me as your girlfriend ... You, uh, you can.'

# 46

# July 2019

*23 Years Old*

After a beautiful lunch at Baressie, Dylan drove us to the Botanical Gardens. The day remained bright and blooming as we walked together towards the garden. It wasn't all that busy like I thought it would be, considering it was school holidays.

'How are you liking the date so far?' Dylan asked, kissing the back of my hand, his warm breath sending warm tingles through my body.

'Very much so,' I replied. 'This has been incredible.'

He beamed at me.

We started on the path, looping through the gorgeous greenery and river of flower beds. Dylan spotted an area that was partially secluded and in the sun. It didn't take long before I was being pulled towards it.

'Come on!' he exclaimed. 'Before someone takes it.'

I laughed and started jogging, even though no one was present. It was nice to see him in a different context, apart from work and his friends.

He took his coat off and placed it on the grass.

'Afraid of a little dirt?' I joked as he sat down on his coat.

'Ground's cold,' he replied.

I playfully rolled my eyes at him and sat down beside him. The coat acted like a barrier against the cold grass and dirt. Dylan scooted closer to me, like a moth to a flame, holding me. I enjoyed revelling in the feeling. This is a sensation I've never felt until now. Like that saying, isn't it, "Home is where the heart is"?

Adding to my problems, his five-year plan matched up perfectly with mine. Neither of us had any intentions of ever leaving Adelaide. He was reconsidering his choice in Orthopaedics, now opting to be a General Practitioner, and one day own a clinic. After some serious consideration from placements and lectures, I was considering psychiatry. As much as I loved kids, I think psychiatry was a better suited area of interest for me. I now had a newfound passion, and one that would still allow me to work with children.

'What are the popular kids asking on these dates?' Dylan asked.

'Oh, so the girls were right, been a while?' I joked. 'Ya know, I don't think I even know what your hobbies are. How has that not come up in conversations?'

'Dunno. Guess it's kind of inferred, like you cook, read, and distil gin. Does practicing my suturing count as a hobby?'

I laughed, picturing him sitting in the dark with a bright light. Hunched over a fake skin, or a banana, with a suturing kit, practicing before bed every night. If you don't practice, you lose it, I suppose.

'Definitely not,' I said.

'Damn.' He paused momentarily to think. 'I enjoy the occasional horror read. I will also play the occasional computer game, but I'd rather cook, bake and read. You?'

'Well, you've seen my never-ending array of books,' I half joked. 'Let's see, what don't you know ... I sew. Haven't done it in a while, but yeah, I'm a mean tailor.'

'Oh, wow. That's different. Still lead footed?'

'And how. I'm very precise too.'

'Like you're cooking?'

'I'm not that precise with my cooking. I'll have to show you what I'm like when I do my Calamari Risoni. Would pair nicely with the red wine you just bought me.'

'Getting a little ahead of yourself there?'

'Hey, this is going pretty well, or ...' I trailed off for a dramatic pause. 'Are you a player, Doc?'

'Absolutely not, I'm just playing with you, 'course I'd like to. Tomorrow night?'

'Now who's keen?'

'I'll take that as a yes.'

We sat in a comfortable silence, looking out to the rest of the botanical gardens. I hastened to be between his legs. It was far more comfortable ground than the tree root that kept poking me no matter how I adjusted my sitting position. His arms enveloped me and pulled me closer to his chest.

'I could stay like this forever,' he whispered in my ear.

'So could I,' I replied.

I could feel the rise and fall of his chest deepen, and the tensing of his muscles.

'You okay?' I asked, craning my neck to look at him.

Being this close to his face was surreal. His eyebrows were perfectly sculpted. His face was clean, not a single pore was visible. His eyes were a gorgeous deep ocean blue. I could get lost in them any day of the week.

'Y-yeah,' he replied. I caught his gaze going from my eyes to my lips. 'Can I — Can I kiss you?'

'Yes,' I breathed out.

His lips were warm and soft. Gentle. Dylan pulled me closer as we moved in sync. I could taste the wine and the tomato taste of the Bolognese.

'Wow,' he said.
'That was ...'
'Yeah ...'

Our heavy breathing was the only thing I could hear. No more rustle of leaves, or distant chats of people, or the chirps of the various birds in the area. It was just us, and I was all too aware of it.

We pulled away to catch our breath. I turned back around and pressed my back to his chest.

'I can stay like this forever,' he said.

'You're so cheesy,' I laughed, turning my body so I could peck his lips.

'You didn't just say that.'

I felt him shift behind me. His hands moved up to my armpits.

'No, no, stop,' I giggled as he started tickling me.

'Tell me I'm not cheesy then.'

'Hmm.' Dylan paused. I shook my head. 'Never.'

'Guess I'll never stop then.' His fingers grazed over the sensitive areas of my sides.

'Can we go for a walk around the gardens?' I asked giggling.

Dylan stopped, 'Sure.'

He helped me off the ground and dusted off his jacket. Dylan took my hand in his and led me towards the speckled concrete path that followed the perimeter of Main Lake. The grounds were huge with large sections of well-manicured lawns, and well-groomed trees. Flowers were scattered around giving pops of colour amongst the gorgeous greenery.

I let go of his hand for a moment to do up the buttons of my coat as the breeze picked up.

'Sorry,' I said.

'Cold?' he asked.

'Yeah.' He immediately took his jacket off, wrapping it over my shoulders. 'Is it obvious that I come from the Northern parts of the country?' I asked.

'No,' he scoffed. 'It's fine. Better than getting hypothermia.'

'Now that is very true.'

I leant against my apartment door, a hand instinctively tracing my lips.

'Oh my god,' I breathed out.

It was the most amazing day but felt anticlimactic when he kissed me goodbye. Almost as if there was a lack of closure hanging in the air.

I placed the two bottles of wine that Dylan bought me in my liquor cabinet.

A knock at the door startled me. I waited a moment before looking through the peephole.

'Dyl?' I asked as I opened the door.

His lips were on mine in an instant.

'Call me "Dyl" again,' he breathed against my lips.

I said his nickname again, and he pushed me against the wall, kicking my apartment door shut. One arm wrapped around my waist, the other placed near my head holding his bodyweight. His lips left mine and started sucking on my neck. The tiniest gasp that escaped my lips made him stop.

'I'm sorry, I —'

I ached for his touch again.

'It's okay,' I replied.

'No. You're —'

'I'm what?' I moved towards him, trying to gauge his emotions.

'You wanted to take things slow.'

'Making out is fine. I would've stopped you once it was getting a bit much,' I said. 'Promise. Why don't you stay for a bit? I can make us some tea?'

He nodded, and I flicked the kettle on before joining him on the couch.

I wasn't going to lie, part of me didn't want it to stop. If there was anybody who I felt safe with, it was Dylan. All of today, he had proven to me that I had settled for someone who made me feel nostalgic for my Nyctophilia. Kaleb was the living darkness that existed in my head rent free for a decade before we met. I took solace in the feeling; settling for the comfort of the darkness he brought over my life.

Meanwhile, Dylan was the opposite. He complimented my true personality that had been tucked away behind the shadow's delusions. Not once did I have that devil on my shoulder or in my head tell me otherwise. I had no desire to self-sabotage, otherwise I would have started to fall back into old habits back in week six of term one. My therapy sessions were working, and I was reaping the benefits. I had a guy in my apartment wanting to spend more time with me despite us having spent the entire day together.

'I'll be right back, I'm getting a little warm,' I said, patting his leg as I got up.

The temperature in the apartment was not the right climate to still be in pants, long-sleeved turtleneck, and coat. I could feel myself starting to sweat. It was, however, the perfect temperature to get away with wearing oversized t-shirts and shorts. He knew he wasn't getting any tonight, but that didn't mean I couldn't have fun. My bra came off with all my day clothes, fully embracing the feeling of comfort.

I walked back out just as the kettle had finished boiling.

'What sort of tea do you want?' I asked. 'I've got everything from black tea to green tea, to peppermint, to chamomile, to everything in between.'

'Peppermint please, Mic,' he said. The nickname just rolled off his tongue. Shock went through me that I forgot I was mid-pour momentarily. Boiling water spilled over one mug. I quickly damage controlled and wiped up the hot water as safely and quickly as I could. 'Need help, Mic?'

There was that nickname again.

'N-No, thanks. I'm about ready,' I replied. I filled part of the boiling mugs up with cold water and headed over to the couch.

We fit together on the couch like a puzzle.

*I deserve this.*

Working on myself opened the door to the opportunities that Kaleb was trying to keep me away from. My new med school friend group, which consisted of around twelve of us, had planned a trip to Fiji for the end of year celebration.

I was thriving down in Adelaide in a way that made my parents proud. On our last video call, mum said she was happy to see my social media showcasing how happy I was, knowing that I was never one to hide behind false advertising online; all real.

Just like that, Dylan and I were hip to hip on my couch, sitting in silence and drinking tea. The weight of his hand on my thigh kept me grounded; this was real life, I was not dreaming. For the first time in my life, since I was eight, I got to be happy.

'I could get used to this,' Dylan mumbled into my hair.

'So could I,' I replied.

The smell of peppermint tea wafted through the air. I could feel it ingraining in my brain, to remember this moment. The feel of his body beside me was incredible. I never wanted it to end.

He put his mug on the coaster and pulled me closer towards him. I could smell his strong woody cologne, the hints of bergamot and cedar combined with the aromas of peppermint from our teas. It was an interesting mix, but I wasn't complaining.

'What are you wearing? The cologne,' I asked.

'Oh uh, can't remember the name of it but the brand is Burberry,' he replied.

'I like it, subtle.'

The feeling of his hand in my hair gave me tingles all over my body. This was deeply intimate. I felt myself melting into his touch. Not to mention, the tingles were nostalgic, sending me back to when girls used to play with each other's hair in primary school.

'Can I stay the night?' Dylan asked, drawing me in closer.

'Hon …' I trailed off, trying to find a reason for him to go back to his apartment, forgetting the obvious fact that it was far too soon. Though, I found myself thinking about waking up beside him with Ferni at our feet.

'I saw that smirk, come on, share.'

*Openness and honesty leads to a healthy relationship.*

'It's too soon, got it.' He sat us up and looked at me. Pain and understanding in his expression. 'You went through something horrible. I don't want you to feel pressured into anything. I like you, I really do.'

With no hesitation I put my mug of tea down on the table and reached up to touch his face. 'Dylan …' My thumbs stroked his cheeks. 'I'm not going to sit here and compare you or today's date to him, as it's not comparable. If this was any normal situation, I'd be saying "stay". Even though I know you respect my boundaries, I am terrified that if I push myself too much, I can start to self-sabotage at any given minute.'

Watching him tear up was surreal. All day I felt like I was walking on air. Not to mention, he was taking photos of us, and me alone, all day. The more I got to know him, the more I wanted to be with him.

In that very moment, I was nearly forgetting my "no sex" policy that I had made very clear an hour ago. This was a new position for me, for the first time in my life I had control. I did not have to abide by rulings nor was there that pesky voice wanting to succumb to the darkness again.

*Was I free?*

'You are the strongest and bravest person I know. Watching you grow this past year has been unbelievable. I'm jealous of your ability to be resilient and stand up for what you believe in,' Dylan said, tears glassing over his eyes, threatening to spill out any minute. 'I know you're still healing, and that you'll have bad days. No matter what, I'll be there. I am just a flight of stairs away.'

He leaned down and kissed me. I was powerless as I let my body melt into it, giving him my full body weight.

# 47

# July 2019

*23 Years Old*

I slept for maybe an hour before I woke up. The thrill of the day still repeated itself in my head, but so was the desire for self-sabotaging. It was as strong as the fears that rolled around in my brain too. I was once again alone with my thoughts. No more serotonin to keep my thoughts at bay.

As I stared at the beige linen curtains I reached for my phone on the side table next to the bed and called Aster.

'Babe, do you know what time it is?' she groaned into the phone.

'You're the one who answered!' I replied.

'Wait, it's midnight! Did you —?'

'No,' I said. 'Today was ah-maze-zing, but I'm scared I'll wake up and all of this just goes away.'

I knew what my subconscious was afraid of.

'How about you tell me about today, and I'll tell you if you're being silly.'

'Are you diminishing how I feel?' I said, despite knowing she wasn't. Instead, it was my brain on a war path.

*Just let me be happy, please? I deserve happiness.*

'Oh God, no, hon!' Aster said. 'I just mean, I'll make sure you aren't in your head, and that you are, instead, fearing going back to what your brain has deemed as normal.'

'Oh.'

*Well that's another way to look at it, I suppose.*

'Okay, so tell me, what has gotten your stethoscope all tangled?' Aster asked.

'I don't know. Like he started with taking me to the winery — the one I like. Learned that he's a very physical person,' I said. 'I'm certainly not complaining, physical touch is literally my primary love language.'

'So a lot more than when you guys were friends?'

'Yes.'

'So what happened to make you question?'

'Called me his girlfriend as soon as the woman taking us on the tasting introduced herself.'

Aster squealed into the phone, causing me to pull my phone away from my ear and put it on speaker. 'That's so —'

'— It took me by surprise. I liked it, but it was sudden ...' I said, cutting her off.

'Hon, spell it out to me. If today was so great, and you like him, and he treated you well, what's going on?'

'I don't know. It's ... You remember how I told you about that Valentine's date that Kaleb took me on?'

'Yes ... Where are you going with this?'

'It sort of felt like that. His hugs and kisses felt like home, the passion and the safety ... Kaleb gave me no reason to fear him or question him. The red flags were there, and I ignored them.'

'So you're comparing apples to oranges then?'

'No. It's like my brain is waiting for the drop,' I said, flicking my sheets and blankets off my legs. 'Am I seriously waiting for the red flags?'

'I don't know, maybe,' Aster said.

I groaned and started pacing around my room, phone in hand.

'Why do I feel like I'm going insane?' I asked.

'Hon, you suffered a huge amount of trauma. Speak to your psych, but I think this might be classed as your usual,' she said. 'Now stop pacing, make yourself a chamomile and sit on the lounge while I talk to you.'

I stopped pacing and sat down on the lounge with my plush teal throw blanket wrapped around me.

'Right, Kaleb was charismatic, I'm not going to lie,' Aster said. 'If he wasn't drilling holes into your skull at the games night, I'd have been thinking there was nothing wrong with him. You were not insane, he knew how to manipulate.'

*That's true.*

I frowned and nodded.

'Dylan, on the other hand,' she continued. 'He's sweet, doesn't have a God complex, is friends — scratch that — he's best friends with nurses. He can admit his mistakes and apologises. He is handy and can look after you if you're having a shocker of a day. I think that man is actually in love with you. The dude's been pining for a while. Guarantee you! Dude, I can go on.'

*The stolen glances. Or when our eyes lock onto each other within a crowded nurses station or patient room.*

'Thank you,' I said. 'My subconscious is deciding that I am not deserving of such a great man.'

'Oh but see, that's where it's wrong. No one is more deserving of happiness than you.'

I laughed, 'Thank you Aster.'

'You're very welcome, now, get some sleep.'

'Shall do. Goodnight.'

I didn't go to bed though, well at least, not straight away. Dylan had sent me the photos from earlier and I couldn't help but scroll through them all. The way he looked at me — it was something like you'd see in a film or show. This wasn't the face of a man who wanted to hurt me, he liked me and wanted me to be happy. If I continued to wait for the red flags, I'd be waiting for a long time for something that is never going to come.

# 48

## September 2019

*23 Years Old*

The smell of chai tea filled my apartment as Dylan poured the boiling water into the mugs.

'Instead of going out, mind if we stay in tonight?' he asked, sitting down beside me on the couch, handing me one of the mugs of steaming tea.

'Yeah, sounds good, I can teach you how to make my famous handmade gnocchi,' I replied. It was a much better plan, considering I was comfortable in one of his many long sleeve t-shirts, and a pair of my black exercise leggings. There was no way I was getting out of them.

Right on cue, Dylan's stomach grumbled.

I chuckled, 'Bring your tea, we'll start now.'

'But I just —' He stood back up. 'Can't argue over your gnocchi.'

This was highly domesticated. Not to mention, his hand never left my body as I got the ingredients out of the fridge and pantry.

'Can I ask you something?' Dylan said, while I still prepped the area to cook.

'Of course, hon,' I replied, my head in the cupboard searching for a large mixing bowl.

'Why do you flinch whenever I touch you?' I stood up straight, wrong bowl in hand. 'You, you don't have to answer. I just ... did he ...'

*I flinched? I thought I didn't.*

'H-How long have I been doing that?' I asked.

'Not long, couple of weeks,' he replied.

*Shit.*

'Shit,' I repeated out loud. 'I'm so sorry. I-I didn't realise.'

'No, no. It's okay. I mean it isn't. Just ...' He paused, groaning as he tried to find the right words.

My cheeks burned. This wasn't easy. Nothing about this would ever be easy. The fact Kaleb still lived rent free in my subconscious was concerning. Then again, I guess this meant I was healing. Something was triggering me, and instead of ignoring it, Dylan wanted to raise it.

'Open and honest right?' I said.

'You don't have to tell me,' Dylan said.

'I have a feeling it's a muscle memory response in thinking that you want something each time you touch me,' I said. 'I know it isn't, especially since nothing's happened ... It'll pass.' I quickly put the bowl down and walked the few steps to close the gap between us. My hands reached out to his shoulders. 'I know that you're not him.'

Dylan laughed, 'Time heals.' He leans down and pecks me on the lips. 'I —'

'I know what you're going to say, and I know you won't hurt me. That's why I'm about to show you my secret gnocchi recipe. Though I do need to mention, if we break up, I will need to kill you. You cannot share this with anyone.'

I grabbed the correct bowl from the cupboard and got him to start peeling the pumpkin.

'*The* pumpkin gnocchi?' Dylan asked.

'Yes,' I replied as I turned on the oven.

He handed me the pumpkin, freeing him from his duties, for now. I cut the pumpkin into cubes, putting them straight onto a baking tray. His arms snaked around my waist, and his soft hair tickled my neck.

'Right, in about forty minutes they should be roasted and soft,' I said. 'In the meantime, wanna start dicing the mushrooms, please?'

'Sure, or maybe, I just want to spend a little more time, hugging my *girlfriend*.'

'You can do that while we wait for the pumpkins to cook and after the 'shrooms are diced.'

I went back over to the couch, my now lukewarm chai tea greeting me as I took a long swig from the black mug. Dylan playfully sulked away as he pulled the fungi out of the fridge and started dicing them.

This was how it was meant to be. Us cooking together, laughing. Having an absolute blast. He put the scraps into the bin and started to wipe down the bench. The smell of my lemon scented spray 'n' wipe filling the air. Just as he lifts his head, I quickly snap my head back towards the television.

'What?' Dylan asked, catching me out.

'Nothing, nothing,' I said quickly, but he cocked an eyebrow. 'Just admiring you. Thought you wanted a hug?'

His eyes lit up, and he immediately ran over, sliding in behind me on the couch and pulled me backwards so I could lean against his chest.

'You know what I like the most about this?' I asked.

'No, what?'

'I can be myself, not just around you, but Bia and Nat too. Like you guys complement my personality.'

He hummed into my hair. My hand rested on his knee. The six-o'clock news played softly in the background, neither of us paying attention to it. His fingers combed through my long, thick brunette hair causing shivers to run from the top of my scalp down my spine.

'Can I braid it?' Dylan asked. 'I'm pretty good, my sisters forced me to practice on them when we were kids.'

'Oh, yeah, sure.'

My hair hadn't been played with since I was in primary school. It was something I truly missed. Only difference was that this was incredibly intimate. It was just him and me, our perfumes mixing in the air.

'Got a hair tie?' Dylan asked.

'Uh no,' I replied. 'I'll hold the end, if you go into the bathroom, open the mirror cabinet, there'll be plenty of hair ties in a plastic container.'

'Okay.' He passed me the end of the braid and went to my bathroom. 'Got it.'

He tied it off as tight as it would go, and I raised my hand, running it over the braid. There was not a single bubble or missing strand.

'This feels incredible, holy shit!' I said. 'They taught you well.'

We continued cooking and I had him rolling out the pumpkin gnocchi. Flour went everywhere. It was a right mess, but we had fun. Just like being back home with my family, the kitchen was full of laughter and smiles.

I had the sauce going on the stove, and Dylan once again had his arms wrapped around my waist.

*I hope he never lets go.*

'This smells amazing,' he said.

'Thank you. Next time, it's all on you.'

'Yes ma'am.' He took the spatula off me. 'You've done enough, put your feet up.'

'But I —'

'Now, Mic, please. It's almost ready.'

There wasn't much point in arguing. I headed back to the couch and finished the rest of my tea.

*I could get used to this.*

Dylan brought over his favourite white wine and two glasses to the dining table as he waited for the meal to cool down a little before serving.

The strong scent of tomato and herbs emulated from the marinara sauce, and the combination of the chorizo sausage and pumpkin was unreal, better than I've ever made by myself.

'My God, this smells amazing,' I exclaimed. 'Gotta taste it to confirm, but I think this may just be the best dish I've made, with your help of course.'

'It does smell even better,' Dylan concurred. He loaded my plate with a large serving of gnocchi. 'So, what movie shall we watch tonight?'

'Well you know how you've said you've never seen *Grease*, and I almost had a heart attack?' He nodded reluctantly. 'Well, 'bout time we changed that.'

His smile dropped, eyes bulged.

'Ugh fine.' He exaggerated with a laugh and eye roll to top it off. 'It is your turn to pick anyway.'

If this was in my default scenario, he never would've agreed. He would've forced me to watch yet another sci-fi film or documentary on health. But this wasn't my default, if he wanted to compromise he would've. Instead he was letting me have my way.

There was a feeling seeping through in the pit of my stomach that I couldn't quite describe. It wasn't anything nefarious, in fact, it was the opposite; it was very different to all the gloomy feelings that I've had for almost the past two decades.

'Thought your sisters would've made you watch it,' I said as he finished loading his plate.

'Nah, they weren't big on musicals.'

'Well, shame for you, I love them. Next pick of mine will be the *Sound of Music*, mark my words.'

Dylan groaned, causing me to laugh into my glass of wine.

'Fine, but hope you like horror films,' he said.

'Dammit,' I laughed and took a mouthful of the dinner. 'Holy shit. This is so good!'

The sauce was rich but not overpowering, I could still taste the sweetness of the pumpkin and the spicy Italian sausage. It was by far the best dish I had ever cooked, though I couldn't take all the credit. Whatever Dylan or I did, to the sauce, elevated the flavours. Each individual flavour and texture complimented each other perfectly.

'Goodness, what did we do?' Dylan asked.

'I have no idea.'

'You cut me off before, when we were talking about Kaleb.' He took a swig of his wine. 'I just wanted to say that if you want to talk about it …'

'I know, thank you. Just that, there's a lot. I really don't want to get into it. If anything, therapy has helped me realise that I was in it because that was how I saw myself. Unlovable. Disgusting. Worthless.' I took a swig of wine, trying to combat my suddenly dry mouth. 'I don't anymore. I'm more than the boxes my past put me in.'

'Unlovable? Mic …' He gently lowered his spoon down to the side of his plate and grabbed my hand.

'Oh, I know that's untrue.' I fought hard to keep a playful smile from growing on my face.

His eyebrows raised and gaze set on mine, eager to hear more. 'Oh, yeah?'

'Yeah.' My tight smirk burnt my cheeks. 'Me. I love me.'

Laughter erupted from the both of us. Tears streamed down my cheeks, unable to control myself.

'Done?' Dylan asked.

'Yes, thanks.' He removed my plate from the table. 'I could've done that.'

'Nonsense, let me do the dirty jobs while I'm here.'

'Should just bring Ferni over then you could stay the night.' I realised what my suggestion was. My hand flew to my mouth. Heat rose to my cheeks.

*Am I ready for that? Or anything close to.*

'I-I,' I stuttered.

'Do you want me to spend the night?' My cheeks burned. 'McKenna?'

*Ugh. Why am I like this?*

'Maybe?' I replied, finally forcing my brain to remove my hands from my mouth. 'How about we decide, after I make you sit through *Grease*?'

'What, you think I'm going to change my mind?'

I shrugged and walked over to my DVD and CD stand to grab the movie from my collection, putting it into the player.

'Mic,' Dylan said softly as I sat down beside him on the couch. 'Thank you for being honest.'

'Thank you for wanting open and honest communication, and for listening.'

# 49

# October 2019

*23 Years Old*

I thought I'd have gotten used to sitting in this dark cold waiting room by now. Except I hadn't. The receptionist typed away in the background as the uncomfortable black plastic chair caused me to hunch forward.

'Just had a meeting with an officer about Kaleb.' Aster said on the other side of the phone. 'I reckon you'll be getting a call soon. They're racking up a lot of evidence to arrest him.'

'Awesome,' I whispered into the speaker. 'Yeah, Constable Button did call me the other day to say that there was new evidence presented.'

'Yeah, lots happening here bro. I'll keep you posted, but an arrest should be happening soon.'

I looked up to the clock above the reception, 'Shoot, I gotta go. Xenia will be here soon.'

'Okay, "kick therapy's butt", girl.'

We ended the call just as Xenia's bright pink hair entered my peripheral vision. 'McKenna,' she called, and I followed her down the hall to her office.

The soft forest atmosphere and woody scents relaxed me as I entered. The beige sofa enveloped me, as I sunk as far as I could into its cushions. 'How are you doing?'

'The police officer handling my case said that they are getting close to arresting him.'

'Wow, that is excellent news. How do you feel about that?'

'I think it's great. I kinda forgot about it, if I'm being perfectly honest. Life's been good recently.'

'"Forgot about it"?' she asked.

'I guess, I mean, as we spoke about it a session ago, Kaleb is still in the back of my mind, but he's no longer my priority. Medical school, Dylan, my job, and my friends are my top priorities.'

'I do want to go into this good stuff in a minute, but I want to get a deeper understanding here. Do you feel like you're compartmentalising at all?'

I thought for a moment. 'I don't know.' I leaned forward. 'To be honest, since I reported him and moved, I've felt somewhat free. I mean, I can't exactly let this man continue to govern me. Like when Dylan touches me, even though it's non-sexual, I flinch. It's been getting better since we last spoke, but I just ...' I sighed as I paused to collect my thoughts. 'Part of me wonders what will happen if I get no closure.'

'So you're distracting yourself instead?' Xenia asked. 'What you've gone through is massive, and I know we've spoken heaps about him and your past abusers. But if you've forgotten about the investigation — I'm concerned you're not processing but rather ignoring.'

'Maybe I'm subconsciously ignoring. To me, I'm just trying to move on. When I notice a trigger, sometimes Dylan notices it first and he raises it. Then I, or we, deal with it.'

'I'm glad that you have that support. Sounds like a massive change of pace,' she said. 'How's that working for you?'

'Oh, it's been great,' I said happily. 'The communication has been wonderful, scary—'

'Of course,' Xenia piped in. 'It's not something you're used to.'

'No, and he knows that. Dylan is patient with me, and I know he won't be upset with me if I raise concerns or if I have to talk about Kaleb. As I said, he notices things and helps me work through the triggers. Except, his touches never bothered me in the beginning. Now they make me flinch or jump, but how he treats me is with respect. I don't get it, why now?'

'We've talked about repressed memories, right?' she asked.

'Yes,' I said.

'Well, at the time, when we did the EMDR, we talked about triggers and how new triggers could come up that may've been suppressed.'

'Right,' I said hesitantly.

'While you might feel more comfortable, considering you've been with Dylan for a few months now. It's starting to get serious, and it's natural to progress. So what I think is happening is more of a delayed trauma response. Your body is now remembering that a simple hand on the back or kiss is your partner's way of saying "I want sex" or "I'm bored, and I want you to entertain me". But that isn't Dylan. Consciously, you know that, but subconsciously, your mind flicks back to Kaleb.'

'So what do I do?'

'Keep sticking to your routine and journaling, but you also have to start acknowledging your trauma. Have you done that? I know that you would have had to acknowledge Kaleb, but do you remind yourself that you are a victim?'

'No, and wouldn't that excuse my behaviour?'

'No, no, I mean that each time something triggers you, you understand why it does. You were abused by several teachers, causing you to be a selective mute, and struggled to stand up for yourself as a result. It allowed your peers to twist the very few words that left your mouth when you did try. They knew you would never stand up for yourself until the very last minute. And that's just scratching the surface. Everything in adulthood, starting with Kaleb, stems from the psychological conditioning and impact as a result of the childhood abuse.'

I bore a hole into the white shaggy rug as I processed what she was saying.

'If I use your words from a previous session, you became a "metaphoric punching bag" during your schooling, so that was bound to have significant impacts,' Xenia continued. 'Most adults, unless in an industry where they are faced with perpetrators or victims, won't fully comprehend what emotional abuse is or how it can impact a person. What you've been able to accomplish has been incredible. I know that sometimes it feels like you're stagnant or going backwards, but you're very strong, McKenna.'

'Oh, well that explains why I now cry in the bathroom or start over apologising,' I said. 'I normally could handle it. Dylan even commented about how I handled his boss who berated me whilst I just started my job as a registered nurse. I didn't cry or over apologise, I stood my ground.'

'These feelings will be raw for the time being, but now that you're aware of them, I'm hoping it'll be easier for you to manage.'

'I think so.'

'So let's dive into the issues surrounding intimacy,' she said. 'From what I'm hearing there's nothing Dylan's saying that triggers you, just the physical intimacy?'

'Correct,' I replied.

Last appointment it was established that intimacy was contingent on my emotionality. While I was open with Dylan, I couldn't fully let him in given how this information had been used in the past.

'Last session we established that you felt you were ready despite getting out of a serious but abusive relationship seven months prior. As well as the fact that Dylan has taken care of you and recognises when he inadvertently crosses your boundaries.'

'What —'

'Let's go right back to the beginning, what was the first time you experienced a crossed boundary in your life?'

I thought for a moment. It was a fairly simple question, except I hunted through almost two decades worth of crossed boundaries.

'You have the answer don't you?' I tried to joke. 'I wanna say grade three?'

'Yes, and from there boundaries were repeatedly crossed, despite your parents respecting your boundaries?'

'That's correct.'

'You've been together for a few months. Have you felt any pressure from him? Whether that be sexually or even in communication?'

The word 'no' left my mouth quickly.

'So what do you think is stopping you?' she asked.

'I'm not sure. We spend a healthy amount of time together and apart. We involve each other in our hobbies. If I take him out of the equation for a moment, and really dig, I think it's my entire life that's stopping me. I'm happy, but I've been happy before and I've been burned because of it, because I got comfortable. Sex for me is ... I don't know how to describe it.'

'Try me.'

I played with my long cardigan that I had draped over my lap. 'As you know I used to use masturbation as a form of self-harm, finding a way to mimic my period cramps. I don't know if what I shared with Kaleb was ... I don't know, sex is sex isn't it?'

'Depends on how you view it,' she replied.

'Helpful,' I scoffed and looked out of the window to the River Torrens.

Xenia shifted in her seat. 'How do you view it?'

'I'm not sure.'

'Do you have a sexual relationship with yourself that's healthier than when you were self-harming?'

'I'd like to think so. I'm honestly not sure.'

She hummed in response and flicked through the session's notes. 'I'm going to give you both homework. Some physical and emotional connecting exercises to ease into giving into the urges.' I leant forward to take the piece of paper off her with the list of joint and solo activities on it. My cheeks flushed with that ghastly unforgiving shade of red.

'Thank you.'

The cool spring air greeted me as I stepped out onto my balcony with my iced mango tea and journal. My head still reeling from the morning's psychologist appointment.

It was one thing to move on from the abuse and be with someone who valued me as a whole. It was a whole other thing to open up the conversation involving sex, when I knew now that it involved a lot more trust and emotional input than just the physical components of the act.

Just as I was learning what sex meant to me, Kaleb had ruined it. Only keeping me around to fulfill his biological urges rather than as a loving act between two people. He didn't care whether or not I finished, just as long as he did. Solidifying my own belief that an orgasm was a reward, the very one that I ingrained at the age of fifteen.

'She has a point, I guess,' I said to myself.

'Who has a point?' Dylan asked, startling me.

'I really gotta take back my spare key, or maybe put a kitty bell on you,' I joked.

'Ha. Ha. Ha. Very funny,' Dylan replied, rolling his eyes in the process. 'So, who has a point?'

'This,' I handed him the paper, half-filled in homework exercises.

'Oh.' He stared blankly at the page. Awkwardness filled the air. 'Uh-huh.'

I tried to study him. Read his micro facial expressions, but there was nothing. Only his eyes moved, following the words on the page. 'Some of these we could do now.'

'Like —' My ringtone cut me off and the awkward tension continued to rise.

*Saved by the bloody bell.*

'Hello, McKenna speaking.'

'McKenna, it's Officer Button,' the voice replied.

'Oh hi,' I replied, putting the phone on speaker and signalling to Dylan to keep quiet.

'I am calling to let you know that we have arrested Kaleb,' he said. Dylan smiled down at me, pumping his fists in the air. 'He will face the Magistrates' Court on Thursday next week, for the pre-trial, pre-committal hearing. Will you be able to make it? If not, the Court could potentially arrange for a video call. As a primary witness, you will need to be there.'

'Uhh, let me just check my calendar,' I said as I went through my phone. 'Yeah, that should be fine, I'll book flights pronto.'

'No problem, the Court will be in contact with you for the details, and you'll be given the case number.' He paused momentarily, and I could hear the sounds of his keyboard. 'Do you have any questions?'

'No, no,' I said. 'Just, thank you so much.'

'No problem at all. Take care, McKenna,' Constable Button said.

'You too, bye.'

'Bye.'

I put my phone back onto the table and started to laugh uncontrollably.

'That wasn't a response I was expecting,' Dylan said. 'You okay?'

'Y-yeah,' I replied, as my laughter died down. 'Let's go out and celebrate! There's that French place we've been dying to try down the road.'

'Sounds like a plan. I'll be right back, pick you up at six?'

'Sounds good.'

Dylan headed back to his apartment.

'What the fuck do I wear?' I asked myself as I headed down the far end of the balcony to my bedroom. It wasn't a fancy place, but one where jeans were not part of the attire.

**Me:** *What do you wear on a date where you're likely to have sex after?*

**Aster:** *WTF. Black pumps, a dress with a zipper, and of course, good underwear. Otherwise, clothes would likely be ripped.*

**Me:** *Why would they be ripped?*

**Aster:** *Babe, that man is an absolute saint. But you've been together for how long now? Done absolutely nothing beside make out. I wouldn't be surprised if he gets a little feral.*

**Me:** *Ugh gross!*

**Me:** *This okay?*

I sent through a photo of one of my mini black A-line dresses that stopped at the knee. It was my go-to dress and was one of my favourite handmade creations.

**Aster:** *For any other occasion, I'd say yes. This isn't that occasion. What about that cute burgundy dress? The one with the high slit, comes down to the ankles. The Asymmetrical straps.*

Back into the depths of my wardrobe I went, pulling out the faux sheer burgundy dress. It hugged my slim figure nicely, leaving nothing to the imagination. As I put it on, I adjusted the only adjustable strap slightly, before I slid the slider of the zipper up, the grinding of its teeth locking loud in my ears.

I sent back a picture to Aster, who reiterated to pair the dress with my dainty black strappy heels.

**Me:** *Sounds like a solid plan. Also have other news. Will call you later xx*

**Aster:** *Oh you better. Have fun!*

With my heels fixed tightly to my feet, and makeup fixed, I headed out to the living room to wait. Xenia's homework list sat on the coffee table.

'Ready to go?' Dylan asked, opening my apartment door.

*Damn.*

He was dressed head to toe in black and white. The white button up shirt was tucked into his black pants and held in place by a black belt.

'Yeah,' I breathed.

'Holy shit,' he said, taking my hand. 'You look drop dead gorgeous. Can we, um, can we — can we skip dinner?'

*Yes, please.*

'No.' I grabbed his hand and led him out of my apartment.

# 50

# October 2019

*23 Years Old*

As we walked back inside my apartment. Dylan was quick to flop onto the couch, pulling me down with him.

'Ah,' I yelped in surprise.

'Okay, that was by far the best dinner ever,' Dylan exclaimed, flopping down onto my sofa.

'For sure,' I replied. The piece of paper from Xenia sat face up on the table. Its first point of the homework was to share something traumatic from our childhood. 'Can we — Can we talk?'

'That homework?' I nodded. 'Yeah, okay.'

'It won't, like, trauma bond us?' Dylan asked.

'No, unless we had a similar or shared trauma, then maybe, but that's a whole other complex issue,' I replied. 'It's only meant for us to let each other in a little more and feel more connected.'

'So we can't just skip a step?' he joked, leaning into me to point at the next item on the list.

'No,' I laughed.

'Okay, okay,' he said, leaning back against the couch. 'I'll go first.'

'Sure,' I said, turning to face him.

'You already know that I was bullied, but what I didn't share was that it went beyond name calling and getting my head dunked in the toilet. You know, the typical nerdy treatment.' Dylan laughed dryly, trying to lighten the mood. 'When I moved from the UK to Brisbane, as you know, I was fifteen and bullied quite a bit due to my ways from back in England. What I haven't told you, or even previous exes, I mean it's embarrassing ...'

I moved closer to him, taking his hand in my own.

He smiled at me weakly as he continued. 'I had a crush on a girl, not really popular. She was a math whiz, nerd, but insanely gorgeous. Anyway, she knew I liked her, everyone did. One day, she thought it would be a bit of fun to ask me out. Of course I said yes, thinking nothing of it.' He swallowed. 'Did it suddenly get hot in here.'

'It's okay, you don't —' I started.

'No, no, it's okay,' Dylan cut in. I nodded. 'She, um. You won't laugh?'

'I won't, I promise.'

'She had invited me to a party, and it was her idea to play a game. It was like seven minutes in heaven but one of us was blindfolded?' He dropped my hand to cover his reddening face. 'She shoved me into the closet, only I was kissed by *someone* other than *her* ... It was photographed and sent via MSN to the whole school. So a couple of hundred, maybe more, saw me kissing a guy. My. My first was —'

*Oh shit.*

I quickly moved to sit next to him, holding him. No amount of words could express my concern and sorrow. Dylan was quick to reciprocate, wrapping his arms around me and leaning his body into mine, his head on my chest.

'Thank you,' he whispered. His head drew back against my chest as he took a deep breath and continued, 'I didn't date until med school. Same girl for two years until graduation when I found out that day she was cheating on me,' he said into my chest.

'That's horrible,' I remarked. 'I'm so sorry Dylan.' I kiss the top of his head.

'You know, as much as I love Bianca and Natalie, when I met you, there was just — I don't even know, it was something about you that made me feel like I could trust you.'

'I get that. I feel the same about you.' I kissed the top of his head again. 'Thank you for telling me.' He leaned up to peck my lips before leaning back into the corner of the couch. 'Guess it's my turn then?' I chuckled. Unfortunately, for me, there was a whole book full. Sometimes it felt like I was at a standstill, but then I'd realise that I was having fewer depressive episodes prior to therapy.

'Take your time, if it's too much, we'll leave it for now and come back to it when you're ready.'

'Nah, it's fine, I'm going to take you to 2004, where the victimisation started when I was eight years old.' I turned my body to face him. 'I was emotionally and psychologically abused by my grade three teacher, Mrs McConnell.' Dylan moved closer to me, his knees touching mine, and hands rested on my legs. 'She used me as a scapegoat for students around me talking. Even if the students were on the other side of the room. She didn't care. She would hold my exam papers up to explain that all questions needed answering despite a plethora of unanswered questions. Classmates would later tell me most of my questions were wrong and they hoped I changed them. I felt stupid. I felt like I was worthless. It followed me to high school where I still wasn't given an education like my peers. They could ask questions, even silly questions, and they'd get a positive response. I would ask a question that a B or A student would ask, and all I got was: "pay attention McKenna or sit outside". Or I was gaslit into believing my work was good, only to find out that they had contradicted themselves. I was told I would never get higher than a C-minus.'

'Mic.'

I waved my hand, signalling to him that I was fine, despite me starting to choke up. My mouth ran dry, but I remained strong.

'It was the catalyst for peer bullying, and I spent the rest of my schooling life being in this labelled bubble of an easy victim for teachers and peers to bully me. Only a handful of teachers actually wanted to teach me and would answer my questions to better my education. I can count them on two hands. They're the ones I'm grateful for. Know why I dyed my hair blonde?' He shook his head. 'When I was fifteen, I dyed it because I was called a "dumb blonde" by a couple of teachers. A fucking disgusting stereotype. Ugh. I mean I was a kid, but the fact I kept doing it ... It was like a form of self-harm. Kaleb preferred blondes, he also called me stupid and a dumb blonde. He fetishized it, and I'm fucking ashamed I played right into the offensive stereotype.'

Somehow I had managed to get through that with dry eyes. Maybe it was the fact that I knew I was safe with him, or the fact that I am stronger.

'What a *charming* woman,' Dylan said sarcastically. 'I really want to call her something else, but I will refrain as I know how you feel about it. My God. I'm so sorry McKenna. I don't know what to say, I mean, if you look at why people abuse it's usually jealously, but how — how can someone who's roughly our age, or even older, be jealous of a child?'

'I have absolutely no idea. Maybe I was just an easy target,' I shrugged. 'Besides it doesn't really matter anymore. She's not worth it.'

'No she is not. Besides joke's on her and all the other horrible teachers. You became an incredibly beautiful, stoic, funny and highly intelligent woman. Each study night I attend, you put me to shame, and I'm qualified! You're fucking amazing. I love you.'

The words tumbled out of his mouth, and those three words hung in the air.

'You sure you're not just saying that because I'm your girlfriend and you have to say that?' I joked, trying to ignore the awkwardness that they produced.

'Oh definitely,' he bantered.

*You can't ignore it anymore.*

'Since, we're being vulnerable,' I said. 'I love you too.'

He leaned forward, his soft lips grazing mine.

'Wanna spend the night?' I asked. 'You have a day off tomorrow right?'

'Yes, I'll go grab Ferni then.'

'Yes! Absolutely!'

'That was far too eager.'

Dylan patted my knee as he stood up to leave, but I felt myself stop him. Grabbing his hand and pulling him back.

'Actually,' I said, looking up at him. 'He can wait a little longer. I feel like we could tick off some of the other things on the list.'

Dylan kissed me again, pushing me gently back into the couch. We let the cushion take most of our combined body weight.

'Are you serious?' he asked, his eyes darkened.

There was not a single doubt in my mind. I tangled my fingers in his soft curly brown hair, 'I didn't get dressed up for nothing.'

He laughed and kissed me again.

'Just, before we do,' I said. 'I'm getting there. Obviously I wouldn't be studying med if something in me didn't click. I'm better now. I'm no longer letting my past govern me, I'm taking my life back. I'm not afraid to take a risk if it means my life gets better.'

'I'm not going anywhere,' Dylan responded. 'You're an inspiration. Truly.'

I leaned into him. Kissing him. 'Thank you.'

He was on top of me once more, this time with more need. His hands roaming along my bare legs and up my body as we made out.

I brought my hands down from his curls to his white button up shirt.

'May I?' I asked, fiddling with the top button.

'Absolutely.'

I undid the buttons down to his belt, my hands resting on the buckle, just as he stood us up to gain access to my back. The zipper to my dress hissed as he pulled the slider down. The garment pooled at my feet.

# 51

# November 2019

*23 Years Old*

Every day this week Dylan had come over, he even had clothes thrown on the couch in the study. It was like he lived here, especially since Ferni sat on my lap as I studied.

'He'll be here soon,' I said to the small dachshund. The door clicked open and in walked Dylan. 'Speak of the devil.'

Ferni leapt from my lap and sprinted to his rightful owner. Except, Dylan ignored him. He ran his fingers through his hair and sadness visible in his gaze.

*Oh, God. He's breaking up with me.*

'Do you know a Harriet?' he asked.

'Sure I know a few, why?'

I tried to dig around in my brain. His forehead was glistening with sweat, his fingers fidgeted with each other. Dylan kept his gaze off mine.

*What could this Harriet have said to cause such a reaction?*

'She, uh, she said that you used to bully her in primary school. She said that —' He choked on his words.

*There it is. What did she say to him? I know that he was bullied, but this reaction is too much.*

'Unbelievable.' I slammed my laptop lid down. 'I'm sorry?' I turned away, my hand pinched the bridge of my nose. 'She's still doing this?'

'What?'

I took a couple of deep breaths and walked towards him, calmly asking, 'What exactly did she say?'

'Just that you used to kick her out of the group at lunches and often threw her under the bus when teachers called you out on it.'

*What the actual fuck? Of course that'd piss him off.*

Rage boiled through me, but I tried to respond calmly as I could. 'Are you serious?'

'I don't believe her, considering our talk, but she was so ...'

'Believable?' He nodded. 'Yeah, she was like that when we were kids too. Our friendship wasn't exactly pretty and will take days to go through with you as there's a lot.'

'So she's lying?'

'Oh absolutely.'

'I can see that it's brought up some old feelings.' I nodded. 'I'll order some pizza and crack open a bottle of wine, and you can tell me everything.'

'Wow, so is she the nurse?' I asked.

'Yeah,' he replied. 'I truly thought I did something to her to make her treat me like absolute shit. Turns out, she just wanted me. I mean I feel like I should be flattered but what she's done ...'

I laughed, 'Oh no, you're totally right. What she's done not only jeopardises the care of patients, probably delaying their scan, but also I mean, I've never seen you so ...'

He was visibly shaken. Hands trembling as he started to organise the takeout. I couldn't blame him. This was meant as a ploy to throw a spanner in the works, but the trust between us was great. He understood my boundaries and respected them, an even more so since our chat a couple of weeks ago.

I pulled the half-finished bottle of wine from the fridge and two glasses while I waited for Dylan to finish the order. He was pacing around the kitchen, tapping on the screen.

'Did you want me to do that?'

'No, it's okay, thanks though,' he replied.

We've been more attuned to each other. As Xenia stated, this was a true partnership, and I was falling more and more in love with Dylan as time went on.

I sat down on my sofa and waited as Dylan changed out of his scrubs. It was a bit of a surreal feeling that my past was still haunting me. Watching me. She could have said nothing, instead she lied to my boyfriend, as if he'd believe her.

'How did she know about me?' I asked as he came back out of my bedroom.

'I'm not sure, she doesn't have me on social media, and we're both hella private,' he replied. 'Maybe word of mouth? Or she's seen us together?'

'Plausible, but I don't look like I did back in primary school,' I said.

'Well, Natalie has basically curated her own Facebook and Instagram to look like a fan page for us.' He laughed. 'She has almost every nurse in the hospital as friends.'

'So true,' I snorted. 'You know despite this not being an easy conversation, I find it funny how considering how big the country is, that Harriet and I have somehow ended up back in the same place.'

'It's one mighty coincidence,' he laughed, pouring the wine into the glasses. 'Still it is a wonder how and why she felt compelled.'

'I don't know if what I'm about to share is because she may hold onto some grudge and wants to be petty, but I have a feeling it's jealousy,' I said. 'I mean, damn, Dyl, look at you.'

Dylan giggled. 'So, give me the tea.' He jumped to turn to face me, using the arm rest of the sofa as a back rest.

Dylan was the biggest gossip; couldn't keep a secret even if he tried. It was a breath of fresh air sometimes. He often shared stories of how a radiology department nurse would often screw things up just so he'd have to go down to radiology to sort whatever it was that needed sorting.

'I've told you about Rebecca, Bec, and how manipulative she was.' I took a swig of the very full glass of wine while I thought. 'She used me as a scapegoat if I didn't do what I was told. I was scared of her, but so was Harriet. She wasn't as heavily bullied like I was, so she could've left at any time, yet she stayed despite being kicked out for no reason.'

I paused to take another sip of the very full glass of wine. Ferni took the opportunity to run up his ramp and jump into my lap, catching me off guard that my wine almost spilt as I drew it back from my lips.

'Oh wow,' Dylan said.

'One lunch, Harriet got kicked out, and like always, I sat with her. Except this time, I went to go get water for her and I was stopped by a teacher ...' I took a mouthful of the wine, letting the alcohol slowly burn down my oesophagus. 'She called me over, and Bec had already thrown me under the bus saying that I was the one that kicked her out —'

Dylan cut me off. 'Wait, how did the teacher believe her?'

'Because Bec had a following of two others. Bronte and Tyler. They were more of Bec's friends, not mine. Bronte and Tyler did what Bec said, because if they didn't, they'd end up like Harriet. Except Harriet didn't stand up for me, she let me go to the Principal.'

'Oh my God! That's fucking disgraceful! So you stayed because —'

'Because of Bec's coercive nature. Sure I had other friends, but like I said, it'd gotten physical a few times, so I was beaten into fear.'

'Fuck me, I am so sorry. That's horrible.'

He wasn't wrong. Whilst I may have gotten over the incidents, the fact that Harriet still believed her version of events and tried to drive a wedge between Dylan and me was diabolical. I had no words for this grown adult woman's behaviour.

'The only person who would stand up for me, other than myself, was Oliver, but he was a floater.'

'Floater?'

'He'd jump from friend group to friend group. We became best friends in high school.' I took a swig of my wine before continuing. 'Nice bloke, or so I thought. He was part of that friendship group that ditched me and decided to befriend Kaleb.'

'Oh yeah,' Dylan replied. 'Can't believe how awful people can be.'

He reached out to touch my leg. The soft skin of his thumb moved smoothly in a circle on my calf.

The intercom buzzed.

'Why don't you go talk to Harriet?' he asked as he got up.

'I guess I could, would be interesting to hear her reasons why,' I replied

'Might give you some closure too.'

He left the apartment to get the pizza, and I grabbed my phone, immediately searching up Harriet on Facebook.

**Me:** *Hey, can we meet for coffee? Seems like we need to have a conversation.*

# 52

# September 2008

*12 Years Old*

I didn't know what Bec's goal was after kicking Harriet and Oliver out for the fifth lunch in a row. As much as I despised Bec, I stayed, unable to find my voice to stand up for myself, despite being vocal in my stance in support of my other friends.

Harriet was always left out, and I couldn't understand why she didn't leave. Unlike me, she wasn't dragged into concrete bleachers or gripped until her arms turned bright red. Instead she was told to sit elsewhere or made to sit a few metres away, watching us play. I tried to stand up for her, but my efforts were ignored. All I could do was sit with her until I was dragged back, or guilt-tripped back to the group.

'Why, Bec?' I asked. 'What did they do now?'

'Can't you see how buddy, buddy they are?' she asked, pointing at the two sitting in the concrete, laughing amongst themselves.

'Boys and girls can be friends. Nothing wrong with that.' Bec pulled a face. 'What?'

'He's not part of the group,' she replied.

*Oh, so that's the problem.*

'How's that any different to Thomas and me? We're friends, he occasionally hangs with us?' I stated.

'They're dating. And he's not *our* sort of people,' she replied.

There was nothing that suggested to me that there was anything romantic going on. Then again, what do I know, I was only twelve years old.

'They're just good friends, Bec,' I reiterated, convinced that Bec was seeing things. 'Also, what *are* "our sort of people"?'

She didn't respond, only scowling in the direction of Harriet and Oliver as she peeled her orange.

I got up from my seat and waltzed over to Oliver and Harriet, plonking myself down on the cold, hard concrete. The stink-eye from Bec seared into me but I didn't care, as I continued to eat my lunch in laughter with Oliver and Harriet.

'Sorry about Bec,' I said to Oliver. 'I don't understand why she does this.'

'It's okay,' he said.

Oliver floated between multiple friendship groups amongst the grade, and it pissed Bec off whenever he joined. I liked it though, it meant that Harriet had a friend to sit with her whenever Bec kicked her out. As much as I tried, I was always dragged away, leaving my friend to sit alone.

As predicted, I felt my ponytail and yanked upwards, forcing me to my feet.

'Ow!' I yelped.

'Why do you sit with that skank when I make it perfectly clear that she isn't welcome?' Bec said.

*Because she's my friend too. Maybe we'll start our own group and leave you out.*

I remained quiet, my legs turned to jelly. Her face was getting redder by the second as she stood towering over me. A whimper escaped my lips, and I scurried back to my original seat next to Bec.

The whistle from the teachers sounded, and the children across each campus made a dash for each of their respective play areas. I dawdled behind Bec, Bronte, and Tyler, letting me partner with Harriet as we walked down to the senior oval.

'What do you reckon we'll play today?' Harriet asked me.

It was always the same made-up game or a game of sticks or red rover. Really, it was whatever Bec wanted to do.

'No clue, probably the same thing we do every day,' I replied.

I watched on as a group of boys, I sometimes played with, finished setting up a miniature touch footy field.

'I wish I was playing with them today,' I muttered.

'Why? Boys are gross,' Harriet said.

I laughed weakly, 'Yeah, they are a bit, but they know how to play and makes me better for when I play club.'

Harriet shrugged and jogged to catch up with the girls who were already down in the far corner setting up for a game of sticks. By the time I made it over, Bec was already annoyed with Harriet because she didn't put a stick in the right position.

Harriet tried to reposition, following Bec's instructions, but it only made it worse.

'Bloody hell Harriet!' Bec exclaimed. 'Just go sit out.'

I cringed and followed like clockwork, racing to ensure my friend was okay.

'You don't have to sit with me,' she said, tears in her eyes. 'You'll get in trouble too.'

'I know, but I don't care,' I replied. 'I want to make sure that you're okay.'

'Thank you.'

'All good.'

We sat in silence, while I let her cry into my shoulder.

'Rebecca!' I heard yelled from behind me from Mrs O'Connor. Nothing good would come of it if I got up from my position.

'McKenna!' My name was called.

*Never mind.*

'Here we go,' I muttered.

*You were comforting a friend. You did nothing wrong. You were just comforting a friend.*

'Yes Miss?' I asked as I headed over.

'I'm just trying to get to the bottom of why Harriet was sitting by herself?' she replied.

I looked over to Harriet who dodged my gaze.

'I-I —' I stuttered.

'I'm not going to continue to play this game with you McKenna,' Mrs O'Connor said.

*You did nothing wrong, you sat with her and Bec kicked her out. You can tell her, she'll believe you.*

'Bec kicked her out,' I rushed out. 'I-I-I —'

Mrs O'Connor rolled her eyes, 'S-s-*spit* it o-o-out girl.'

*Is she seriously mocking me?*

I looked to Harriet who had followed me over, but instead of voicing up, her mouth was pulled into a tight line. Bec snickered beside me, a sound that made my heart drop to my stomach.

I fumbled over the words, only stuttering out more sounds.

'Here's a note, take that to Mr Truches' office.'

I snatched the blue paper, tempted to tear it up in a huff. It was unforgivable. There was no means of true justice or motion to stand up for myself when Harriet denied all claims that I made.

For the umpteenth time this year, I walked across the oval and through campus to the old red brick building. Navigating my way through its dark corridors to the Principal's quarters until I was face to face with the dark reddish-brown timber doors.

My raised fist hesitated before it collided with the solid timber.

'They should be with me,' I mumbled. 'Why do I always take the fall?'

The door opened.

'That's a very good question,' Mr Truches replied.

'Sorry, sir,' I stated, looking down at my feet.

'Not to worry, come in, come in.'

He moved aside, letting me sheepishly walk to the seat in front of his desk.

'Tell me what happened,' he said.

Despite the rumours shared amongst students over the years, Mr Truches was an incredibly courteous man. He always seemed to care but whenever I left his office, I'd be back in there within a week.

No information was seemingly passed to my teacher, or to my parents. Nothing was ever done. Every day, I wished for death, afraid of what sort of hell was lying and waiting for me.

Most days I thought about jumping off the balcony at home, would I make it to the pool or to the concrete. Most days I imagined what this world would be like if we could die from embarrassment; I would've died four years ago at the hands of Mrs McConnell.

# 53

# November 2019

*23 Years Old*

Deep regret sat in the pit of my stomach as I followed Dylan to the main cafeteria of the hospital. Harriet was already waiting, sat out at a roadside table in the rising sun.

'Well it looks like you have a coffee already,' Dylan said to me.

'Awesome,' I replied. 'Text me when you reckon you'll finish, and I'll come pick you up.'

'Sure.' He pecked me on the lips. 'Good luck. Talk to you later, Mic.'

'Bye, Dyl.'

I headed out the opposite side doors and towards where Harriet was sitting, overlooking the car park.

She was just as I remembered, just ten years older. Her dirty blonde hair tied back into a high messy ponytail. Her fake tan wasn't noticeable until I got closer, although it didn't have that slight tinge of orange that I remembered girls in high school having.

'Hey Harriet,' I said as I took my seat across from her.

'Hey,' she replied. 'Bought you a coffee.'

Harriet pushed it towards me.

'Thanks,' I said. It was a thoughtful gesture that I didn't exactly anticipate coming from her.

The breeze had a nasty bite to it as it blew past. Her long ponytail swatted her in her face. Before it came back around, she threw the ponytail into a bun and sighed, 'He told you didn't he.'

'He doesn't exactly have a poker face, nor can he keep anything from me,' I joked.

'Noted.'

'Can I ask why?' I wanted to get straight to the point. What was said, was said, but it stung. It was the fact that she was holding on to a lie and had to say it to my partner. 'I — I'm not mad, but you and I both know what *actually* happened.'

'Honestly?'

'Mmm. Please.'

'I'm jealous. You're in medicine, you get to work part-time with no double shifts *because you're in med*,' she mocked. 'Plus, you scored the doctor that everyone hoped to date.'

'Harriet ...'

'I'm sorry, I wasn't thinking.'

'Clearly,' I scoffed.

I worked hard to give myself a break, heal and allow others in on my terms.

'Jealousy doesn't explain why you never stood up for me. I always stood up for you, *and* myself when I reached breaking point. Bec would get the jump on me and because I was selective mute, it was easy. Why Harriet? You wouldn't have done this if it was Bec dating Dylan and studying medicine with work hours that were actually feasible.'

She stayed silent.

'What exactly do you want from me?'

'I honestly don't know —' she replied.

'So trying to drive a wedge between a girl you haven't seen since primary and a doctor you barely see, unless you, and this is coming from him, cause some reason for him to head to radiology?' I turned to look at the car park, trying to get the breeze to aid in getting my hair out of my face. 'If it's support you want, I can see what I can do, but —'

'Why does he like you, I mean —'

'Harriet, stop. We're not in primary school anymore. We're both near mid-twenty-year-olds. If you're unhappy with your life, start over. Go back to school, get a Master's or find something else. Don't start wishing for my life, because news flash, I shouldn't be here. I worked my arse off to undo what I've been through since grade three, including what you and Bec, plus the other two did. And if you can't see that, then that's shameful.'

She stared at me blankly.

'Judging by that look, you still thought I was some push over selective mute.'

She turned away from me, looking out to the car park, her eyes glassing over. I sighed and held out my hands to her and softened myself as best I could.

'Look, I am willing to help you Harriet, so what is it you need, and I can see what I can do.'

There was silence.

'Okay, well ... Um, th-thanks for the coffee,' I said. 'I wish you the best. If you need anything, feel free to reach out.' I stood up and took my untouched coffee with me as I navigated my way back through the corridors to where I had entered from with Dylan.

As much as the old me wanted to tell my supervisor what transpired, I was no longer *that* petty. However, if this scenario were to happen again, I wouldn't be so nice about it and would be taking it up with whomever I needed to pass it on to.

My past no longer defined me, it was a part of me that had made me the woman I am today. Knowing how great I felt after ditching the toxicity I had in my life. I could no longer tolerate it anymore. There was no room for it. I deleted various social media platforms, keeping Facebook and Instagram for my family and the handful of friends I had.

For the first time in well over a decade, I was happy.

'Hey, you okay?' Dylan asked, intercepting me at the hospital exit. 'I'm on my way to outpatients.'

'Oh, uh yeah, she was jealous,' I said, following him down since it was in the direction of my car. 'I think she wanted something but couldn't tell me. Jealousy was definitely a contributing factor.'

'Wow,' he said.

I nodded and leaned into him.

'So it's me right?' he joked.

'Oh come on.' I laughed, shoving his shoulder. 'In part, yes, but I think it was also because of how "successful" I am.'

'Double wow, so what are you going to do now?'

'Left the window open, so if she wants to reach out, she can. Maybe it was something that was embarrassing, or maybe I came across a little abrupt? I don't know.'

'I'm proud of you, we'll talk more when I get off work.'

'Enjoy outpatients.'

He gave my hand a gentle squeeze before I headed straight to the car park.

I was proud of myself.

Standing up for myself used to be a weakness. I used to always take the blame, becoming a blubbering mess, or I would take a risk in asking a question to boost my education, but more often than not, got shut down.

Now, I was no longer taking bullshit. Therapy was working out for me.

# 54

# January 2020

*23 Years Old*

I glanced up at the Cairns Magistrate Court, unsure if I could proceed. There was always the option to withdraw my statement, but now it was too late.

*Could the court read it out instead?*

Dylan stood behind me, his hand on my back. 'You'll be okay. I'll be right there in the room with you.'

'Thank you,' I said stiffly.

'Are you sure you don't want us to come with you?' mum asked.

My back straightened, and I looked between her and dad. 'I'm sure, this isn't — I thank you both for your support, but no. This isn't — You'll be waiting outside with Aster. It's a closed court so there's not much you can do.'

'Okay sweetheart.' Dad kissed my forehead. 'You're so brave and I'm — we're — very proud of you. We'll find a cafe and wait for the three of you.'

'Sure,' I replied. 'Thank you.'

'Love you, honey.' Mum gave me one final hug before I followed Dylan and Aster into the dark building, stopping briefly to proceed through security.

The waiting area outside our court room was quiet, eerily quiet, and dark. Almost like they wanted to make everyone uncomfortable. Dylan placed his hand on my leg, grounding me.

'I think the grey pin-striped power suit was a poor choice. I don't feel very confident.'

'Hey, hey,' Dylan said, leading me to sit on a cold hard oak-stained timber bench. 'Look at me. You have achieved so much. You're an incredible nurse, and you're blitzing through medical school. Any department and hospital will be lucky enough to have you. You've been through so much, you deserve to be happy.'

'I did stand up to Harriet,' I muttered.

'See, and you don't believe you're confident.'

I laughed, 'Okay, maybe I can do this.'

'I've got you,' he whispered, giving me a hug.

Aster grabbed my hand and whispered, 'As do I. Just saw him outside, looks like he's 'bout ready to poop his pants.'

I chuckled lowly.

'Speak of the devil,' Dylan said.

My stomach churned and a wave of nausea hit as I watched Kaleb walk right past us. His mum, whilst teary eyed, still bore a death stare at me. Trying to hold myself together was a challenge, but I embraced the anxiety like an old friend.

*Why did I do this? I can't do this. This is bullshit.*

The good memories started to whirl around my brain, ignoring all the bad things he did.

*This is wrong. He did nothing wrong.*

'This is bullshit,' I mumbled, leaning forward. My elbows dug into my thighs, my cool hands covered my face. 'Why did I do this?'

'Do I need to remind you of the put downs, and stalking?' Aster asked. 'That's why. Now, chin up, you've got this.'

I wanted to stop after the committal hearing, but after all the time wasted. The fear that he had caused me. He deserved to be in front of that Magistrate, just as much as I deserved to have my voice heard.

'Thank you,' I replied.

My lawyer, Martin, walked down the hall. 'I'm so sorry I'm late.'

'Don't be,' I replied. 'Just — I know that you've gone over a bunch of times but what —'

'Just sit, listen and follow the instructions,' he said. 'He can't hurt you.'

I nodded. After numerous conversations since the day I found out that Kaleb was charged, Martin put me at ease. Despite him only being in his mid-thirties, he had plenty of experience and ran his own firm.

Martin led Dylan and I through the heavy soundproofed door and signalled us to nod towards the Coat of Arms above where the Magistrate was due to sit.

'Sit in one of the seats there,' Martin whispered to Dylan.

Dylan squeezed my hand softly as I headed towards my seat beside Martin. I pulled out the blue mesh-covered cushion chair from the desk. It felt like those plastic school chairs only covered in rough mesh fabric. No lumbar support whatsoever.

*So much for the cushion.*

My hands clasped together with a thin layer of sweat separating them.

'All rise!' The Court Officer called.

My chest grew heavy as I slowly rose along with everyone else. My throat felt like it was closing on me. I zoned out, trying to focus on the wall behind the Judge.

Voices mushed together. My fingers playing with the excess of my belt, my eyes locking onto various objects around the room. Nothing about this felt real. Goosebumps formed along my bare arms. I tried to remain still, but my legs continued to bounce under the table.

*I wish I had my jacket.*

Kaleb sat there. Happy as can be. A smirk etched on his face as his lawyer talked to the Judge. I remembered the first time I saw that smirk.

> *Kaleb reached out for the permanent rose gold choker that was wrapped around my neck. 'A reminder that you're mine,' he whispered so low that I was convinced I was hearing things.*

'I'd like to call McKenna Carrington to give her victim impact statement,' the Court Officer said.

'McKenna?' Martin said, tapping my shoulder.

'Mm?' I responded.

'Your statement,' he said.

'Oh right,' I replied, standing up. The pieces of paper shook between my sweaty hands.

'I — I. Mm.' I took a deep breath. 'I met Kaleb in one of my first-year university elective units in June twenty-fifteen. He was funny, handsome, and everything I wanted in not only a friend but boyfriend. For the first twelve to eighteen months, everything was perfect, until it wasn't. My birthday in March twenty-seventeen was when the abuse started, with a purchase of a permanent necklace in a sketchy home. Despite me showing clear discomfort and use of a safe word, he pushed me through the home. He bought me a necklace, not just any, but a permanent one with a pendant of a padlock and his first initial.'

My eyes locked with Kaleb's momentarily as I paused to give myself a break.

*Don't look at him. Look to the Magistrate.*

'A-At the time, I thought it was innocent, but shortly after was when the put-downs started. "You're not good enough to be a nurse". "You're too sensitive". "If you can't handle stress, how will you be able to deal with doctors on a power trip?" I was convinced he was right, despite me being a straight high distinction student. February twenty-eighteen was the start of the escalation: scribbled and torn textbooks, notes destroyed, and he smashed my glass desk. A couple of months later he sent a series of threatening text messages and called the police. This was when he further escalated, by stalking me in Adelaide, and again when I arrived home.'

My mouth went dry, and I tried to swallow, but I couldn't, choking out, 'H-Have you ever felt like you are g-going to d-die? My safe place, about five kilometres north of my home on the other side of Earl Hill, turned into a death trap. Who knows what would've happened had I gone. I can only imagine my life could have been ended. Instead I was followed home and had an image sent of me at my gate, and threats of releasing the images of a boudoir shoot I had done for him shortly after our one-year anniversary.'

I looked towards Kaleb who rolled his eyes at me. My finger shook the paper as I turned to the next page of my statement.

*Why did I do that?*

I could hear my heartbeat in my ears.

'I don't think there is another word out there to describe how I was feeling because, horrified, petrified, scared, don't even come close. I have been in therapy for a year. I have struggled to believe that I am good enough for medical school and that I will make a great doctor. I constantly feel that I am not good enough for the life that I have now, that I am not worthy to be the girlfriend to my current partner. Whenever I tried to do the right thing for Kaleb, he moved the goal posts every time to ensure I got punished. I was used and abused. Instead, it took three strangers to sense that something was wrong, my now best friend, my current partner who was a co-worker at the time, and an Uber driver. In fact, it was the Uber driver who asked me if the rose gold choker was a collar that really got my brain working. It was my co-worker who showed me how a man is supposed to treat a woman.'

I paused, wiping my sweat drenched hands against the rough fabric of my pants.

'Your honour. I'm not here seeking revenge. I'm here to hold that man accountable. My mental and physical health have suffered significantly because of him, and I am finally taking my life back from the fear and control that he instilled in me.'

You could hear a pin drop when I sat back in my seat.

'Alright, let's head for a fifteen minute break, I will review the evidence,' the Magistrate said. 'Sentencing will be after.'

I rushed from my chair and dashed to the exit, only pausing momentarily to bow my head to the Coat of Arms. My legs carried me across the hall to the bathroom, collapsing in one of the stalls.

'Kenz?' Aster called.

I responded by puking into the bowl.

'Shit,' she said and grabbed my hair, holding it off my face.

'Thanks,' I croaked before I threw up again.

'That's okay, I got you.'

She stayed with me until I was ready to get back up.

'Let me get you some water, stay here,' Aster said.

I gave her a weak thumbs up.

The door squeaked open and banged closed.

A few moments later, it squeaked open again as Aster ran in with a cup of water.

'Thanks,' I said, taking a sip of the cool tasteless liquid.

'You're welcome,' she said. 'The men want to make sure you're alright to go back in for sentencing. If you don't, Martin said that he can try to talk to the Magistrate to just have Dylan in the room.'

'I'll talk to them,' I said, shuffling to the basin to wash my hands.

We exited the bathroom, and Dylan was right at my side. 'Are you okay?'

'Yeah, yeah. I'm fine,' I replied.

'Do you want to be there for the sentencing?' Martin asked. 'I can see if you can have Dylan fill in for you.'

'I should be okay. I would like to see what happens,' I said. 'There shouldn't be anything left for me to throw up.'

I forced a laugh, but nobody else did. Concern stained their faces, and as we're called back in, I felt like I needed to throw up again.

'Shit,' I yelped and dashed back into the bathroom.

Nothing came out and I walked back out.

'It's just sentencing. It's fine, you're fine,' I muttered to myself as I pushed the heavy door and bowed once more.

'All rise!' The Court Officer called.

*Just in time.*

I made it to my seat just as the Magistrate made his way back into the room.

'I've reviewed the evidence,' he announced as he sat back at his desk. The sound of papers ruffling filled the echoing room. 'I hereby declare that I find the respondent guilty on the account of domestic violence. I find the respondent guilty of stalking. I find the respondent guilty on the count of threatening to distribute intimate images.'

I turned around sharply to look at Dylan.

'I hereby sentence Kaleb Brewer to two years, for domestic violence; four years, for stalking, and three years, for threatening to distribute intimate images,' the Magistrate announced. 'These are to be served consecutively, with the possibility of parole in three years. Court is adjourned.'

The gavel collided with the desk, and Martin held out his hand to me. 'Congratulations, McKenna,' Martin said as the Court Officers placed Kaleb in handcuffs.

I wiped the sweat from my palm onto my pants, before I shook his hand. 'Thank you.'

The three of us bowed our heads and walked out of the courtroom.

'So?' Aster jumped.

'Nine years in total on three separate charges,' Dylan said.

'Oh my God!' Aster replied.

'Let's get out of here,' I said.

Kaleb's mum's wails filled the dark quiet corridors as she exited the courtroom.

'She looks pissed,' Aster said. 'Let's move it.'

We headed out of the Supreme Court and walked down the street to a hole in the wall café, hidden amongst the trees and bushes.

Mum and dad sat in a quiet shaded corner.

'How'd it go?' dad asked.

'You should've seen the look on his face,' Dylan said. 'As soon as the first "guilty" verdict came, his smirk was completely abolished.'

'Good, bloke deserves it,' Aster said.

'That he did,' I concurred. 'Ugh, does anyone have mints or lollies or something, I can't wait until my juice comes to rid the taste.'

Both shook their heads.

'No,' they said in unison. 'Sorry.'

'I do.' Mum fished inside her bag, pulling out a stick of mint flavoured Mentos.

'Thanks,' I said, taking one off her, just as our drinks came. 'Hmm, before you take a sip. I just want to give you all a little toast.'

'Oh you don't –' Dylan said.

'Oh but I do,' I replied. 'I just want to say a massive thank you all. I know, I know. I say it too much. But seriously, I am grateful for your love and support. You mean a lot to me and to be able to have the courage to finally get some justice was incredible. I couldn't have done it without you ... And Bianca and Natalie too, of course. Seriously, thank you.'

Dylan pecked my lips. 'I love you. I will always be there for you. Whatever you need.'

'Same here, honey,' Aster said. 'I may be a decent amount of kilometres away but thank God for smart phones and Zoom.'

We clinked our glasses together, laughing as we took our first sip.

'We're so proud of you,' mum said. 'And it was great to finally meet you, Dylan.'

She gave me a smile and a sly thumbs up. Blood rushed to my cheeks as I smiled back at her.

I quickly messaged Will, who immediately wrote back, "*Congratulations, McKenna. Love you. Coming to Adelaide next week for a conference, meet for coffee?*"

'Everything okay?' Dylan asked.

'Yeah, just letting Will know,' I replied. 'He's coming to Adelaide for a conference next week. Figured I'd invite him to stay at mine and take him to that Italian place we like.'

'Sounds like a plan,' Dylan said, kissing my cheek. 'Can't wait to finally meet your brother face-to-face.'

As I sat back and enjoyed the celebrations, I felt every lingering weight leave my body. For the first time, justice finally prevailed.

# Acknowledgements

A huge thank you to my mum who was my very first reader, my alpha to be exact. She has read this almost as much as I have and never got bored. Thank you so, so much. Love you to infinity.

Thank you to my book coach, Ema, who helped me formalise my outline and take the mess that is my brain and turn it to reality. Without you, this book would never have had eventuated the way it did.

To my amazing team of betas, and those who read it as part of my entry to the Queensland Writer's Centre "Publishable" competition. Your detailed feedback was amazing and I hope I executed your comments accordingly. A massive thank you to my writing mentor Mark, thank you for your feedback and industry insight.

CJ, my legend of an editor, thank you so, so much for your hard work and positive commentary along the way. I laughed and I cried. I'm so grateful to have worked with you.

Finally to my cover artist, Stephen. Thank you for being a great friend and for bringing my vision to life. No words can express how grateful I am.

# About the author

Australian author, Astrid Fick, is from South-East Queensland, where she writes across multiple genres, predominantly literary fiction with ties to other genres such as romance and crime. Her stories raise awareness for various topical issues, with the main one being domestic and family violence. She enjoys bringing her tertiary education in Criminology to life, hoping to provide comfort and relatability to readers who may be going through something similar to her heroines. ▯When she isn't writing (or studying), Astrid enjoys spending time with her family and doing her plethora of hobbies.

Subscribe to Astrid's newsletter for monthly updates:

# Content Warning

- Domestic violence
- Child abuse
- Mental health
- Science experiment — rat dissection
- Self-harm
- Stalking
- Suicide ideation

www.ingramcontent.com/pod-product-compliance
Lightning Source LLC
LaVergne TN
LVHW051216070526
838200LV00063B/4914